The Flatpack Observer

Roger Kent

Acknowledgements

I would like to express my sincere gratitude to Rob Gregson, and Robert Wingfield of The Inca Project. Without the support and assistance of the two Robs, Flatpack would still be rattling around in my brain with a 'maybe one day' label attached.

In addition, my thanks go to the Stortford Scribblers Group for enduring sizeable chunks of Flatpack at each of their fortnightly meetings and for offering valuable feedback and encouragement.

The cover painting is by Viviana Elise Zamorano (www.vivelisestudio.com)

The sketch of the grernock is by Roger Kent.

Copyright

This novel is a work of fiction. Names, characters and locations are the subject of the author's imagination and any resemblance to actual persons, living or dead, locations or objects, existing or existed is purely coincidental.

It is sold subject to the condition that it shall not by way of trade or otherwise, be lent, resold, hired out, or otherwise circulated without the writer's prior consent, electronically or in any form of binding or cover other than the form in which it is published and without a similar condition including this condition being imposed on the subsequent purchaser. Replication or distribution of any part is strictly prohibited without the written permission of the copyright holder.

Copyright © 2022 Roger Kent

All rights reserved.

ISBN: 9798811237098

For Dad

Contents

1. An Encounter of the Malleable Kind	1
2. A Vacancy in Vagrancy	9
3. Derek has a Bad Day	14
4. Fourteen and a half Degrees from the Horizontal	18
5. Wagging, Tugging and Growling	23
6. Ridley's Practical Carpentry	27
7. Flatpack in the Morning—Vagrant's Warning	31
8. Puffs, Pancakes and Wooden Sandwiches	35
9. Lady Sucks the Blues	42
10. The Facts in the Case of Squire Gossard Malleable	45
11. There will be no Nipples this Year	50
12. The Water of Life	52
13. Tea and Pinochet	53
14. The Coarseness of Strainers	59
15. Oscar	67
16. The Three Fields, (Part 1—The Wheat Field)	68
(Part II—The Furnace Field)	77
(Part III—The Welsh Field)	81
17. The Colossus of Rump Hill	89
18. A Primrose by any Other Name	93
19. Naked in the Nettles	102
20. Oscar Revisited	112
21. Plié on the Pie	117
22. Falling Asleep without a Goat	134
23. Swell-O-Soil	142
24. The Cirrus of Pestilence	146
25. The Year of the Big Forget	157
26. Play that Funky Elevator Music White Boy	162
27. Liberating a Jeffrey	171
28. Didn't We Have a Lovely Time	177
29. A Traditional Flatpack Wedding	186
30. Poppy Knapweed's Fragrant Romance Bookshop	196
31. Trouser-Pressing Matters	204
Appendix	214

1. An Encounter of the Malleable Kind

All was tranquil leafiness in the B257 rest area that September afternoon; the late summer sun bathed the short length of ill-maintained asphalt in a warm glow of approval. Apart from the infamously-premature horse chestnut, the encroaching trees were still sporting their lush, green summer fashions believing, as they did, the words of a wise elder; 'Rushing into a seasonal wardrobe change is a sign of weak character and an immature root system.'

Unaware that they were being watched by a grey squirrel on a damson-stained stump, a group of blackbirds were on a quest to locate the last of the blackberries. The brambles were tangled and spiteful, but the prize was worth any number of battle scars.

A fly-tipped fridge-freezer had become the home to a family of hedgehogs who were dozing in the root vegetable compartment. The discarded appliance did little to spoil the scene. Indeed, it would have taken the roar of an approaching Mercedes-Benz E-Class Cabriolet to shatter the glass on this picture of rural pleasantness.

There was the roar of an approaching vehicle and a Mercedes-Benz E-Class Cabriolet veered into the lay-by, shooting gravel in all directions. The driver managed to steer around the fridge, but completely misjudged his car's proximity to an overgrown *Poncirus Trioliata*, and there was an excruciating squeal as the thorny limbs dissed the highly-polished paintwork. Once at rest, the engine purred, then all was silent.

The driver's door opened and a pair of high-gloss slip-ons with pigs-bristle stitching and personalised detail stepped out. These were followed by an ostentatious charcoal pinstripe, tailored to fit the athletic physique of its occupier. The man turned and hurled the door with tremendous force towards its frame. Surprised, but unwilling to be provoked by this display of petulance, the door responded with a dignified *flmph*.

Edward St Claire leant against his car, head bowed, muttering obscenities, his handsome face unusually flushed. The distant hum of another car cut through his ruminations; he thumped his car's roof. 'Why can't everyone just leave me alone to think?' He spotted a gap in a roadside hedge and leapt through it, only to be faced by a steep incline. 'Oh come on, haven't I suffered enough today?' He started to climb, grasping at saplings, fighting with nettles, tripping and venting his frustrations through his hugely-expensive soles. Finally, he reached a grassy plateau and dropped to his knees.

Before him, a vast spread of luxuriant green extended in all directions but his own. Far away, a thread of water trickled from a lake, the surface broken only by a forgotten rowboat, before lazily winding its way through gently-heaving fallow meadows with wild, undisciplined hedgerows. Then on it tumbled over mossy boulders, through a random sprinkling of bleating sheep and an ocean of wheat, the ears of which waved to a modest gathering of granite-grey, crossroad-clinging cottages. After dancing through a field of ox-eye daisies, the stream disappeared into woodland.

Edward saw none of this; all he could see ahead was humiliation and ruin. As in the early stages of digesting a particularly heavy pie, he was just beginning to assimilate the unhealthy consequences of his recent actions, and indigestion was the least of his concerns. He replayed the day's events over and over in the vain hope that they would somehow improve with repetition, which they did not. 'That stupid, stupid girl!' He thumped the ground. 'Why couldn't she keep her damn mouth shut!'

Before he could continue his rant, he was interrupted by a voice behind. 'Ah Edward, there you are.'

Edward jumped to his feet and turned to see an unfamiliar man, plump and with a high-shine pate, ascending the hill by the same unforgiving route that he had just taken.

'That really is... one... sod of a hill,' the man struggled to say. Once on the level, the full impact of the climb took effect. Bent over, sweat dropping to the ground, lungs fighting to extract sufficient oxygen from the air, he raised a finger to be allowed a moment to recover. Edward waited, feeling at a disadvantage, an emotion to which he was unaccustomed and didn't like. He used the time to study the man from head to toe in an effort to make a connection.

He had rounded and ruddy features that suggested a jovial disposition and a tendency towards over-indulgence, features that spoke of late nights with cigars and brandy, of genial company, leather sofas and stilton.

I'll bet he's never seen the inside of a gym, Edward thought, flexing his pecs.

A half-Windsor knot dangled beneath an open collar.

Many years since he's been able to comfortably button that up.

There was a yolk stain on his breast pocket.

No doubt his fat wife served up a Full English this morning, eugh.

Below, his shirt struggled to remain buttoned around an ample waistline. Single-pleated, low-slung suit trousers were belted below the stomach, and these broke lightly over grazed wingtip oxfords.

What a revolting sight. He looks like one of those enormous gasping fish you see on the cover of angling magazines, held aloft by some prat in waders... he'll probably have a heart-attack at any moment.

Finally, the man straightened up. 'You must excuse me, Edward, I'm afraid old Maxie isn't the athlete he used to be!' He offered a moist hand. 'Atticus Malleable, but do call me Maxie - everyone does, you know.'

Edward hesitated then took the hand, intent on giving it the briefest of shakes. 'And why do they call you that?'

Maxie enclosed Edward's hand in both of his and began a vigorous pumping motion. 'Now that's a very good question, and I have to say it's always been something of a mystery to me. I suppose people find 'Atticus Malleable' a bit of a mouthful, and 'Atty' would just sound, well...silly. Whereas 'Maxie Malleable' sort of dances off the tongue, don't you think? On the other hand, I suppose it could be an affectionate reference to my girth - I'm certainly no 'Mini' you must agree!' He laughed. 'Oh, and don't trouble yourself to recall our previous meetings, there haven't been any.'

Edward wrenched his hand away and wiped it on his trousers. 'So... how come you know me?'

Maxie glanced over Edward's shoulder. 'My word!' he exclaimed, 'Isn't that magnificent - I can see why you came here.' He took a step forward, flung his arms wide as if to beckon the meadows and fields to step forward and embrace him, and recited:

'Come we to the summer, to the summer we will come,
For the woods are full of bluebells and the hedges full of bloom,
And the crow is on the oak, a-building of her nest,
And love is burning diamonds in my true lover's breast;
She sits beneath the whitethorn a-plaiting of her hair,
And I will to my true lover with a fond request repair,
I will look upon her face, I will in her beauty rest,
And lay my aching weariness upon her lovely breast.'

He turned back to Edward. 'Do you know John Clare?'

'Err...I don't think so, does he work in Corporate Accounts?'

Maxie threw his head back, exploding with laughter. 'Does he work in Corporate Accounts?' Oh Edward, dear boy, that's wonderful!' The explosion quickly subsided. 'No, John Clare was a nineteenth century poet, a contemporary of Byron, Wordsworth and Keats. Not as highly regarded as those literary giants of course, but a great favourite of mine. Do you have a personal preference amongst the Romantic Scholars?'

Yeah right, as if.

'I don't have time for that sort of thing.'

'Now that's a pity - you're missing out there you know. They may have been a group of drug-dependent hedonists, but they wrote some pretty damn fine verses between them. Still, after the events of today, I'm sure you'll have plenty of time on your hands to catch up on your reading. I shall be interested to know which of them takes your fancy.' He took a step back and considered Edward. 'Yes, I definitely see you as a Coleridge man...'

'Hang on, hang on... What do you mean, 'after the events of today'? Who *are* you?'

'Oh, all in good time, Edward, but first I must ask - how is Veronica? Has she fully recovered from that nasty fall?'

Edward could feel his fingers closing. He gave the man a cold stare. 'My wife is fine.'

Maxie looked genuinely relieved. 'Oh I *am* glad to hear that. When I heard about the accident, I was concerned that she might have actually *fractured* her tibia. Now that would have meant a plaster cast and... well you know Veronica; I think she would go stark-staring mad if she couldn't get out to squander your not-inconsiderable income on handbags and all that designer silliness.' He gave Edward a playful jab in the ribs. 'And how are your children? I hear they're both at university now.'

'What the hell's that got to do with you?'

Maxie thought for a moment. 'You know, you're absolutely right, Edward – it has nothing to do with me at all - I'm really only making pleasantries. As it happens, I already know that you've talked Ptolemy into studying Business Management rather than Textile Design, and that he's joined the Socialist Workers Party to show just how much he resents you for it. Kids eh - who'd have them? I've got five incidentally. Oh, and I hear that Veronique has dropped out of that accounting technician course to get a certificate in Makeup and

Fashion. I detect Veronica's influence there – you must be *really* thrilled! Excuse me if I ask a personal question, but what possessed you to give your children those appalling names?'

Edward took a very deep breath then let the air out, long and slow.

Manage the anger, manage the anger.

'Veronica chose the children's names, I was... busy.'

'Yes,' Maxie chuckled, 'I guessed as much... absolutely awful! Do you know, I've never understood why, with an infinite number of lovely names to choose from, anyone would burden their child with a trendy variation on their own name. It shows such a self-indulgent lack of imagination, wouldn't you agree?'

Edward neither agreed nor disagreed; his fingernails were digging deep crescents in his palms.

'And as for 'Ptolemy,' well, you need to have half a bag of Victoria plums in your mouth to even pronounce it right! Now don't get me wrong, Edward, I find your wife a damnably attractive woman, but I do feel that she must pile her bowl high with pretentiousness whenever she visits the salad cart.'

Don't hit him. Remember; control yourself – control the situation – then take control.

Edward thrust his hand forward for a valedictory shake. 'Well, Mr Malleable—'

'Maxie, please.'

'Okay then... Maxie,' Edward spat the nickname out, 'it's been a pleasure to meet you, but I have a webinar to attend at five thirty, so if you'll excuse me...'

Maxie looked down at the hand, then directly into Edward's eyes. 'Now you're not being entirely honest with old Maxie, are you?'

'What do you mean?'

'Well, my understanding is that you won't be attending any meetings or conferences, online or in person, for the foreseeable future. Forgive me if I'm not completely word-perfect, but I believe Charles Mason's words to you were:

'Don't sit down Edward, I will make this very brief.

Firstly, I do not want to hear any excuses, nor do I have the slightest interest in your side of the story. What I do want is for you to clear your desk and get out of my building as quickly as possible. Security are waiting in your office to escort you out of the building, and I shall expect you to leave your ID card and parking permit at reception.

'You are being dismissed on the grounds of gross misconduct and are not, therefore, entitled to a severance package of any kind. I have given our legal team advance warning of your departure, and they will happily tie you in legal knots should you have the affront to appeal the decision.

'As you know, Edward, I have considerable influence in this industry, and I can say with confidence that no other company within the sector will employ you, unless of course you foster a hankering to push a post-trolley around.

'Lastly, if I hear that you have come within ten miles of any member of my family, I will arrange for an acquaintance of mine, Mr Chisel Grimes to give your flashy car one of his none-too-subtle midnight-makeovers. Do I make myself clear?'

Maxie put his thumb and finger to his chin. 'I think that was about it. Did I leave anything out?'

Edward, whose face had gone as white as a bleached sheep in a blizzard, said nothing. Maxie's preface about possible inaccuracies in his rendition had been completely unnecessary - every word of the verbal assault, every mannerism, every gesture had been as the original.

Maxie laughed. 'I thought it was an outstanding performance - articulate, forceful and yet remarkably restrained in the circumstances. You have to admit – Charles gives good sacking! Now, Edward, I don't want you to think that Maxie is here to pass judgement on you, because nothing could be further from the truth. It is certainly not my place to point out the folly of your...how should I put it... little dalliance. We've all been tempted from time to time, haven't we?' He leaned forward and whispered: 'Although I wouldn't admit as much to Mrs Malleable.' Returning to full volume: 'Of course, I'd never do something quite as crass as to polish plums with Lysette Mason at her own engagement ball – you really must have taken extended leave of your senses that evening! It's a bit like that murder game, you know – Edward St. Claire...in the library...with the Chairman's daughter.' He laughed at his own joke. 'Anyway, as I said, I'm not here to pass judgement—'

'Then why the hell are you here?'

'Why...to offer you a job of course!'

* * *

2. A Vacancy in Vagrancy

'To offer me a job... you?' Edward gave an incredulous laugh.

Maxie smiled. 'Yes, I thought you might find that amusing, but don't worry—this isn't some menial, dead-end office job, and no—it doesn't involve pushing a post-trolley around. What I'm offering you is a truly outstanding opportunity where someone with your qualities can really shine in a fast-moving, dynamic environment.'

Edward eyed the man warily.

Have I misjudged the fat fool?

He folded his arms. 'Oh really, okay then - tell me about this *outstanding opportunity*.'

'Of course, of course! But first I do need to give you a bit of background... shall we walk a little?'

Edward held up his hands. 'No! Look, I've had a really bad day. Can you just tell me what this is all about?'

'Oh come now, young man – just a wee stroll. If I stand around for too long, I find that my bowels seize up.'

Edward winced and began walking.

'Three weeks ago,' Maxie began, 'an extraordinary meeting of the Flatpack on the Meander village committee was called to discuss a number of pressing items which, according to our Chair, could not wait until the regular biannual meeting. Oh! Look at that!' He bent down and picked up a large conker, buffed it on his shirt and held it up to the sun. 'The seed of the *Aesculus Hippocastanum*... and what a magnificent specimen! Do you know, I had a forty-three-er as a boy, earned me a lot of respect in the playground I can tell you - other boys would run and hide when they saw me arrive with my mighty weapon dangling.' He put the conker in his pocket.

'Now where was I? Oh yes – those 'pressing items.' He drew quotation marks in the air. 'Well, my personal view was that some of those 'pressing items', he repeated the gesture, 'could *indeed* have waited until a later date. In particular, I couldn't see the great urgency to review the village-green grass-cutting rota, and neither did I consider the distribution of the monies raised from Doug Punitive's sponsored shout to be all that pressing, but there you are - the Chair was insistent.'

Edward shifted from foot to foot.

'Even Councillor Mrs Git from the Greengrocers, who is normally as quiet as a mouse at our meetings, objected to missing her Shove-the-Slack tournament in order to debate the need for padded seating in the Cottage Abattoir—'

Oh, for Christ's sake...

'Look, I don't mean to be rude, but could you just tell me what the job is?'

Maxie raised his bushy brows. 'My – you are champing at the bit aren't you! I am impressed; I do like a man who's eager to get started! But you will have to be a bit patient, young Edward - I wouldn't be doing my job if I put the carthorse before the... err... before the... err...' He closed his eyes and held the bridge of his nose, 'Nope, it's no good – I can't remember that particular cliché, but you know what I mean don't you? Now where did I get up to?'

'You were about to tell me what the job is.'

'Was I?' Maxie's brows went from raised to furrowed. 'I don't think so.... no, wait - I was telling you about the extraordinary meeting, yes that's right. Now, there was one item on the agenda that we all agreed required urgent resolution, and that was the task of finding a replacement for dear old Ichabod Groove who passed away recently.'

'Oh, I'm sorry to hear that.'

His loss...

'Thank you, it was very sudden I have to say; one minute Ichabod was sitting outside The Weaver's Slouch catching some rays and enjoying one of Annie Gibbet's splendid greengage *tartelettes au gratin*, and the next, he was flat out on the village green having breathed his last.

'It was a while before we realised that he had actually departed; he was something of a drama queen and did have a penchant for simulating his own demise in places of public recreation. It was really only when his dog, Mr Lean, started licking Ichabod's face and he failed to respond that we realised something was wrong.

'Well, of course, Annie felt terrible. She was convinced that she'd poisoned him and swore that, once she'd finished doing the catering for the funeral, she would never bake another soft-fruit-based pastry.'

Edward was only half listening; his head was full of questions.

How the hell does he know me... and Veronica... and the kids? And how on earth did he know what slap-head Mason said to me?

'Anyway, getting back to the meeting, our Parish Clerk, Ethan Spurious reported that there had been a disappointing response to the advertisement placed in The Flatpack Observer, with only two villagers applying for the job. Between you and me Edward, I think the response would have been considerably better if he'd placed it under 'Situations Vacant,' rather than listing it in the 'Potted Herbs' category. In fact I made that very point to the Clerk.'

'Did you really?' Edward spoke the words with as much obvious disinterest as he could muster, in the vain hope that the windbag would take the hint.

'I most certainly did, and his explanation was that there were insufficient funds to place an announcement of Ichabod's death in 'Births, Deaths and Marriages,' and a separate advertisement for a replacement under 'Situations Vacant,' so a decision was made to amalgamate the two matters into a single notice. But then there were disagreements about the appropriate category in which to place the combined notice. In the end, it was felt that 'Potted Herbs' was a good compromise, and—'

Edward could take no more. 'Oh for God's sake, will you please just get to the point!'

Maxie looked startled, but then nodded his head. 'Yes... you're quite right, Edward, quite right - I do have a habit of prevaricating. It's something Mrs Malleable is always pulling me up about.' He smirked at a recollection, 'Like that time—'

Edward glared at him.

'Sorry, must keep my mind on the business in hand. Okay... Ethan went on to say that both applicants had been rejected, one because she was wearing an offensive hat, and the other because he was a border collie.

'Now, Edward, I do need to explain at this juncture, that Flatpack is a self-sufficient community; we grow our own, marry our own and bury our own, and when a job vacancy arises, we endeavour to employ our own. On this occasion, however, it was clear that we would need to fill the post from...' he paused for effect, '...the outside! So a motion was passed that Maxie,' he put his hands to his flabby chest, 'in his capacity as Senior External Recruitment Co-ordinator, should identify a suitable individual, get them to take the bait, then 'reel 'em in!' He performed a desperate charade of a fisherman landing a large fish, which caused his shirt to ride up and his trousers to slide down revealing a well-worn flowery undergarment.

Edward cringed and turned away.

Maxie hitched up his trousers as if nothing had happened. 'So I left the village on the following Monday and began making enquiries. I won't bore you with the details of my methods...'

Well, there's a first.

'...except to say that I spent the next few afternoons sharing some splendid pots of Darjeeling and rediscovering my passion for fondant fancies. By the Friday I was able to report back that I had found a suitable individual; I told the committee all about you, your background and strengths, generally 'bigged you up to the max,' he drew the quote marks in the air again, much to Edward's annoyance, 'and by the end of the conversation I could hear gooseberry-wine corks popping at the other end of the telephone.'

There was a pause.

'Is this the point at which you *finally* tell me what Ichabod Groove's job was?' Edward asked wearily.

'Oh yes, didn't I say? Ichabod was our resident Vagrant.'

* * *

3. Derek has a Bad Day

Edward rubbed his forehead. 'Did you *really* just say 'Vagrant'?'

'Yes Edward...'Vagrant', Ichabod was our official Gentleman of the Road... our Bum if you like.'

'So let me get this straight, you're offering me the job of a penniless tramp?'

Maxie looked hurt. 'On good lord no! Not penniless, dear me no! I'm actually rather pleased with the remuneration package that I negotiated on your behalf; the committee have agreed that you can start on a basic salary of,' he paused for effect, 'twenty-three thousand Brogues per annum!'

'Brogues'? What do you mean 'Brogues'? You're going to pay me in shoes?'

Maxie burst out laughing. 'No, no, no... Pah! That really would be an idiotic way to operate, wouldn't it? No, the currency of Flatpack is the Brogue. There are twelve Slacks in a Danish, and twenty-four Danish make one Brogue, do you see? Now, you will find that some of the older shopkeepers still price their wares in Cringes, and this is despite that particular coin being withdrawn from circulation several years ago... together with the Half-Dock and the Gregory. Would it help if I jotted this down for you?'

'Oh no, I'm memorising every word.'

The sarcasm was lost on Maxie. 'Good, good. Now, a Cringe was equal to one Brogue and five Slacks. It was a pointless and confusing coin, and I for one was glad to see the back of it, but you would not *believe* the outcry when its withdrawal was announced! There were protests and demonstrations, some of the villagers even staged a sit-in at the town hall would you believe! They plonked themselves down, linked arms and chanted: 'I whinge... you whinge... we all whinge to save the Cringe!'

'It was all fairly good-humoured to be honest, but after a couple of hours on that hard wooden floor, tempers began to fray and teacups began to fly. At that point, somebody had the good sense to call in Mrs Pynching from the Nursery School to try and talk some sense into the protesters.

'Now, Fuchsia has an impressive track record in resolving village disputes; she uses what she calls her 'Three A's technique', that's Abuse, Arbitration and Anchovies. It's a kind of carrot and stick approach, highly unorthodox but certainly effective. Do you know, she had those sentimental old fools eating out of her hand within thirty minutes of her arrival! Not only did they consent to the withdrawal of the Cringe, but they even agreed to pay for the damage caused by the flying crockery. And all they wanted in return was the re-introduction of the Adequate Shilling and the promise of a 'Farewell to the Cringe' street party!'

Maxie paused and looked at the younger man who was staring into space. 'Oh.' He slapped his forehead. 'I forgot to give you a copy of the job description and contract.' He sunk his hand into his right trouser pocket and bought out a collection of fluff, boiled sweets and the conker. An examination of his left pocket produced a dubious handkerchief and a look of mild concern.

'Aha!' He thrust his hand into his shirt breast pocket and withdrew some crumpled papers. These he unfolded and flattened against his leg before passing them over.

Edward stared at the crowded, hand-written pages. Odd groups of words jumped out at him from the big blocks of text:

'A constant, reliable presence.'
'To instigate, exaggerate and circulate gossip.'
'A soothing source of sage counsel.'
'A good working knowledge of squirrels.'

A tide of redness surged up his neck.
'So, what do you think, Edward?' Maxie asked.

Edward let out a brief, involuntary chuckle. 'What do I think? he asks.'

He looked up from the papers, his face now crimson.

'I'll tell you what I think... Maxie... I think that someone really hates me! I think that it simply wasn't enough to see me get unceremoniously sacked this morning; this person wanted to find a way to make me feel small, really small. And what better way to achieve that than by sending the message that Edward St. Claire, former highflying sales executive, is now only fit for the job of a smelly village tramp!

'Let's face it, you have to be pretty vindictive to go to all the trouble of fabricating this ridiculous story, then employing some ham actor to deliver it.' He indicated Maxie with a gesture of derision. 'And even drawing up a vagrant's job description and contract, now that shows real contempt!

'It's actually quite an impressive achievement, to have organised this farce in the space of a few short hours... I'm intrigued to know who thought it up. It clearly wasn't you, Fatty; I've no doubt you just needed the work to fund a drink problem, although I do hope this person is paying you well; your performance today has really been most outstanding!'

He slapped the job-description against Maxie's chest and applauded, putting as much sarcasm as he could into every clap. 'I'm just sorry that no-one else was here to enjoy the show...' He stopped. 'Or were they? I wonder...'

He picked up a stick and marched over to a huge, solitary bush, the only significant piece of vegetation in the vicinity, and took an almighty swipe at it. 'I know you're there!' he shouted. 'The show's over, you can come out now!'

He parted the leaves and peered in, then turned back at Maxie, his eyes filled with rage. 'Of course, it's David Miller, isn't it!'

Maxie opened his mouth to respond, but Edward had returned his attention to the bush.

'Come on, Dave, this is your moment of triumph; surely you want to come out and kick me some more!'

A further wild swing.

'You never did equal my figures did you, you little worm? I saw you at your desk night after night, desperately phoning people in a pathetic attempt to catch me up! Do you want to know why you could never match my sales Dave? Well I'm going to tell you; it's because, Dave, you simply haven't got it - you don't have what it takes! It's all about charisma, Dave, a quality that you completely lack!'

These last words were accompanied by another assault. The bush, Derek, was getting a bit miffed by this point and resolved to retaliate should the attack continue.

'There's nobody there, Edward.' Maxie rested a kindly hand on the younger man's shoulder. Edward recoiled at the touch in a manner more suited to an amorous advance from a rabid tarantula.

He composed himself with an embarrassed cough and set off to make an examination of the far side of the bush. 'Oh he's there all right...' He disappeared around the back. 'That slime-ball wouldn't miss this.' There was the sound of more random thrashing.

After several minutes he re-emerged. 'Yeah...well, he's probably too busy moving his stuff into *my* office.'

4. Fourteen and a half Degrees from the Horizontal

Edward threw the stick to one side. 'What a mess... what a bloody-awful mess!'

'Something the matter?' Maxie asked with an air of genuine concern.

'Oh nothing much, I have no job and no prospect of finding another, my wife is going to drag me through the divorce courts, I'm going to lose my car and my house, my friends will disown me and my kids will hate me even more than they do already, that's all.'

Maxie raised his eyebrows. 'Ah yes... consequences, Edward, consequences. Isn't that a terrific word, 'consequences'? It has such a lovely rhythm - rather like a folk dance; dum - de dum - de dum - de dum - de con - se quen – ces dum - de dum - de...'

Edward glared at him.

'Dum de dum de... You know, you're a very lucky man.'

'Ha! How do you figure that?'

'Well, you're not actually going to have to face up to any of those consequences that you've just articulated. You are simply going to disappear.... poof!' He mimicked the discharge of a disappointing firework.

'Poof?'

'Like a snowflake on a spaniel, and nobody will have the vaguest idea where you've gone or what has become of you.' He leaned in. 'Not even the formidable Veronica.'

'Oh, you don't know my wife - she'd find me wherever I go.'

'*Not* ...if you come to Flatpack!'

'Oh really! So what's so special about this Flat Pack? Where is it anyway?'

Maxie raised his eyebrows. 'Oh not far, walking distance... I can show you the route if you like.' He took Edward's arm and turned him to face the stunning panorama.

Edward pulled his arm away. 'Will you *please* stop touching me!'

Maxie held his hands up. 'As you wish, Edward, as you wish. Do you know, that's exactly what Mrs Malleable keeps saying to me... she doesn't mean it, of course.'

Bet she does.

'Now let me show you the route; firstly you need to make your way to the bottom of this hill – it's a pleasant stroll providing you navigate the splats.' He looked down at Edward's gleaming shoes. 'Those really are a splendid pair; it would be a crime to see them caked in sh... manure.

'After about ten minutes, it's a good idea to break into a trot – you're going to need a good run-up to jump the river.'

Edward opened his mouth to speak, then realised that he didn't care enough to pose any question.

'Next, climb up the bank and you'll find yourself on the edge of Farmer Rosser's oat field. Now, tell me, can you see that five-bar gate?' He pointed to the opposite side of the field.

Edward nodded.

'Well you may be tempted to cut through the crops to reach it, but I strongly recommend that you resist the urge. Stick to the outer edge, and when you do reach the gate, you'll notice that some young scamp has carved the words 'Farmer Rosser is an absolute tosser,' into the wood. Now, normally I wouldn't condone such vandalism but, having had a colourful exchange with Farmer Rosser when I myself took a short cut through his barley field, I have some sympathy with the sentiment.

'Anyway, climb over the gate, turn right and after a few paces you'll come to an old stile. Be careful – it's very wobbly and there are some spiteful blackthorn bushes on either side which are capable of ruining a perfectly serviceable blazer... as I discovered to my cost. I wasn't Mr Popular that night, I can tell you.

'There's an animal track on the other side which will lead you through a delightful wildflower meadow, past a line of poplars and into a small wood, do you see? The locals call it Skinner's Copse after a young lad who went missing in the area and was never seen again... such a sad story.

'When you come out the other side, you'll see a heart-shaped lake directly in front of you; there are usually some elderly sheep paddling in the shallows. And that, my friend, is the source of the Meander.'

Edward peered into the distance. 'So where's the village?'

'Why, right next to the lake.'

Edward looked again. 'Well I don't see it.'

'Pah! I should hope not! Can you imagine all the undesirables that would descend on the village if every Tom, Dick and Edward could see it! No, obviously you can't *see* the village – due to the angle.'

'The Angle?'

'Yes, fourteen and a half degrees from the horizontal to be precise.'

Edward shook his head, 'You've completely lost me.'

'Yes... I'm not surprised, but don't worry – it will all become as clear as a cucumber in no time. Listen, do you mind if I sit down, I'm not used to standing for long periods - I'm more of a well-cushioned recliner and pouffe man myself.'

'You surprise me,' Edward muttered under his breath.

'Pah!' Maxie pointed at him. 'You have a quick wit young man – I like that!' He lowered himself onto the long grass and kicked off his shoes to reveal a sturdy, well-darned pair of socks. 'Ahhhh, that's a treat.' He wiggled his toes. 'Do join me, Edward.'

'I'd rather stand.'

'Oh come now, humour old Maxie.' He patted the grass.

Edward looked at the spot indicated. Then, leaving a much wider gap than the pat had allowed, sat.

'Now, where was I? Oh yes – the angle. Tell you what, let me give you a demonstration.' Maxie positioned himself in a kneeling position facing Edward and placed his hands on either side of the younger man's head.

Many years before, Edward had attended a corporate stress-management workshop at which a grey-haired man in a matching grey suit had made a presentation entitled, 'The primal 'fight or flight' response to real or perceived threats'. Edward had spent the duration doodling an unkind caricature. Afterwards he consigned the memory to a rarely-visited region of his brain's Limbic Experience-Library, labelled 'Boring and Useless'.

Oh my God – he's going to kiss me!

Edward leapt to his feet with an expression of absolute horror.

Maxie emitted a sigh of irritation. 'Edward... how am I supposed to demonstrate something to you when you leap about like a naughty schoolboy? Oh... I see, you thought...oh, good God, man, I'm not a pantywaist, you know! Now sit!'

Edward lowered himself... slowly and with a fist clenched behind his back. A smile played on Maxie's lips as he replaced his hands. 'I must remember to tell Mrs Malleable about that, how she'll laugh!' He tilted Edward's head down towards his left shoulder.

Meanwhile, the memory of the fight or flight presentation was preparing for its afternoon doze when it was snatched from the Experience Library and transferred at great speed to the pre-frontal lobe where it was subjected to a frantic interrogation. Based on the results, Edward was now doing equally-frantic deep-breathing exercises.

Maxie removed his hands with great care, like he had just put the final touch to a playing-card pyramid. 'There we are; fourteen and a half degrees from the horizontal, marvellous. It's remarkable what you can achieve with a rudimentary bit of geometry, don't you think?'

'I wouldn't know.' Edward was just relieved that Maxie was no longer touching him.

'Oh, and one other thing that I must mention; you will be required to adopt the name 'Jack' upon your arrival in the village, and the children will refer to you as 'Mad Uncle Jack'.'

'Any particular reason, or simply to add to my humiliation?'

'Oh, just tradition, Edward; it all started about a century ago when the incumbent was very, very mad indeed, and in his case the nickname was entirely appropriate. He only ever used two words - 'cumbersome' and 'twat', and would form huge sentences that, to him, made perfect sense. I've tried it myself, and you end up saying 'cat' and 'twumbersome' after a while. Now, Edward, if you'll excuse an old man with a weak bladder, it's my turn to go round the back of that bush.'

He stood up and winced. 'Ooh! I really should have resisted that third glass of *Le Baiser du Blaireau*, but it did go *so* well with the game platter.' He made hurried strides towards Derek.

* * *

5. Wagging, Tugging and Growling

Left alone, Edward dropped his shoulders and returned his head to the vertical. He felt weary, as though his brain had been stretched beyond its normal limits of elasticity.

The workshop memory trudged grumpily down the spongy corridors to its quarters. It was aware of an unusual stillness in Edward's head; there were no electrical pulses carrying manipulative sales initiatives, no competitive interplay between the hemispheres, no storming session in the *parietal sulcus* and, most surprisingly, no lecherous images of Mandy from Payroll. The only sound that echoed around the chambers was 'Whir-heep, tickaticka, chee-har, chee-har, chakchakchak.' In the absence of any mental activity, Edward was being forced to listen to the mating dirge of a Mexican Curve-billed Thrasher, the dreariness of which needs to be heard to be fully appreciated.

Far off, Edward could see two figures crossing a field. They were accompanied by a blur of joyous vitality that charged around them, leaping its own height off the ground before racing off into the distance only to return moments later like a guided missile. Then war - man against wagging, tugging, growling animal to determine rightful ownership of a drool-sodden tennis ball.

Edward smiled and remembered Oscar.

He stroked the tall grasses, allowing them to tickle his palm, then plucked a top-heavy strand and held it up.

Summer tree

Pinching the shaft, he ran his thumb-nail and finger up its length, capturing the lilac seeds.

Winter tree... bunch of flowers

He flicked the seeds into the air

April showers

He placed the grass between his teeth - a familiar crunch and taste, then tapped the grass up and down with his tongue.

Nearby, clutching one of several blades that were gathered together by a foam of cuckoo-spit, a tiny hopper stretched its back leg. Edward copied the movement, and hundreds of identical insects leaped into view... then blended.

It must be those creatures that produce those balls of froth.

This train of thought came to an abrupt halt.

What the hell! Why am I thinking this garbage? Who gives a toss about grasshoppers? He kicked out at the grasses.

'You're starting to feel again!' Maxie called out as he returned from the bush wiping his hand on his trousers and looking smug. 'I knew you would!'

Edward stood up and brushed himself down. 'You don't know anything about me.'

Maxie smiled. 'I think we've already established that that isn't true. One thing that I most certainly do know is that you're going to make a splendid vagrant.'

'Oh will you stop going on about that sodding vacancy! It doesn't exist and neither does your stupid, invisible village!'

Maxie looked quite shocked by this outburst. He ran his fingers through his long-absent hair and continued in subdued tones. 'If that is what you believe, Edward, you'll be wanting to head off home then...'

'Yes, I will.'

Oh God, now he's sulking because I've insulted his precious imaginary village.

'But before you go, I would like to tell you a brief story.'

Oh for f...

'Some thirty years ago, after many previous attempts, the villagers finally succeeded in convincing old man Kafuffle that he needed to take on an apprentice. He's a proud man, is Maynard, he's been running the brewery single-handedly since his father died, and has produced some truly outstanding ales over the years.

Actually, I believe it was Maynard himself who came up with the slogan: 'If you want to avoid a most violent scuffle, then mind that you don't spill my pint of Kafuffle!'

'So, at the next committee meeting, the board discussed the matter and took the unusual decision to employ somebody suitable from 'the outside'. Similarly unusual was their pronouncement that the job of recruiting a trainee be assigned to a young man with no previous experience. Well, the boy was thrilled to be given such a responsible task. "I'll be back with the perfect man... or woman within three days," he announced, and saluted as he left the room.

'And, true to his word, three days later the boy strutted up Rump Hill with Jenny Darwin, a nineteen-year-old Fine-Art Graduate, at his side. Oh, how the villagers cheered! The boy thought his chest would burst with pride. I was that boy, Edward...'

Oh what a surprise.

'... and since then I've never looked back; I've brought in a schoolteacher, a haberdasher, a cattle-wench, two bridegrooms,' he counted the jobs on his fingers, 'a bastard, a bobbin-winder, three vicars, a gentleman... oh, the list goes on and on. I even employed our resident comedian!' A look of regret came over his face. 'Although that hasn't proved to be one of my biggest successes... rather took my eye off the ball there, you might say.

'Anyway, the point is that I've never been surer of a candidate's suitability than I am of yours, Edward. Believe me - I know a tramp when I see one!'

'Yes, but...' Edward began, but a smile was now tickling the side of his mouth, and despite his best suppressive efforts, it was determined to develop into a full-blown grin. He tried imagining dead kittens, but that didn't work. Worse still, he could feel the warning-tremors of an imminent giggle in his lower belly. He bit his cheek, but the laugh burst through his lips with unstoppable momentum - a primal, child-like sound, quite unlike the practised professional laugh he used when closing deals. 'Well Maxie, on that note...' He tried to talk through it but his voice just went all silly and high pitched. 'I'm going back to...' His shoulders shook and his lungs demanded more oxygen. 'What's left of my life...' A further surge of hysteria made it impossible to continue.

Needing no encouragement to join in, Maxie was soon belting out a hearty accompaniment.

At last, Edward regained control and extended his hand, feeling strangely euphoric. 'Goodbye Maxie, I hope you get the treatment you clearly need.'

Maxie clasped the hand firmly with both of his. 'Take care, Edward... and don't forget - fourteen and a half degrees from the horizontal!'

'As if I would!' Edward called behind him as he walked back in the direction of the B257.

* * *

6. Ridley's Practical Carpentry

Edward was deep in thought as he picked his way down the improvised path to the B257. On reaching the road he turned left.

Veronica's bound to have had a call from Gloria or one of the other brain-dead bimbos in marketing... I'll have to assume that she knows everything by now and come up with a good story. I just need to keep it simple, play it down, tell her it's all a big mistake... she's pretty gullible. Maybe suggest that she goes on another shopping trip with Hazel... that would get her out of my hair for a while...give me time to charm my way into another company. Mick owes me a favour...if he can get me into Trinity, I can work my way up quickly enough... plenty of decent skirt in that place as well...

The road bore to the right. Edward fumbled for his keys as he turned the corner... then stopped dead. Only yards from where he stood was something quite inexplicable, and something that cut through his thoughts like they were warm butter. It was impossible, it was absurd, it was... the end of the road! And not a gradual-petering-out-into-a-dirt-track kind of end, that would have made a degree of sense; this was an abrupt, unquestionable end to the tarmac. Mature trees leaned towards him from beyond, like buffers at a terminal.

But this is ridiculous...

He turned his back on it and powered in the opposite direction.

After several minutes of purposeful pacing, there was still no sign of his car; the road stretched out in front of him, straight and featureless. Edward stopped and put his hands on his hips. He looked all around, but it was what he saw in the direction from which he had just come that truly disturbed him; the end of the road was following him!

Never, in all his years of treadmill-pounding had he run quite like he did at that moment; this was no steady cardiovascular workout, but a panic-fuelled flight of fear.

What the hell is going on!

Mile after mile he ran. Maybe it was the uniform blandness of the road or the regularity of the conifers that lined it, but he felt a sensation of going absolutely nowhere. He persevered through the wall until finally, a combination of exhaustion and burning calves forced him to stop. His hammering heart sank as he turned and saw that the extremity had kept pace with him and appeared eager for a further pursuit.

'What the hell do you want?' he gasped. 'Why are you chasing me? What have you done with my car?!'

The end of the road hesitated and retreated a little.

Get a grip man, you're shouting at a lump of asphalt...

Edward began walking again, each step prompting a gravelly echo from behind. After a few paces, his attention was drawn to something light-coloured at the side of the road; a rectangular object with blurred edges and a translucent body. He could make out letters, thin black letters on a white background, but their fuzziness made them impossible to identify. He reached out and, finding cold metal, traced the raised shapes with his finger.

F... l... a...t...

'Oh you can't be serious!'

With a sigh, he tipped his head to an angle of fourteen and a half degrees from the horizontal, and the words sprang into sharp focus:

'Flatpack on the Meander - A warm welcome assured on Tuesdays and Fridays.'

His peripheral vision was filled with slate and granite; busy little buildings all different in shape and design lined the road and tumbled over each other, camp and chatty. From thrown-wide upstairs windows, a tangled waterfall of purple petals cascaded down the side of the nearest cottage, all but obscuring a whisk-wedged notice in a lower window which advised; *'Thursday tea will be on Wednesday. Sorry, no eggs - Simon has a cold.'*

Up ahead, Edward could see a partially-built village within a village; brightly striped tents and stalls, a marquee and flowers, everywhere flowers. In amongst the tents, and similarly bedecked, a gallows complete with noose stood tall. Around the village green, an amphitheatre of gabled, grey stone, washed in the pink-gold light, climbed in terraces to a gallery path. A single spire, dignified and correct, looked down.

This is completely impossible...

A large sleek cat appeared from behind a hedge, strolled up to Edward and began circling his legs, rubbing its face in an affectionate manner against his trouser, and purring loudly.

'Oh piss off, you scabby animal!' Edward kicked the cat to one side.

The cat steadied itself and gave Edward a cold stare, its tail swishing from side to side. 'Well that's just charming,' it said. 'I try to give you my best feline welcome and what do I get in return? Abuse and a physical assault!'

'Christ!' Edward recoiled.

'Oh it's much too late to bring up religious references, Jack; the damage has already been done!'

'No... I mean, I'm sorry... I didn't realise—'

'That I could speak English? No, well, I don't suppose you did.' The cat put its paw to its chin. 'And maybe I should make allowances for that... but that doesn't excuse your behaviour – we have a tradition of mutual respect around here... and laws to reinforce our traditions!' The cat paused, then continued in calmer tones. 'Anyway, let's put this unfortunate start behind us, shall we? I'm Hexagon and I'm what's left of your welcoming committee. You can call me 'Hex' if you like, but I'd rather you didn't – I do so dislike epithets. If you'd arrived an hour ago, there were quite a few villagers here to greet you, but you were very late and they all drifted away; there was a lot of grumbling about last-minute preparations for the big day.'

'But... you can speak...'

'Oh, all cats can speak, Jack; it's just that most are content with their single-word vocabulary and have no ambition to better themselves – I'm not like that. I mean, can you imagine how difficult it would be if you had to convey all of your needs, feelings, opinions and so on using just one word?'

'Err... very hard I would think.' Edward's head was spinning like the sails of a windmill in a violent gale.

'Too damn right! Fortunately my master, Atticus, is very perceptive; he recognised early that I had a desire to develop my vocabulary and coached me with the help of a copy of Ridley's Practical Carpentry. It's no great literary work, but I'll bet I know more about drills and corner-clamps than most oriental shorthairs of my age. I hear you're a big Coleridge man...'

Edward shook his head in an effort to restore some sanity. 'No... I'm not...that's not right... none of this is right...'

Hexagon looked concerned. 'You must be tired. I expect you've had an exhausting day, and tomorrow's not going to be any less demanding, I can tell you. Come on, I'll show you to your... err... lodgings. Follow me.' The cat walked off down the road, head and tail held high.

Edward hesitated, then felt something nudge his heel. 'Okay, okay, I'm going!'

***

7. Flatpack in the Morning— Vagrant's Warning

In the kitchen of number 27 Tantamount Street, Melanie Cartilage was applying dark, uncompromising marmalade to toast when her husband Rollace poked his head around the door.

'I'm just going to sing dear.'

'Okay Rollace, don't be long.'

Still in his pyjamas and with wood-blocks in hand, Rollace Cartilage climbed the stairs, entered the bathroom, opened the window and squeezed out onto the flat roof of his workshop. He took a deep breath of sweet morning air.

Three doors away, Barbara Knipflit poked her sleeping husband in the back. There was no response - a further poke. 'Wake up Miles, he's singing again!'

'Wh... What?'

'Rollace is singing that bloody-awful song about cowboys again!'

Miles Knipflit rolled onto his back and sighed. 'I can hear that, Barb; what exactly do you want me to do about it?'

'Well tell him to stop it! He knows the council's position on the performance of songs about spittoons and tin baths before ten.'

The sound of Rollace's whip-crack-away wood-block effects echoed across the village and entered the ears of Danvers Quiescence, thereby terminating a rather pleasant dream about Jenny Darwin from the brewery, and almost causing Danvers to fall off his branch. It would only have been a short drop of course, the grass below was lush and, well... it wouldn't have been the first time. He opened his eyes and was dazzled by the sun reflecting off Dahlia Brûlée's open bedroom window. Inside, Dahlia was sewing open-cup mushrooms onto a cotton sheet. She pricked her finger and let out a most uncharacteristic expletive.

The Flatpack Observer

On hearing the pained exclamation, the Reverend Carsten Spankie lowered his copy of *The Observer* and placed it carefully on his manicured lawn.

Caroline Spankie approached with a tray of tea and macaroons. 'What on earth was that?'

'Oh, that'll be Dahlia sewing open-cup mushrooms onto a sheet; I've told her many times that she should use common inkcaps or scarlet elf cups - so much safer.'

'Those red ones that we saw on our walk in the copse would be pretty; they always make me think of goblins and elves—'

The Reverend puffed his chest out. 'Fly Agarics, the home of the fairies they say, but it's the wrong time of year for flys.' He took a mouthful of macaroon and a mischievous smile appeared on his face. 'Maybe we could suggest that she uses shallots.'

'Shallots?' Caroline laughed. 'Oh Carsten, you are naughty!'

The sun listened in to this conversation until it got bored and turned its attention to Rump Hill, Flatpack's main thoroughfare, where it noticed that the village had a new arrival.

#

Edward opened one eye; a large fish was leaning over him.

'Aaargh!' He scrambled backwards into the shop doorway.

'Ah, you are awake, Jack, excellent!' the fish said. 'Listen - can I get your thoughts on this poem?'

It stepped back to reveal two red-stockinged legs with a pair of carpet slippers, and cleared its throat:

'Lord knows the madness of Millicent Thrush,
A vision in cinnamon, velveteen crush,
She married a turbot - a turbot called Herbert
And feeds it on bagels and pineapple sherbet.
She walks into town with a shoe on her head,
And sews up her nose with a needle and thread,

She sings about gizzards and Ilchester Cheese,
Then listens intently to everyone's knees.
For luncheon - banoffee with feathers and dung,
A glass of emulsion to steady the tongue,
Then home 'cross the meadows past berries of straw,
The tears of the willow, the thorn of the haw,
A supper of gravel with slices of 'cumber,
And several pies to ensure perfect slumber.

Now, I know what you're thinking, Jack.'

'You do?'

'The meter is a bit clumsy in line eleven, isn't it? Still, never mind, I have several hours to work on it. Thanks for your help, have a nice Grunt.'

Edward watched as the fish walked up the hill, continuing to recite the piece with flamboyant fin-gestures. It turned left into a side road and, apart from three pigeons, Edward was left alone. The pigeons stood in the middle of the road staring at him with unblinking curiosity.

Directly opposite, 'Your Dead Meat' was closed and shuttered, with a colourful poster affixed that encouraged the reader to, 'Come and join the St Gruntle's Day fun - it should be a bit better this year.' Next door 'Hettie and Lettie's Herbal Heaven', a much larger enterprise, was in darkness behind some frilly nets. As there were no pavements, the shop doors opened straight onto the road, the surface of which resembled the topping of a particularly stodgy apple crumble.

Edward looked back at the pigeons who continued to gawp with such intensity that he felt compelled to ask: 'What?'

He was quite relieved when they failed to reply. It then occurred to him that the birds were in fact looking beyond him at the shop door. He turned and read the words *'Flatpack Pies - The Pies that pack a Punch!'*

The Flatpack Observer

* * *

8. Puffs, Pancakes and Wooden Sandwiches

'Eh...what?' Edward awoke once again, this time with the aid of a forceful shake and a woman's voice.

'Good grief, Jack, there you are - we've all been waiting for you!' She took Edward's arm and pulled him to his feet, then stepped back to consider the new arrival. Edward wobbled and struggled to remember who and where he was. In front of him, a stocky woman in coarse tweeds and brown lace-ups that looked far too tight, was inspecting him. She furrowed her forehead, and her dense eyebrows met in the middle. 'Oh this won't do,' she tutted, 'this won't do at all!' A large clothes-brush appeared and Edward's crumpled jacket was subjected to a vigorous pummelling. 'I blame Maxie, you know; he knows how important the handover of new arrivals is, and yet I find you asleep in my shop doorway with no mentor or schedule. It really isn't good enough! And why he couldn't have brought you in a week ago is beyond me - today of all days!' She returned the brush to an inside pocket, straightened Edward's tie then finger-combed his hair to one side. 'Well, that's the best I can do, come along.' She locked Edward's arm in hers and marched him off down the hill.

'What's going on… there was a fish… it recited poetry…who are you?'

'I'm Annie, and the fish was… Renston.' She raised her eyes to the heavens and shook her head. 'Honestly, a funeral director in a red herring costume – how undignified is that? He wears it every year you know – nobody knows why. Oh, and those godawful poems… did he recite 'The Grernock' to you?'

'The Grernock?'

'Hmmm... obviously not, you'd know if he had – it goes on for about half an hour. He calls it his 'cautionary verse,' - I call it silly, self-indulgent nonsense. He tried it out on me once – half-way through I pretended to have an urgent batch of mutton puffs in the oven. You had a lucky escape there!'

She's the poisoned-pie woman...

'You're Annie Gibbet...'

'Yes dear, and you're our new Jack.'

'I've heard about your tartlets... and the name's Edward by the way.'

Annie beamed. 'They are rather good if I say so myself. I was going to stop making them after that silly business with your predecessor Ichabod, but they are *so* popular... and at one brogue, five slacks a time, they simply leap off the shelf!'

Edward looked around at the deserted village. Down a side-street he could see Hexagon curled up on a welcome mat, an open book at his feet. Nearby, a huddle of children were playing jump-rope and jacks in the sunshine, their abandoned pram having spilled its hand-knitted occupant onto the road, button-eyes and a stitched-kiss mouth. Bunting criss-crossed the road from the pub-sign for The Anxious Flounder, (a depiction of a fish with a pint and an expression that spoke more of inebriation than anxiety,) to, at the far end, a pear-laden tree with nets stretched underneath to catch early fallers. In windows, on walls, trees and doors, the St Gruntle's Day poster filled every space.

What have I done to deserve this?

'Where is everyone?'

'At the Parakeet of course, which is where you should have been an hour ago!' Annie upped the pace. As they passed through the aroma of a hurriedly-cooked and consumed breakfast, Edward became aware that he was extremely hungry. He started to hear voices, many voices - the unmistakeable buzz and bubble of an expectant crowd filled with excitement and anticipation. They turned a corner and were faced with a large green building with a sloping grass roof and a red beak protruding from the front. High on one side, an illuminated sign read 'The Flatpack Parakeet – the place with the groove and a mowable roov.' In front, a precarious-looking stage had been erected utilising an ancient farm wagon, several hay-bales and some fence-panels, with a sackcloth covering to disguise the perilous nature of the construction. Twenty rows of hard wooden chairs faced the stage, each of which was occupied by at least one villager's backside.

The crowd hushed as Annie hurried Edward up the centre aisle. He could hear whispers:

'He's over an hour late, you know.'

'Hedley will be furious.'

'That reminds me, we must get some more celery.'

Annie pointed to a single vacant seat in the front row and shooed Edward towards it; the chair was located between a smart middle-aged woman and an elderly, completely-naked man. Edward was horrified. 'I can't sit there! There's a....' but Annie was already squeezing her way down Row G, offering polite apologies as she went.

'It's okay,' the naked man piped up, 'it's reserved - Jack always sits here.' He indicated the word 'Jack' written in crayon on the chair.

Edward could feel a burning sensation on the back of his neck and realised that a couple of hundred pairs of eyes were willing him to sit down. With great care he perched on the lip of the seat, his legs pressing against those of the woman, the alternative being unthinkable. The naked man turned to face him and offered his hand. 'Trite.'

'What?'

'Bedford Trite, a pleasure to meet you, Jack.'

Edward eyed the man with distaste as he shook the one naked part with which he felt comfortable. 'It's Edward actually... and the pleasure's all mine.'

The Flatpack Observer

A gaunt, grey-faced man shuffled to the front of the stage, a stick in one hand and several grimy sheets of paper in the other. He surveyed the audience with barely-concealed contempt. 'What a bunch of losers,' he muttered, then hacked in a disgusting manner.

'So, do you fancy a chuckle!' he bellowed into the microphone, and nodded to a boy who was sitting at the side of the stage. The boy was feeding his delighted gerbil with huge pieces of fruitcake, and missed the signal. The man mouthed something unrepeatable and administered an impatient poke with his stick, which caused the boy to drop both cake and rodent as he jumped to his feet. He held aloft a large sign bearing the prompt, 'Give us a chuckle Chuck!'

There wasn't a sound from the audience.

Ah yes, now this must be the resident comedian that Maxie regrets bringing into the village. Looks like he's about to die on his feet... should be good for a laugh.

The comedian smouldered and mouthed the words, 'Inbred Cretins.' There was a creaking sound as he forced a smile to form on his face. 'Thank you, it's great to be here and to see so many familiar faces. Hey, there's Annie Gibbet.' He pointed to row G. 'I had one of her pies for my breakfast this morning, and guess what - I'm still alive! Now I call that a result!'

He paused for the expected laughter, but none was forthcoming.

'But seriously, I think Annie's pies and tarts are great - so much more effective than rat poison! They're not so much 'The pies that pack a punch' as 'The pies that pack a violent bodily assault!'

There was the rustle of a sweetie being removed from its wrapper, but otherwise nothing. Then a single peal of hearty laughter, easily recognisable as emanating from Maxie Malleable, filled the void.

'Thank you... oh look - there's Mrs Plenteous from Plague Cottages.' He indicated a blooming young woman in row L. 'I hear she's expecting another child - this'll be her eighth you know. I certainly hope this one's better looking than her daughter Felicia.

Honestly, that girl is so ugly that Farmer Rosser pins her picture to his scarecrow!'

A tangible atmosphere of brooding resentment was hovering over the heads of the genteel assemblage like a drizzle-laden cloud.

'And as for the mayor, that man has so many chins, he looks like he's staring at you over a stack of pancakes!'

A frail voice at the back was heard to ask, 'Did he say pancakes?'

'Yes Mother, pancakes.'

'Oh... I'd like a pancake.'

Charlie glared at the audience like a tank commander taking aim at an opposing army, then scanned his last sheet before crumpling and discarding it. 'Well, you've been a wonderful audience.' The words appeared to stick in his throat like a ten-minute boiled egg. 'I'm Charlie 'Chuckles' Radweld, and I'm now going to pass you over to a man who needs no introduction, which is lucky because I've completely forgotten his name!'

Nothing.

'Your mayor... Hedley Gerald-Headley!'

Even before Charlie had finished introducing the mayor, the audience was on its feet, applauding, cheering, whistling and waving flags. A band started playing and children began dancing on the margins. A banner which read, 'There's only one Mayor Gerald-Headley! (as far as we know),' appeared from nowhere, then a chant of 'Hed-ley! Hed-ley! Hed-ley!' began, accompanied by the stomping of feet. An angry wave of purple flowed up Charlie's neck; he gave the crowd a last withering stare and stormed off the stage, kicking over his chair as he went.

After what seemed like an eternity, the mayor got to his feet, and the crowd erupted. The man was easily identifiable by his red civic robe and a ridiculously-large chain of office, items that he wore over a hairy three-piece suit with a huge knotted tie, the tightness of which had created a glistening overhang of neck fat. The outfit was topped off by the most tragic comb-over that Edward had ever seen. Clearly enjoying the hero-worship, the mayor walked slowly towards the microphone, stopping at the half-way point to do a strange robotic dance which produced a roar of laughter from the crowd, and caused Edward to cringe.

What a prat!

He looked around - every person with the exception of himself and the woman at his side, was leaping about like idiots, even Bedford Trite... Edward wished he hadn't looked.

Having milked every last drop of adulation from the crowd, the mayor did 'calm down' gestures and the villagers returned to their seats. He waited until there was complete silence before speaking.

'Friends, families, fellow pack-men and women, committee members, children...dogs.'

A smattering of laughter.

'Once again, I, your mayor, am here to open this, our annual celebration of the Grunt!'

Cries of 'Whoo!' and 'Go Hedley!'

'Can it really be twelve months since I last regaled you with my considerable ideas and reflectives on the morn of our special day? Hard to believe, I accept, but accept it we must - a year has indeed passed us past and here I stand once again, ready to inspire and provoke, to excite and stimulate you with a few brief words of wiseness.' A large well-thumbed pile of notes contradicted any suggestion of brevity.

'Now, I'm sure you will all remember my speech that I made at the opening of Mrs Precarious-Wildflower's splendid wooden-sandwich exhibition, in which I made some excruciating observations about life in our beloved village. 'We are a community,' I said, 'and at the centre of our community is the letter 'U'.' He paused, presumably to allow his audience to recall his previous speech.

'Well, since that day, many of you have come up to me and asked, 'Mr Mayor, what did those fine words mean? You must tell us more.' So, I am going to take this opportunity to expand my idea, clarify my words and exasperate a little.' He turned a page.

"'U' is at the heart of the word 'community', and you! And you! And you!' He jabbed his finger at random villagers. 'Without 'U' there would be no community; indeed we would be a commnity, and I don't think any of us would want that.'

There was a murmur of agreement and a shout of 'certainly not!'

'But also, dear friends', the mayor leaned on the podium, 'there is an 'I' in community. But who is this 'I' of which I speak of? Is it I, your beloved mayor? Is it Mr Radweld here?' He gestured to the overturned chair. 'Maybe it's Mrs Yawn from the chemist or one of Mrs Plenteous' children. The truth is, that we are all 'I's and 'U's in differing measurements, and that is as it should be.

'And yet... I remain troubled that there is only one 'U' in community. I have given his matter much soul-scratching and have an important announcement to make: from this day forthwards, we will be replacing the 'I' in community with a second 'U', and I firmly believe that our communuty will benefit from this change.'

He stepped back and waited. The villagers turned to one another and there was a rumble of muted debate. Occasionally, a discernible comment would poke its head above the rhubarb:

'An interesting idea.'

'Certainly has his finger on the village pulse.'

'But will it work in practice?'

A noticeable rise in pitch suggested that rapturous approval was imminent and, sure enough, the audience were soon back on their feet.

The mayor beamed, and turned to his next page. 'Now... many years ago, I found a parsnip at the side of the road...'

There was a ripple of recognition as would greet the opening bars of a familiar song, and a sigh of 'Oh for God's sake' from the woman sitting next to Edward. She squeezed his leg and leaned in towards him. 'Have you heard enough yet?'

* * *

9. Lady Sucks the Blues

Edward turned to face the woman;
Hmmm... not bad, I guess... a bit old but well preserved... clearly quite fit... half-decent breasts... not worth turning on the charm though... her breath's a bit floral... and what's the deal with those blue teeth?

'Let's take a fern break,' she whispered. 'Follow me.'

Taking his arm, she led Edward, crouching as they passed the stage, down an alleyway that ran the length of The Parakeet, then round to the back of the building.

Edward looked back. 'He'll notice we've gone—'

'Ha! Like you care!' The woman leaned against the back-wall of the night-club and began rummaging in her handbag. 'Anyway, the fool's just started the parsnip story so he won't notice anything for the next seven or eight minutes. He goes into a world of his own when he's telling that one!'

Edward looked around; they were standing in a deserted square. Apart from an ageing bench, three pristine dustbins and an olive tree, the roots of which were straining to break free from a wholly-inadequate pot, it was featureless. 'You've heard it before then?'

'Oh yes, he tells *that* story every year, usually more than once. In fact, he makes pretty much the same speech every year, give or take the odd stupid announcement or dreary anecdote.' She produced a small silver case, flipped it open and offered it to Edward. Inside were several delicate blue flowers.

'Err...no thanks.'

The woman shrugged, chose two flowers and crushed them between her fingers. She rubbed the resulting mess into her gums, then sucked in air through her teeth and closed her eyes. 'God, I'm going to need a lot of this stuff to get me through today.'

That is so gross...

'So why do you continue to come?'

She opened her eyes and turned to face him. 'Edward, the mayor's wife does not get the option of staying away!'

Edward stifled a laugh. 'What? You're married to that... to the mayor?'

'I'm glad you find it funny, but yes - I'm Angela Gerald-Headley... for my sins. And now you're wondering why this glamorous beauty is hitched to that deluded old bore.'

'Beauty' is pushing it.

'Something like that.'

'Well, believe it or not, Churchwarden Gerald-Headley was considered quite a catch twenty years ago - I thought I'd done really well for myself, and most of the villagers still think so. Anyway, that's enough about me, I want to hear what you think of your new home, Eddie-boy.'

'New home? This place? I'm not *staying* here!'

'Yes, you are, Edward!' This was said in the tone that a mother might use when informing her young son that, despite his theatrical cough, he *was* going to school. 'You see this,' Angela did a sweeping gesture, 'this is your whole world now. I know it's ghastly, but you're just going to have to get used to it.'

'Why, because those simpletons have decided that I'm going to be their next resident tramp? I don't think so! Once I've had something to eat, I'm outta here!'

'Oh really.' Angela folded her arms. 'And how exactly do you plan to do that?'

Edward walked to the centre of the square and looked all around. From what he could see through the gaps between the buildings, the village was completely encircled by steeply-rising fields dotted with spherical sheep.

Can't be that hard... can it?

'I plan to put one foot in front of the other. I managed to walk into this dump and I'm quite capable of walking straight back out again! I'll make my way to the next town and get a cab home from there.'

Angela rested a hand on his shoulder and gave him a sympathetic look. 'Oh you poor love, do you really think I would still be here if it were that simple? There is no 'next town' Edward, and all you will find beyond those fields are more fields. The only reason you were able to enter the village in the first place was because you availed yourself of the angle.'

'What do you mean?'

'I mean, you tilted your head to fourteen and a half degrees from the horizontal, didn't you?'

Edward shrugged. 'Maybe.'

'Not a good move, Edward. You were shafted from the moment you did that. I expect you're curious to know what the angle is all about.'

'Not particularly, but... if this angle got me in...'

'Oh, don't raise your hopes there, Edward; it's a one-way ticket. Yes, it gets you in, but that's it. I've spent many frustrating hours standing at the edge of the village tilting my head from side to side like some simple-minded idiot. Trust me, it doesn't work on exit.'

A piece of grass floated down from the Parakeet roof and landed on Edward's shoulder. Irritably, he brushed it away. 'But what about Maxie, he seems to come and go as he pleases?'

'Ah yes.' Angela's expression darkened at the mention of Maxie's name. 'Atticus... our self-styled External Recruitment Co-ordinator... or the twat with the cat as I prefer to call him. You're quite correct - he does, but then Atticus knows the secret... and guess what - Atticus ain't tellin'! Let's sit down for a minute and I'll tell you the whole story.' She gestured to the elderly bench. 'And I promise it's a better one than the Parsnip Story!'

* * *

10. The Facts in the Case of Squire Gossard Malleable

The bench groaned as the pair sat on it, both just off mid-centre.

Angela flipped open the silver case once again. 'You see, Atticus had an ancestor, the Squire Gossard Malleable. A bit of a rogue by all accounts; when he wasn't beating his servants and squandering the family fortune, he was fathering twenty-seven illegitimate children.' She chose another flower and worked the crumpled bloom into every corner of her mouth, then wiped her fingers on a discoloured handkerchief. She shuffled closer to Edward, to the point where their knees were touching.

Yeah, yeah, yeah, I get the message - you've got the hots for me. Hardly surprising really – I bet the mayor's more interested in writing stupid speeches than in servicing the Lady Mayoress.

'One winter evening,' Angela continued, 'frustrated by his lack of success with the blacksmith's wife, the Squire broke into Kafuffle's cask-room and set about drinking it dry. In the early hours of the following morning, he burst forth through the cellar doors in a foul, ale-fuelled rage and staggered around the streets hurling stones and unholy abuse up at the bedroom windows. Well, of course none of the villagers dared confront him in such a state, and the barrage of invective and missiles continued for quite some time... but then it stopped quite suddenly, mid-curse. A few brave faces peered out, but there was no sign of the Squire, and neither did he appear the following day, or the next.'

'So, where had he gone?'

'That's the point - nobody knew.' Angela spat out a blob of blue spit; Edward shuddered and then noticed the abundance of circular blue stains around the square.

'As the weeks went by, the villagers came up with a number of explanations: that the Squire had been flattened beyond recognition by a single enormous hailstone, that he had fallen down one of the many potholes on Rump Hill, even that he had spontaneously combusted due to the strength of Kafuffle's Winter-Warmer. Either way, they weren't sorry to see the back of him, and didn't feel in the least inclined to organise a search. It must have come as a big disappointment when he reappeared just as suddenly, laden with valuables of all kinds and flatly refusing to discuss his recent whereabouts. Anyone who did have the cheek to ask where he'd been, found their rent quadrupled overnight.'

Edward was wondering where this was leading and what it had to do with him, when his thoughts were interrupted by a roar of laughter from the other end of the alleyway, followed by enthusiastic applause. 'I think your husband's finished the parsnip story.'

Angela rested her hand on his leg, leaned forward and listened. 'No, it's ok, he's just reached the 'flying cassock' section, that's about the mid-point.' She raised her eyes and looked lustfully into Edward's. 'Do you know that you have very defined leg muscles?'

Edward stiffened, not entirely comfortable with a stranger, albeit a woman, examining his muscle grooves. 'I've been doing a lot of work on my quads recently.'

'Ah… down the gym no doubt – we don't have such luxuries. Mind you, Edward, I manage to keep myself fit… in other ways.' She winked.

Edward was keen to change the subject. 'How come you don't call me Jack like the others?'

'Why should I?' She took her hand off his leg. 'It's not your name, and I can't be bothered with their stupid traditions! Now, come on, I need to tell you the rest of the story or we'll run out of time.'

She took a deep breath. 'Okay… so, once again, the villagers' sad little lives were disrupted by this foul-mouthed lech and his crude behaviour. I have to say, he actually sounds quite fun - we could really do with someone like that in Flatpack these days, someone with balls who could shake some life into this dreary place... how about it Eddy, do you fancy the job?'

Christ, she doesn't give up...

'I told you – I'm not staying.'

Angela sighed and gave him a look of regret. 'Ah well - worth a try... anyway, after a few more drunken incidents, the villagers found themselves wishing that the Squire would just disappear once again... which he obligingly did!

'Now, this time an uneasy calm followed; few clung to the hope that he had gone for good and, sure enough, he soon reappeared with two bulging sacks and a self-satisfied grin.

'After that, his behaviour sank to new lows - one Sunday he marched into church during the morning sermon, urinated in the font, then sat at the back heckling and throwing acorns. Later the same day, he exposed himself to the baker and his wife, and demanded that all future loaves be baked in the shape of his manhood, and threatened them with heavy fines for any that didn't flatter him.'

Angela paused to pick at her teeth; she withdrew something with a cobalt hue and flicked it away. A wide-eyed sparrow flew down from the olive tree and hopped around the morsel several times before departing with an expression of disgust.

'The day before a posse of Flatpack's finest strung Gossard up from a sturdy oak, he confided in his one legitimate son Hallard that he had discovered a kind of gateway that led from the streets of Flatpack to another world, one of curvaceous women and limitless riches. On the night of his first disappearance, he had stumbled through the gateway quite by accident and found himself on the streets of a town that clearly wasn't Flatpack.'

Edward was only half-listening; his mind was on his escape, and his stomach. He felt hungry and light-headed, and craved an energy bar.

It could be a long walk, I need to get something inside me... doesn't matter what, as long as it's not one of that woman's killer pies... bet they live on crap here – fried food and milky puddings – eugh! Probably haven't discovered...

He was wrenched out of his reverie by the sudden realisation that he was staring down Angela's cleavage, and that she had stopped talking.

'I'm sorry, I...' He jumped to his feet and turned to face the nightclub wall, pretending to be hugely interested in a sign that read, *'The Management encourage you to fern freely in this square. Please respect our neighbours by sucking quietly after 8pm.'*

'Oh, don't apologise,' Angela purred and spread herself out on the bench. 'I'm glad that I please you, young man.'

'No, you don't... I mean, you do... but I wasn't intentionally looking at your –'

'Oh don't spoil it, Edward! Have you any idea how long it's been since a real man paid me any attention?'

Edward said nothing; he read the sign again.

'Well anyway,' Angela snapped the case shut and stood up, 'we need to get back. I'll tell you the rest of the story on the way.'

They walked slowly back up the alleyway. 'So, on the night before he was lynched, Gossard revealed to his son Hallard that, having found himself transported to a new town, he began ingratiating himself with the locals, particularly targeting the wealthy and attractive. Within a few days, he'd charmed his way into their homes, fleeced them of their valuables and virtue, and disappeared into the night. He made Hallard swear never to divulge the location of the gateway to the villagers, but only to reveal it to a single favoured child on his deathbed.

'Now, unlike his giant of a father, Hallard was a man of moderation; a glass of sweet white wine – but never a second, the company of ladies – but never to excess. He was polite and courteous - in short, he was dull. I think he may have made a couple of excursions through the gateway, but only brought back a bottle of elderflower cordial and... oh, I don't know, some drawer liners or something. With his dying breath, he told the secret to his son, and it's been passed down through the Malleable generations ever since.'

'To Maxie?'

'To Maxie.'

Well, that's worth knowing; if there is something preventing me from simply walking out of this dump, I can always beat the secret out of Maxie...

'Let me guess,' Angela said. 'You're now planning to beat up Atticus.'

How did she know that?

'No, of course I'm not!'

Angela gave him a knowing smile. 'Well, good luck there; I've tried

bribing him with everything from fondant fancies to sex.'

They re-took their seats - there were a few disapproving grumbles from behind. Bedford Trite leaned toward Edward and whispered, 'You're just in time for the punch line.'

* * *

11. There will be no Nipples this Year

Edward looked up at the mayor, who was redder in the face than before and clearly approaching the climax.

'There was a twang, and the parsnip flew across the church, narrowly missing Mr Trite on the organ, and completely demolished a tall stack of Ancient and Moderns! Well, I can tell you...' He tapped the podium, then conducted as the whole audience chanted in unison;

'That was the last time I wore braces to a funeral!'

Huge cheers, another standing ovation, tears rolled over cheeks and dripped off aching jaws. Edward heard an emotional voice several rows back say, 'His best parsnip ever!' Neighbours hugged and smiled and laughed some more. The mayor joined in the applause, then turned a page.

'Thank you, but now.... to heavier matters; I have, with regret, decided to cancel The Prominent Nipples performance this year.'

A unanimous, 'Ohhhh!'

'I know, I know, believe me I have debilitated long and hard on this matter; I do understand how much you all enjoyed their set last year, and trust me - I enjoy a bit of crossover thrash metal as much as I enjoy the next man.' He played an air-guitar in a manner so tragic that Edward simply couldn't watch. 'But... it has taken Mr Bacon and his team most of the year to repair the broken furniture and return the mouldings to their former glory, so I think we must learn to treat our town hall with a little more constipation in future. On the plus side, Reg Atkins and his semi-acoustic log band have agreed to step into the Nipples' shoes, so we can still end the day with a bit of a bogie.'

There was a mumble of reluctant acceptance. Angela nudged Edward and handed him a folded scrap of paper. He opened it and read, *'If you want a bit of fun, ask one of them to tell you about the year of the big forget, then watch their reaction.'*

'Next,' the mayor announced, 'it gives me great pleasure to tell you that Maxie Malleable has brought a fabulous new vagrant into our village - he's here in the Jack-seat, stand up Jack - don't be shy! Everybody, give our new vagrant a rousing Flatpack welcome!'

Edward stood up and turned to face his audience - row upon row of vacant, suspicious faces. The applause was polite, but stopped well-short of rousing.

Looks like I'm on probation.

'And Jack will have the time-honoured honour of pulling the lever to hang Dr Jeffries at about five o'clock. A word of advice Jack - you may want to pump the handle a couple of times, your predecessor complained that it was very sticky last year. That was before he died of course.'

Before Edward had a chance to voice his incomprehension, the mayor was winding up his painfully-overlong speech. 'Well, I think that's about it.' He shuffled his papers. 'It only remains for me to say... Have a nice Grunt!'

Thunderous applause.

* * *

12. The Water of Life

An apologetic bell tinkled apologetically above the door of Al Turd's Offy as Charlie Radweld burst through it. He ignored the arrows painted on the floor, designed to steer him past the Vintage Cabinet, the Bin Ends and the Home Distilling Kits, and went straight to the counter. Nobody was there; he snorted impatiently.

'Won't keep you a mo... just rinsing the empties,' a young, enthusiastic voice called out. It was actually rather less than a mo before a fresh-faced lad appeared, wiping his hands on a towel, 'Sorry to keep you waiting sir, how may I be of service?'

Charlie grunted, 'Where's Turd?'

'Oh, Uncle Al's up at the Parakeet like everyone else. He left me in charge to get some work-experience... I'm Timothy', he pointed to his name-badge which was pinned to a crisp t-shirt that bore the slogan, *'Drink Kafuffle's Ales—they get you drunk!'* This message was reinforced by a picture of Maynard Kafuffle giving a thumbs-up sign.

'Huh! I thought he'd know better. Give me one of those.' Charlie pointed at a shelf of bottles behind the boy. Timothy lifted one and read the label, 'The Infamous Shag is it sir? A fine choice—I believe that's Uncle's preferred tipple.'

Charlie slapped a filthy eight-brogue note on the counter, grasped the bottle and turned to go. His hand was on the door handle when Timothy called out, 'Thank you for your custom, sir. Have a nice grunt, sir!'

Charlie turned and fixed the boy with a bloodshot stare. 'If I do', he snarled, 'you'll be the first to know.'

The apologetic bell gave a terminal tinkle before dropping to the floor.

13. Tea and Pinochet

'I don't like the look of those clouds,' Hettie Dalliard announced as she put the final touches to a sugar-lump pyramid.

Twin sister Lettie stopped swirling the leaves, straightened up and scanned the magnificent, azure canvas above their heads. 'I think you may be mistaken dear.'

Hettie sighed. 'Look again little sister.'

Lettie had earned the soubriquet 'Little' by virtue of being born seventeen minutes after Hettie. By the time the twins were twelve, Lettie was the tallest child in school, and towered over her sibling, peers and most of the teachers. The inappropriate nature of the nickname soon became the subject of 'over the fence whilst pegging out the washing' gossip, which in turn developed into full-scale tea-room debate. Eventually, the village council passed a motion outlawing future use, and a notice was placed in The Observer to this effect. Unfortunately, the nickname had stuck and, now in her 70s, Lettie remained 'Little.' Hettie had never had a nickname; her sister called her 'Tortoise' for a while in retaliation for the 'Little' jibes, but this never caught on.

Little Lettie craned her neck, turned a full three hundred and sixty degrees and was about to make a similar statement to her last one when she spotted a small feathery blemish floating harmlessly above the spot where Scurvy the Pirate, (Mr Molar from the confectioners,) was nailing the slogan, *'Yo ho ho and premature tetracycline stains,'* above his brightly-coloured sweeties stall. 'Oh really sister, that little chap won't give us any trouble.'

'That 'little chap',' Hettie explained in a deep burgundy voice that matched her blazer, 'is a cirrus, and you should never trust a cirrus - they are the deceptively-meek offspring of the cumulonimbus. If you see one out on its own, you can be pretty sure that it's not-so-meek parents will soon come looking for it, and before you know it the whole extended family has arrived.'

'An extended family of clouds?' Lettie laughed. 'That's fanciful even for you!'

'Oh! I'm being fanciful am I? Well little sister,' Hettie puffed out her ample bosom, a bosom that more than compensated for her lack of height, 'maybe you will be less inclined to scoff after you hear what happened to me last night; I had a visitor... Maisie Wittering no less! I was just getting ready for bed when—'

'Oh how lovely!' Lettie squeaked. 'I haven't seen Maisie in ages. If I'd known she was coming around, I could have brought over a flagon of my radish soup. Maisie was always so complimentary about—'

'I do wish you wouldn't interrupt me like that, Leticia! You're always doing it you know - you wait until I've got something really important to tell you, and then you start prattling on about your soups or some new hat you've bought or... oh I don't know... something someone said at the watercolour circle... it is a most discourteous habit!'

'Sorry, Hettie.'

'Now will you please prepare a pot of the Urbane Umber and listen to what I have to say.'

Hettie watched, arms crossed, as her sister selected a large brown pot from many that lay on the grass beneath their long-suffering trestle table and began ladling tea into it. 'Okay, so...I'd given Fulton his coley portion and was just about to blow out my candle when there was this urgent rapping on the front door. I nearly jumped out of my skin, I can tell you. 'Who on earth can that be at this time of night?' I thought. So I put on my house-coat and went to investigate, and there was Maisie, as white as a sheet and shaking from head to toe.

'Good Heavens, Maisie!' I said, 'Whatever's the matter?' Do you know, she didn't even answer, didn't say a word; she just stared into space like she was in some kind of trance. Well, I couldn't just leave her out there could I so I took her hand, led her to the best chair and went to put on a strong pot of the Ladies' Squat Bracer.'

Lettie listened quietly, anxious not to incur her elder sister's wrath again. She removed the lid of the industrial-sized kettle and filled it from an equally-huge plastic water container, then placed the plug on the grass, turned the pins downwards and stamped it into the earth; the kettle immediately started rumbling and fizzing.

'When I came back in,' Hettie continued, 'Fulton had curled up on her lap and was washing himself... the way he does. Well, you know Maisie can't stand cats, but I don't think she'd even noticed he was there! Anyway, I put the tray on a side-table and encouraged her to take a sip. 'It's the bracer, dear,' I said, 'one of your favourites,' I said... Still nothing. After a few minutes of complete silence, I thought to myself, *I'm going to have to take the bull by the horns*, and I asked her if Aldous had gone to hamster heaven.

'Oh no!' She suddenly snapped out of it. 'No Hettie,' she said, 'it's much worse than that, it's the bladder wrack you see, it's.... moist! Can you believe that... Moist! It's impossible... unthinkable... I must be wrong... and yet I've checked it... several times, and each time... it was moist! Why, I could have wrung it out... like a flannel... a moist flannel! No, no, no, this can't be right... I must be mistaken... but I'm not... It's moist! Don't you see what this means, Hettie?'

'Well, obviously I knew what it meant, and I was going to remind her that I did my thesis on bladder wracks, thong weeds and dadderlocks, but now I couldn't get a word in edgeways!

'There's going to be a storm, Hettie,' she said, 'a big bugger of a storm.' I'd never heard her use such language. 'The Grunt is going to be ruined... a complete wash-out... rain, Hettie... torrential rain... torrents of torrential rain... and a twister, yes, a twister... like the one I read about in the library... it's going to carry away the tents... and the livestock, and... the mayor – we need to tell the mayor; someone has to tell Hedley about the twister...'

Lettie giggled. 'You do such a good impersonation of Maisie.'

'This is no time for levity, sister! Poor Maisie, she was getting herself into a right old state, so I discretely grated some mellofish scales into her cup and tried to make light of it. 'I'm sure you are mistaken, dear', I told her. 'After all, we haven't had a drop of rain on St Gruntle's Day since 1976!' But she wouldn't have it, just kept wringing her hands and saying, 'the seaweed never lies!'

'In the end she made me promise to consult my breakfast leaves, that was what I was doing just before you arrived this morning; I had my usual cup of Robust Roger, swirled the dregs into the saucer, and wouldn't you know it – the leaves formed into an inverted cluster to the left of the handle!' Hettie looked up to gauge her sister's reaction; Lettie's expression was blank.

'You don't remember what an inverted cluster to the left of the handle indicates do you? Oh honestly, Lettie, have you forgotten everything I taught you?' She reached into a string bag and produced a dark, leather-bound volume of 'Pinochet's lore of Tassiography'. She flicked to the desired page and read aloud: *'An inverted cluster to the left of the handle symbolises a sustained period of stormy and inclement weather. Alternatively, this pattern can predict a dispute with a neighbour over the ownership of an oat-dibbing stick.'*

'So there you have it.' Hettie closed and tapped the book. 'You can't argue with Pinochet. Oh, and just in case you don't think that all these indicators are sufficient proof of the devastation that lies in store, then let me remind you that all of Farmer Rosser's Shorthorn Devonshires were lying down as we cycled past his big field this morning.'

'Maybe they were just hot,' Lettie whispered mischievously into the pot.

'I'll pretend I didn't hear that, Leticia, but I can see you're in one of your contrary-mary moods so I'll say no more on the subject, except that you will come to regret leaving your vest off this morning, you know that you should, *'ne'er cast a clout till August is out.'*

'Oh sister! That's May! Anyway, we're in September.'

'Even so... *'Behind September's manners mild – are tantrums like a sulky child.'*

Lettie suppressed a giggle. 'Well if you're right, dear, what shall we do?'

Hettie walked around the front of the stall and began sticking labels to the table: 'Course Blend', 'Old Flaky', 'Mrs Ward's Hammock' and 'Richmond's Maternal Ankle Tea'.

To the consternation of other stall-holders, the sisters had been allocated the much-sought-after prime-pitch, by the entrance to the green, next to the dung-gate, for a fifth consecutive year. When The Observer first published the stall plan, a number of unpleasant rumours began to circulate. Certain prominent committee members had, it was alleged, received free samples of the ladies' Dwarf-Bilberry Spirit-Lifter through the post, and this had explained the sounds of hysterical laughter, communal singing and party poppers that came from the town hall on the evening when the stall-allocation sub-committee sat. Any suggestion of bribery was dismissed by Hettie as sour grapes, and sales of the spirit-lifter soared as a result of the adverse publicity, (as did those for the ladies' sour-grape soother).

'We shall do, little sister, what we do every St. Gruntle's day - serve tea to our friends, and if the good Lord chooses to refresh us in his special way, we shall be thankful.'

Lettie went back to stirring the leaves. Hettie picked up a clipboard and walked around the front of the stall. 'Pots full and labelled – check,' she ticked the top box, 'cups, saucers and spoons precisely aligned and gleaming – check, milk-jug brimming – check, sugar lumps and buns in pleasing piles – check, little sister away with the faeries as usual – check.'

Happy that all was as it should be, she turned to face the buzzing hive that was the village green. Stalls that had languished, forgotten and unloved in leaky sheds for three hundred and sixty-four days were being subjected to frantic, last-minute cobweb-removal, botched repairs and paint jobs. At the far end of the green, Farmer Rosser was positioning his display of fertilizer-fireworks for his traditional 'End of the Evening Bang'. Hettie could see that the fireworks were already beginning to steam. Landlord Ganglion Reeves was reassuringly petting his donkey Maxwell, having secured the animal to a tree in readiness for children in blindfolds to pin tails on it. The Reverend's wife, Caroline Spankie sat in the pitch next to the tea stall counting garden peas into a large glass jar; a couple of times she lost count, cursed ever-so mildly, and began again. Taped to a tree behind her, a sign read, *'Guess the number of peas in the jar and win a pea.'*

Hettie put her hand to her mouth to disguise her amusement at spotting Ethan Spurious struggling to manoeuvre an over-loaded wheelbarrow across the green towards his *'Vast Vegetables and other Outsized Produce'* display. 'Yes,' she said to herself, 'let it rain – it would take more than a few drops of the wet stuff to spoil this perfect day.' Then her smile disappeared. 'I just pray that the leaves weren't hinting at something more sinister...'

*　*　*

14. The Coarseness of Strainers

The applause from the Parakeet finally abated. Hettie looked up at the sun and her expression showed that she was clearly impressed. 'A six-minute ovation! The Mayor must have really pulled out the stops this year.'

'Hedley does make a lovely speech,' Lettie said.

'He's a good speaker - I'll grant you that; there aren't many who can captivate an audience with a parsnip story.'

'Oh yes,' Lettie giggled. 'The parsnip story – I must have heard it …ooh… twenty times, and it still makes me laugh. Do you think it's true?'

'Of course it's true! Our mayor is an honest man… honest and decent… honest, decent and respectable… and sensible – always wears a vest you know… now you would never catch Hedley casting a clout before—'

Hettie was interrupted by the approach of a pair of red braces holding up the bottom half of a fish costume. Within, was Undertaker Renston Ardlish, a man with the physique of a lightning-struck willow and a face that had no place on such a sunny day. To look upon his features was to step back into the short, bleak days of winter, to feel the pitiless winds and near-frozen rain violating every tissue, to cower under a drear blanket and long for fruit and leaf, for laughter, maypoles and lusty dances.

'Good morning Mr Ardlish,' Lettie tinkled. 'What can I get you?'

A thin crack appeared in the chiselled, melancholy face, from which a contrastingly jaunty voice responded:

'Dear Lady, refreshment is that which I crave,
A cup that revives without intoxication,
A reminder of clippers on towering wave,

The Flatpack Observer

Calcutta to London, a drink for the nation.

"Come to afternoon tea, served with crumpet and scone,
Around four of the clock," read the Duchess' invite,
'Remember your hat, mustn't lower the tone,
We will sit on the lawn if the weather is bright.'

Edward got in line behind Renston.
Oh great, it's the fish-man again!

'A Victorian Lady with Gentleman friend,
A lump or a slice, prey - what do you take?
And how is your mother, is she on the mend?
A pleasant exchange over Battenberg cake.

'But... clink the cup sides, slurp tea from the spoon,
Or, heaven forbid, pour it into the saucer,
Place the spoon on the left, or whistle a tune,
Point with your utensils, oh what could be coarser?

'A crime against England! You would rightly be tried,
And sentenced to hanging until nearly dead,
Then dragged through the streets, to a cart you'd be tied,
Insulted, beheaded and dismember-ed'

Lettie tapped her palm with three elegant fingers. 'That was lovely Mr Ardlish - very nice. Would you like a cup of tea?'

'A cuplet of tea? What a splendid idea,
On a day such as this one should take it with ice,
So much more refreshing than a pintlet of beer,
Though a drop of the hard stuff would also be nice.

'A cuplet of tea? Oh my dear, you're a Saint!

Delicious and Golden, and certain to quench,
A thirst that is making me feel rather faint,
So pour forth from the spout, oh benevolent wench.'

The W-word didn't go down well with Lettie, but she quickly wiped away her expression of moderate offence. 'There you are, the first cup is free.'
'Free?' Renston's tone was one of disbelief.

'My dear, I feel thankfulness beyond expression,
A tear in my eye is now blurring the view,
And do be assured of my utmost discretion -
If they hear there's free tea, you will have such a queue!

'Now talking of tea brings to mind an occasion,
When, as a young man, I was learning to swim—'

Hettie intervened. 'I think seven verses is quite enough for this time in the morning, thank you, Renston. Enjoy your tea.'
The undertaker picked up his cup. His face was reverting to its unseasonal norm when he caught sight of Edward behind him in the queue. 'Why, Jack - how good to see you again. Have you got a moment to listen to me recite The Grernock?'
'The what?'
'The Grernock in the Copse... it's my cautionary verse. I'm sure you'll like it.'
I'd rather die...
'I'm afraid I haven't got time at the moment – I need to find Maxie.'
'Maxie eh?' Renston put his thumb and forefinger to his chin, then struck his performance pose.
'There's no-one more valuable
Than Atticus Malleable –'

'Renston!' Hettie barked, 'Jack wants tea, not poetry! Leave him alone!'

The undertaker ducked as if to avoid a low-flying missile. 'Better go - I'll catch up with you later.' He gave Edward a pat on the back, then added, 'Maybe you'll have some time after you've hanged Dr Jeffries.' With that, the fish-costume and braces ensemble departed.

Edward shook his head, then turned his attention to the tea stall. 'I'll take two of those buns and an espresso. I'm looking for Maxie, do you know where I can—'

'Why, Jack, how lovely to meet you,' Lettie offered her delicate hand. 'I'm Lettie and this is my big sister Hettie. We've been *so* looking forward to meeting you—'

'I'll deal with this.' Hettie stepped in front of her sister, a blocking tactic which had limited effect due to the height differential. 'Henrietta Dalliard, Chief Blender; good to meet you, Jack.' She gave Edward a manly handshake. 'You must excuse my sister, she's not very good with new people.' Hettie studied Edward's face. 'You look tired – slept in a doorway, I expect. Sister – pour Jack a cup of the Pagan Infusion, he looks like he needs it.'

'No really - I don't like tea, I just want to know where Maxie is.'

Too late, Lettie was already handing Edward the saucer with a schoolgirl grin. Their fingers touched and she flushed.

Why does nobody here listen to me!

Edward took a slurp and nearly fell over. Intense, muscular flavours marched around his mouth demanding the attention of his taste-buds, whilst an aroma of smoked herring and recently-forked compost cleared his sinuses like an over-zealous chimney sweep.

What the hell is in there?

Hettie continued to study him. 'That's one of my newer blends, Jack - I would value your honest opinion.'

Edward swallowed and immediately felt euphoric. 'Well, it certainly clears out the cobwebs.'

'You have cobwebs in your mouth? That sounds most unhygienic. Anyway, back to business; you say you're looking for Maxie. I'm afraid I haven't seen him...how about you, Sister?'

Hettie looked up; her sister was floating, hands-clasped in a daydream of admiration for the young man.

'Lettie!' Hettie snapped.

'Oh... err no, I haven't seen him either.'

Hettie frowned then turned back to Edward. 'You could try asking Mrs Plenteous over there, she's the one who's wearing her apron high.'

Edward scanned the tide of bodies that were arriving from the Parakeet; wave upon wave of flowing frocks, once-a-year hats and bouncing prams, a whole family in crayon-themed fancy dress, a tearful toddler on a pony and a stilt-walking clown twisting balloons into dinosaurs. A brief gap allowed Edward to spot a pregnant young woman standing by the striped marquee. He mumbled a thank you to the Dalliard sisters, went to leave, thought for a moment, then went back for his tea and buns.

Taking care not to spill the infusion, he fought his way through the dense throng. As he approached her, the heavily-pregnant woman turned to face him and smiled. 'I know exactly who you're looking for, Jack. Keep an eye on the girls, I won't be a moment.'

Mrs Plenteous disappeared through a flap in the marquee before Edward had a chance to say, 'No, wait... I don't *do* children!' He looked down; a ring of seven expectant faces looked up.

One of the girls was stroking a patch of grass. 'Here, Mr Jack, I've made you a seat.'

'No, *here*, Mr Jack, *mine's* got a cushion'. It was a large flat pebble.

Edward looked back at the marquee - there was no sign of their mother returning.

'Here, Mr Jack!'

'Here, Mr Jack!'

Edward considered making a run for it, then sighed and lowered himself onto the un-cushioned patch. 'This'll be fine.'

The spurned girl folded her arms and pouted. 'I wanted Mr Jack to sit here.'

'Well Mr Jack wants to sit next to me, so there.' There was an exchange of extended tongues. 'Isn't that right, Mr Jack?'

'Actually it's Edw... oh never mind. Anyway, I thought you were meant to call me Mad Uncle Jack.'

'Oh no, we don't know if we like you yet, Mr Jack. Now... I'm Merry, that's Daisy, that's Apple, that's Felicia, that's Catkin, that's Daisy 2,' indicating the huffy girl, 'and that's-'

Daisy 2 burst into 'Merry loves Ja-ack, Merry loves Ja-ack! The other girls joined in.

'I do not!' Anyway Mr Jack is married.'

'Have you got a wife, Mr Jack?'

'Is she pretty, Mr Jack?'

'Has she got big bosoms, Mr Jack?'

All but one of the girls succumbed to a fit of giggles. Apple turned her head to one side and looked up into Edward's eyes. 'You must be awfully sad, Mr Jack.'

'No... why would I be?'

'Because you're never going to see her again.'

'Of course I am! But... for your information, it suits me fine to spend a bit of time away from my wife. We've got a couple of things to... sort out.'

Merry patted Edward on the back, 'Never mind, Mr Jack, you'll find a new wife soon... but I'm only five.'

Daisy 1 raised a finger, 'I know, Mr Jack can marry Miss Pynching from the nursery!'

Edward snorted. 'Oh yes! That sounds like a great idea – me and Fuchsia Pynching. I've always wanted to be married to someone who settles disputes using anchovies!'

Daisy raised her eyes to the heavens. 'No, silly, I mean her daughter Primrose. She's Maid of the Grunt this year.'

Felicia was shaking her head vigorously, the ribbon on the end of her plait dancing like an excited butterfly. 'That won't work, Primrose is promised to Dan McGkroid.'

'Yes, but Dan's got a hairy wart. Mr Jack hasn't got a hairy wart. You haven't got a hairy wart have you, Mr Jack?'

Edward put his head in his hands. 'No, I haven't got a hairy wart.'

'That settles it. Mr Jack can marry Miss Pynching after he's hanged Dr Jeffries.'

'Ooh, can I be a bridesmaid, Mr Jack?'

'Ooh me!'

'Me!'

'Me!'

Seven arms reached for the sky.

The girls' mother reappeared. 'My, you're getting on like a house on fire! Maxie didn't mention that you were such a natural with children!'

'I'm not! I don't even like –'

'Yes, we've got it all sorted out.' Merry gave her mum a big hug. 'Mr Jack is going to marry Primrose Pynching after he's hanged the Doctor... and I'm going to be the Chief Bridesmaid!'

'What a lovely idea,' Mrs Plenteous said. 'That would make a perfect end to the day. Then we can all dance the Gruntle Hornpipe around the blowhole while the petals float down around our heads.'

They're all completely mad!

'Anyway, here we are.' Mrs Plenteous handed Edward a piece of string, the other end of which was attached to the collar of a dachshund.

'What's this?'

'Why, Mr Lean - your dog.'

'What? Oh no – I can't have another dog...'

'Oh don't be silly, Jack – didn't you read the job description and contract? She's a lovely girl, aren't you, Mr Lean?' Mrs Plenteous scratched the dog's head and she purred.

* * *

15. Oscar

A boy stood at the bottom of his garden; at his feet was a deep hole and, in his arms, he cradled a large white box. Above his head clouds, burdened and black, waited for the right moment.

'Come on Eddie,' a woman's voice called through the kitchen window. 'Put the box down now and come in for your tea... it's fish fingers!'

The boy pulled the box closer to his chest and looked up at the dark sky.

A louder, man's voice; 'Oh, for God's sake put the dog in the hole and get inside! Look—accidents happen, you need to get used to it! If I'd known you were going to act like this, I would never have bought you the damn animal... you're certainly never having another one!'

The first drop slapped the boy's cheek.

* * *

16. The Three Fields, (Part 1—The Wheat Field)

Two lengths of double-sided tape hung from the arm of Maxie Malleable's deckchair. He neatly folded a tea-towel into quarters and laid it in his lap. Removing one side of the backing paper from each strip, he stuck them to the tea-towel in the shape of a cross. It was then a simple matter of removing the remaining backing paper and sticking the tea-towel to his head. The application of a little pressure and the briefest of test-shakes later, he laid back, exhaled and closed his eyes. The sun kissed his flabby jowls.

At his feet, the Meander tinkled its merry melody. From some distance behind him, came a cacophony of merriment as the village let its hair down as far as its standards of decency would allow. The indecipherable hubbub was punctuated with cheers of delight, laughter, good humoured groans, the crack of wooden ball on coconut, of conker on conker. A man's voice: 'Well I never! I've won a pea!' Then the tap tap tap of a finger testing a microphone, the crackle of a needle hitting a groove, a scratchy accordion introduction, and a plummy voice sang;

'Old Nick he liked his butter thick,
Oh, butterman, butterman, butterman Nick,
He spread it thick upon—'

There was a howl of feedback and the music stopped abruptly, prompting a mix of cheers and grumbles. Next came a countdown, '5-4-3-2-1... lift off!' More cheers.

Edward, who had spotted Maxie by the river and was marching across the recreation ground towards him, turned his head to see around a hundred balloons, each with a brightly coloured sock attached, rising from bedroom windows into the perfect blue. He shook his head.

Simpletons.

He ignored the footpath that would have taken him via the swings, slide and tea-cup ride. Mr Lean bounced along at his side, showing every sign of being delighted with her new owner.

So this is where he's been hiding out. What the hell has he got on his head?

Before Edward had a chance to ask, Maxie spoke. 'Do you know, Edward, this is my favourite part of The Grunt; the bit between the mayor's speech and the arrival of the procession. I get a few short, leisurely moments to catch some rays, have a little paddle and enjoy my first pint of the day.' He held up a glass of murky liquid. 'I come here every year around this time… it's a little ritual of mine.'

'Oh really.' Edward tapped his foot.

It's a tea-towel!

'Well… you enjoy your *little ritual.* I just want you to tell me where the gateway is.'

Maxie stretched and yawned. 'Gateway, Edward?'

'Yes, you know – the gateway that allows you to escape this place. Please don't deny it – I had a long talk with the mayor's wife; she told me all about your ancestors and the big secret that's been handed down through the generations… blah blah blah. So, do me a favour: just tell me where it is and I'll get out of your hair.'

Maxie opened his eyes and pointed at Edward. 'Pah! Get out of my hair - that's a good one!' He peered at the bulges in Edward's jacket pockets. 'Are those buns?'

'What? Oh… yeah, they're the only thing I could find that passes as food in this place; I got them from those two old women at the tea stall.'

Maxie looked impressed. 'Well, I must say, you made a good choice there; I'm rather partial to Hettie's buns myself, although I must warn you that they are something of an acquired taste. Many people say the same of Mrs Malleable you know – rather drab and uninteresting on the outside but once you get beyond the characterless exterior, you discover something truly special within. Yes, I'm sure you'll find them a most uplifting experience.'

They're only buns for Christ's sake!

'The ladies told me that you'd paid a visit to their stall, and I understand that Little Lettie has something of a crush on you.' He raised an eyebrow.

Oh right, that'll be the one who looks like a giraffe.

'I have to say, they spoke about you in glowing terms... in fact you seem to have made a cracking good start generally. First impressions are really important, Edward, and everyone seems to be very taken with you.' He laughed. 'Especially the Plenteous girls! Oh, and I hear there are going to be some nuptials later.'

'Some poor sod's getting hitched then?'

'Why, yes Edward... you are, to Primrose Pynching.'

It was Edward's turn to laugh. 'Oh Maxie, you'll believe anything won't you! That just ain't gonna happen!'

'Really? Oh I am disappointed... and surprised - the village gossip network is normally so reliable when it comes to speculation of a marital nature... Mrs Yawn from the Chemist must be having an off-day. She really is a marvel you know, Edward; every day she collects up all the fragments of tittle-tattle, filters out any scurrilous or indelicate bits, then releases the juiciest morsels into the community where they spread like the pox! Do you know, if one of Farmer Rosser's Shorthorn Devonshires breaks wind around breakfast time, the whole village knows about it by elevenses. And by the time the story appears in The Observer... well, it's old news. Frankly, I wonder why we bother to have a newspaper at all. Personally I only buy it because Hexagon likes to browse the 'Readers' Rants', but after he's done with it, it goes straight in his litter tray!'

As Maxie rambled, Edward recalled the words of one of the Plenteous' girls to her mother. 'Jack is going to marry Primrose

Pynching after he's hanged Doctor Jeffries.' *What the hell was that all about?*

'Of course,' Maxie continued, 'back in the days before the network was established—'

Edward held his hands up, 'Look…just stop!' He let out a long sigh. 'Are you going to tell me where the gateway is or not?'

'Certainly not, Edward! Why, you could stick a hot poker up my backside and I wouldn't squeal.' He made a thrusting gesture to illustrate. 'Actually, that's probably not true – I imagine I would squeal rather a lot… but,' he raised a finger, 'I would *not* divulge the location of the gateway even if my life depended on it. Is this the point at which you rough me up a bit?'

Edward looked at the fat old man with a tea-towel stuck to his head, wearing nothing more than a pair of highly-polished brown lace-ups which looked suspiciously like ladies' shoes, some scarily-skimpy shorts and a discoloured string-vest, through which curls of silky, white chest-hair poked. He considered his previous plan to beat the truth out of the man and shuddered.

Eugh… that would mean touching him!

'Don't tempt me!'

'Well, I warn you, Edward, I'm a tough old turkey -- did a lot of boxing in my youth, you know.' Maxie stood up and adopted an old-fashioned manly, fisticuffs pose.

Oh this is ridiculous.

'Look… whatever. If you're not going to tell me, I'll find my own way home. I suppose it's asking too much for you to tell me where the road out of the village is?'

'Can't help you there either I'm afraid – we don't have one. Oh… do you mean the road that chased you? Well, if you recall, that road followed you in, and it's been here ever since. Quite a character actually.'

Edward ran his fingers through his hair. 'Ah yes, so it did.' He unwound the string from his wrist. 'Here, take the dog.'

'Oh no! Mr Lean needs a good walk, you take her along.' Maxie sat down again, adjusted the tea-towel and closed his eyes.

Edward looked down at the dog; big, adoring eyes looked back. He said nothing and wound the string back around his wrist, adding a couple of extra turns. 'Well, Maxie,' he said and then, adopting his best belittling tone, 'Have a good Grunt!'

'It's 'Have a *nice* Grunt', Edward, and *you* have a nice walk. If I'm not here when you get back, you'll find me in the beer tent. Tell you what – I'll buy you a pint of Maynard's festival ale – the Gruntle Gulp - it's quite outstanding this year!'

He really thinks I'm coming back. What a prat... 'The prat with the cat' *– Yeah, that just about sums him up.*

#

Two vaguely-curious sheep, who looked as though they'd never made the acquaintance of the shearing shed, stopped chewing as the man and dog passed. They'd seen a man before of course, but this one was more angular and shiny than the one they'd grown accustomed to - the one who made those annoying whistling noises. Also, this dog seemed remarkably chilled and didn't appear to want to chase them around in pointless circles.

Edward was determined to maintain his powerful stride despite the steep incline. It had been a full forty-eight hours since he'd been to the gym, and the resultant softening of his *rectus femoris* leg muscles was causing him concern. Power-walking up this steep hill would help, but what he really needed was a lengthy session on the Bulkitup Vertical Leg-Press Workstation. Not that he enjoyed his daily visit to the gym - on the contrary, he couldn't imagine how anyone could honestly enjoy forcing their body through the pain barrier, performing endless repetitions, spending time in the company of flabby, grunting losers, or changing in stinking locker-rooms where those same losers strutted around with their junk swaying. That said, nothing in the world would induce him to cancel his membership - that hour in the gym meant the admiration of women and the envy of men, so of course it was worth it.

As they approached the top of the hill, the gradient became even steeper; it was like climbing the inside of a giant tea-cup. Edward stepped over the lip and took in the view.

'Oh... you gotta be kidding me!' He turned a full three hundred and sixty degrees, his heart rapidly sinking. 'Oh, come on – this is ridiculous!'

There were no towns or villages to be seen, no roads or railway-lines, no pylons, phone-masts or vapour-trails... just fields - endless sodding fields... with a single dimple – the dimple that contained Flatpack on the Meander. Edward recalled the words of Angela Gerald-Headley:

'There *is* no next town, and all you will find beyond the fields are more fields.'

He dismissed this recollection as he would an insightful comment made by a lower-grade co-worker.

Naah – that's just stupid and impossible. Of course there's a next town, it's going to be a long walk, that's all – not a problem. If I keep going in a straight line, I'm bound to hit civilisation sooner or later.

He peeled off his jacket and tied the arms around his waist. A stench of re-heated sweat assaulted his nostrils. Mr Lean looked up at her owner with wide, excited eyes, and began sniffing and scratching the jacket pockets.

'What do you want dog? Oh... right.' Edward reached inside and broke off a bit of bun which Mr Lean devoured like it was prime sirloin. Edward also took a bite; it was as Maxie had described – drab and uninteresting, like a stale scone. He swallowed it with some difficulty then offered a second chunk to Mr Lean, and nearly lost several fingers in the process. Taking a second bite himself, Edward found this to be a distinct improvement on the first, as a liquid centre filled his mouth with stars.

He looked down at the village and was surprised to see that it was shrouded under a shimmering haze, with only the spire of St Gruntle's piercing the veil. This gave it the soft, sepia quality of an old postcard, needing only the words, *'Having a jolly time in Flatpack,'* to complete the picture. With the exception of the odd throaty bleat, no sounds rose up to Edward's ears, and neither could he discern any movement on the village green. It was a scene of stillness and peace that contradicted the reality that Flatpack on the Meander was a village partying hard. The more he stared at the rooftops, the more convinced he became that he could see right through the buildings to the fields beyond. It was a peculiar illusion but, having had a lengthy conversation with a cat the previous evening, nothing surprised him anymore.

The Meander melted into the haze; Edward smirked and imagined Maxie Malleable paddling in the river with the tea-towel still on his head. 'Well good bye Maxie, good bye Flatpack – it's been really average!' He turned his back and tugged the string. 'Come on, dog.'

Right... head for the sun, no deviations.

#

The pair stepped through a gap, one of many, in a poorly-maintained boundary hedge, and found themselves in a recently-reaped wheat-field dotted with bundles of old-fashioned sheaves waiting to be threshed. A wave of something pleasant, that Edward took to be nostalgia, washed over him. His thoughts drifted back to his choirboy days; the harvest festival service, wheat sheaves leaning against the alter, Christ on the cross looking down on a huge plaited loaf, a sack of muddy potatoes spilling onto the marble, singing 'We plough the fields and scatter' and slipping the communion wafer into his cassock pocket to feed to Oscar after the service.

Edward lowered himself onto the straw carpet, lay back on his elbows and released the string. The second he opened his fingers, Mr Lean was out of the blocks and tearing towards the nearest bundle of wheat. Having demolished this, she began digging and throwing clouds of straw into the air. Then off again – running in joyous circles, her tongue lolling and flapping. A smile stretched across Edward's face.

What an amazing dog she is... look at her go – faster than a greyhound, so full of energy and life.

The wheat sheaves seemed to be glowing under the golden sun. Edward noticed a large scythe lying on the ground next to the nearest bundle.

Why would anyone cut wheat by hand these days? It's like the painting by that Dutch guy who cut his ear off... now what was his name? I'll look it up when I get back... I could even enrol on an Art History evening class. Yes – that's what I'll do – it would be great to learn about the major artists and their work.

I really should improve my mind... Maxie reckoned that I'd like Coleridge... maybe he was right and I should start reading the work of the Romantics. Then I could start writing poetry myself, about, ooh... wheat fields... and small dogs, yes – The Playfulness of small dogs, that would make a great title. Gosh these shoes are so comfortable!

He reached forward and caressed the leather.

That's another thing I'll do when I get back -write to Panici and Russo and congratulate them on their artistry.

His smile broadened further to the point where his face-muscles ached. Nearby, an orange-beaked blackbird chirped its dreary and repetitive song.

What a beautiful sound! Surely that's the song of a nightingale... it must be! Oh why have I wasted my live obsessing over women and money when the world is full of such loveliness? Maybe I should go back to Flatpack - it wasn't that bad...

Deep in Edward's cerebral cortex, behind a door marked 'Default Settings,' an ear-splitting alarm was sounding. An elderly cell looked up from its newspaper and sighed a sigh of irritation. It laid down the paper and wobbled across the chamber towards a sign that read:

'In case of an uncharacteristic behavioural emergency, firmly press the benign lesion below. Fine for improper use: Withdrawal of Fantasy Storage Facility Access Permit.'

Moments later, Edward experienced a sharp, stabbing pain in his head and put his hands to his temples. 'Ow! What the f—?'

The pain subsided, but left behind a clarity of thought.

Something's not right here... why is my face aching? Have I been smiling? And why did I just resolve to write poetry? I hate poetry... and evening classes? In art? Do me a favour! What's got into me?

He looked over at Mr Lean who was still tearing around in endless circles.

And what's got into that stupid dog?

He clapped his hand to his forehead.

Oh I don't believe it – of course! It's those sodding buns!

'Those old witches must have spiked my buns!'

He caught hold of the trailing string and reined Mr Lean in. Then, keeping a firm hold on the string, withdrew the second bun from his pocket and threw it into the distance. As expected, the line immediately went taught. 'Leave it, dog!' he ordered.

* * *

(Part II—The Furnace Field)

Edward was still shaking his head in an effort to clear the bun-induced euphoria, when the pair came upon a fence. It was a tall fence—at least a foot taller than Edward and constructed from thick, vertical, dark-wood planks that seemed to go on forever in either direction. Edward glared at it and shook his head.

This is a sodding conspiracy.

He wasn't about to change his strategy - to continue to walk in a straight line until he reached civilisation was the plan and he was sticking with it, but now he had to make a decision. Should he try scaling the fence? It would be difficult but not impossible... ah, but then there was the dog to think of... no, that wasn't going to work. Maybe he could break down a section by means of a powerful shoulder-charge... that didn't appeal – it was good-quality hardwood and unlikely to yield.

With a view to considering his options, he leaned against the fence, and immediately fell through it. The sense of surprise was quickly overridden by a desperate need to remove himself from the hottest place he had ever encountered. 'Ch-rist!' He jumped to his feet and threw himself back through the man-with-flailing-arms shaped hole that he had just created.

From the relative coolness of the wheat field, Edward peered back through the hole; what lay beyond was less a field, more an arid wasteland, devoid of even the hardiest vegetation. A mosaic of bowed mud-platelets, randomly sprinkled with rocks and rodent-bones, stretched into the shimmering distance. The branches of a single long-dead acacia tree reached for the sky like the fingers of a tortured man. A gecko dashed from left to right before disappearing down a crack.

Edward shuddered.

This is impossible!

He broke off a bit of wood from the fence and rubbed it between his fingers; it crumbled to dust like the flakiest of flaky pastry. Gingerly, he reached his arm through the hole and quickly withdrew it - it was like putting his hand in a roaring furnace.

The time had come for Edward to have a serious talk with himself.

It's a field, Edward, a field – it may look like a desert, but it's not. We don't have deserts in this country for Christ's sake! Therefore it's a field... an absurdly hot field admittedly, but still a field... and I need to cross it. Now man up and get walking!

'Okay... I can do this.' He held his jacket above his head, took a deep breath and... hesitated. The memory of his one-and-only continental holiday with Veronica had drifted into his mind. An opportunity to ogle semi-naked women he had told himself, but the novelty had quickly worn off and the oppressive heat drove him back to the air-conditioned hotel room where he spent the rest of the holiday watching un-subtitled Spanish soap-operas.

Mr Lean was waiting expectantly on the other side of the hole, seemingly oblivious to the extreme temperature.

Look – if the dog can cope with the heat, so can you! If you sprint across, it'll be over before you know it.

He plunged into the cauldron.

The sprint lasted precisely five paces before his legs transformed into a pair of railway-sleepers. The act of inhaling became virtually impossible - akin to sucking on an industrial hair-dryer, and an enormous, clammy hand seemed to be pressing down on him, willing his bones to join those of a thousand small animals on the parched pavement.

God, this is horrible!

Each step was now a massive effort – he had to consciously lift each leg, swing it forward, then stamp it down, and the weight of his arms was such that he couldn't continue to hold his jacket up, and dropped them to his sides. The jacket hung down over his head, limiting his field of vision to a small circular patch of ground.

Mr Lean's cheery face appeared in the circle; she'd found a stick which she presented at her master's feet. 'What? You want to play?' he gasped. 'Are you mad?'

Soon, the conditions under the jacket became unbearable; Edward tore it off and threw it to the ground. Now he was subjected to the full force of the sun, which was marginally worse, but at least it meant that he could look for signs of… well, anything. It was a panorama of utter desolation, the most notable feature being the complete absence of anything that could be described as a feature. His head started to spin.

I'm getting dehydrated… must stay conscious… focus on something…

He reached into his trouser pocket and squeezed hard on his bunch of keys until they dug into his palm. As a focusing technique, this worked really well… rather too well in fact. So focused was he on the self-inflicted pain that he saw neither the boulder nor the gaping crack. The boulder helpfully guided Edward's left foot down the crevice, whilst the abrasive sides of the crack obligingly scraped several layers of skin off his ankles. Thrown forward, his one free hand stung as it clapped against the scorched mud.

'Ow… Shit! For Christ's sake, haven't you had enough fun at my expense?' he shouted at the cloudless sky.

As if to answer the question, a sudden wind blasted fiery dust into his eyes.

'Oh God… Oh God!'

He frantically rubbed and swivelled them round in their sockets as he imagined himself spending his last few minutes alive staggering around this terrible place, burning and blind. To his relief, the vision cleared in one eye.

The relief was short-lived as, in the drama, he had dropped the string and now Mr Lean was missing. 'Dog! Dog!' Nothing. He tried hard not to picture her corpse, flies buzzing around glazed eyes, but to no avail. He tried to prevent the camera from tracking back to reveal his own lifeless body close by, again without success.

'Dog!' he bellowed, then, 'Mr Lean!' Immediately, a familiar face popped up from behind a wildebeest carcass. She trotted over, an unfussed expression on her face. Edward grabbed her and ran... finding a strength born out of desperation and fear, one last act of defiance, one last fist-shake at his maker, he ran. Finally something began to form in his vision... He could see a row of trees.

Despite his frantic state, it registered that the trees were spaced with military precision, each clipped to be identical to its neighbour, and an immaculate, white picket-fence filled the spaces between them.

Oh God, please don't be a mirage!

Closer and closer... he could hear the leaves rustling now, he could see the shade and... what appeared to be a standpipe.

He vaulted the picket-fence, dog in arms, and crumpled into the shade.

* * *

(Part III—The Welsh Field)

Edward was standing thigh-deep in water so clear that he could make out every scale on the back of an angel-fish that was performing a graceful dance at his feet. A curtain of water, as fine as silk, broke and burst into brilliant beads over his broad shoulders. Mandy from Payroll was wading towards him, wearing very little and smiling that smile that had always given Edward the hots. She ran a finger over his defined torso and leaned in to kiss him; her lips were soft and moist, and her breath smelled of... buns.

Oh for Christ's sake...

Edward sat up and Mr Lean rolled off his chest. He was sitting at the edge of a huge field of lush grass, every blade springy and uniform in colour and length. A few fluffy clouds had bubbled up, and a blissful breeze blew Edward's sweat-soaked shirt against his chest. In every way, the climate had returned to the norm for a September day in England. Edward looked behind him; the boundary of the previous field was marked not only by the fence and trees, but by an iridescent wall of heat that rose from the ground to the heavens.

The stand-pipe stood next to the nearest tree. Edward crawled over to it, clapped his mouth round the spout, and turned the handle. Crisp and lightly carbonated, it seemed to be the purest and most refreshing water he had ever tasted. Having extinguished his thirst, he let out a long, deep sigh of relief. 'Thank God... thank God.'

He turned to Mr Lean who was furiously lapping at the stream. 'Well, that was an adventure wasn't it, dog? I did alright though, didn't I ... I had the situation under control – we were never in any real danger. Stick with me dog, and you'll never come to harm.' Mr Lean paused, tongue out, to stare at Edward with an expression of incredulity.

'Right, so, what have we got here? Oh what a surprise - another sodding field!'

He gazed into the distance but could see nothing... except, there was what appeared to be a pencil-line about a mile in length drawn along the centre of the horizon. Of greater interest was a low hum which he took to be the drone of a tractor or some other agricultural vehicle. 'You hear that, dog? That's the sound of civilisation – soon be back in the real world.'

Heartened, Edward stood up and began walking. He began whistling *Scarborough Fair*, one of a number of tunes that he'd taught himself to play on the family piano as a boy. There was the presentation of another stick at his feet and, this time, Edward unrolled the string, picked up the stick and threw it. Mr Lean scurried off on her retrieval mission, little legs a blur and ears flapping.

Mr Lean – what a stupid name. Definitely going to have to change that... she's a bitch after all. Rosie or Lucy maybe. The kids will love having a dog... oh no, wait – they're both at university now. He was reminded of the mess that he was returning to and shook his head.

Nope... I'm not going to think about that now, I'll deal with it later.

Nonetheless, the recollection had applied a heavy weight to his ascending spirits. He felt a sense of unease as he noticed that the pencil line was now more reminiscent of one drawn with a crayon, and was getting thicker at an alarming rate. In addition, the perceived 'tractor' was now humming *The Green, Green Grass of Home*. This had not escaped Mr Lean's notice – she had tucked her tail between her legs and was staying close to her master.

A cloud drifted in front of the sun and the sudden and disproportionate drop in temperature caused Edward to shiver and regret dropping his jacket in the previous field. The cloud eventually moved on, but was soon replaced by another, larger and darker.

The last few blue breaks were succumbing to the merciless encroach of the armies in grey.

A bolt of lightning sliced through the sky and struck the black line; there was a howl followed by a series of uniquely Welsh expletives. Edward stopped dead.

Mr Lean was growling. Edward crouched down to stroke her. 'It's okay, it's okay.' The dog's expression had changed – gone was the ever-present air of vacant optimism to be replaced by that of a wild, threatened animal. She bared her teeth at him and shook her head violently from side to side, clawed at her collar and tugged at the string. There was a snap and she bolted in the direction from which they had come.

'Come back you stupid animal!' Edward shouted at her heels.

'Great... just great!' He turned back to face the object; were it not for the fact that it was still a long way off, he would probably have followed the dog's example, but he hesitated – he wanted to know what it was. It appeared to be a cylinder... a rolling cylinder. It reminded him of the carpet off-cut that had been gathering cobwebs in his garage for many years. The swearing had stopped and the humming, which seemed to come from its entire length, had resumed. And there was a second noise, like... roots being ripped up! Something white was standing in its path and, just as Edward realised that the something was a sheep, it was lifted and swallowed.

'It's the turf...it's rolling itself up!'

To make such an announcement at full volume was ill-considered; the turf hesitated for a moment then thundered towards Edward with renewed purpose, sending up a spray of earth as it rolled. Edward turned and ran. A large rock landed close to him... then another. 'The bastard's throwing things at m—'. The third rock hit him squarely in the back of the head and he went down.

Lying on his front, helpless and dazed, he covered his head with his arms and braced himself. The sound of root-ripping got louder, and louder... but then, as though a window supplied by 'Glazed to Amaze' of 48b Rump Hill, had been blown shut, there was silence, absolute and unblemished. Edward remained motionless; he dared not make a sound, or breathe... or even think. Unfortunately, at that moment, a passing 'worst-case scenario' chose, on a whim, to enter his head via his left ear-canal. Moments later, Edward found himself imagining the turf towering over him; satanic red eyes, made all the more fierce by a plunging unibrow, scanning his body and considering the tastiest bits with a view to tearing him apart. A long, forked tongue licked the bloody lips of a cruel, gaping mouth, and razor-sharp fangs, clearly sharpened for the specific task of tearing him limb from –

'Excuse me.'

The scenario was interrupted by a lilting, slightly camp Welsh voice.

'I hope you don't mind me asking, but why are your rectus femoris muscles so soft?'

Edward was taken aback by the question, and the softly-spoken, unthreatening tone of the voice. 'I haven't been to the gym for two days,' he mumbled into the grass.

'Two days you say? Yes, that would explain it. You know, I've heard that the Bulkitup Vertical Leg-Press Workstation is really good for toning up that particular muscle group.'

Edward found the confidence to glance over his shoulder. There were no red eyes, cruel mouth or razor-sharp teeth, just the predictable underside of a roll of turf; soil, roots, stones and worms.

'It is you!' the turf cried in an increasingly stereotypical Welsh accent, although it wasn't clear exactly where the excited voice was coming from, no obvious orifices presenting themselves. 'You're Jack...' the lilting voice continued, 'the new village vagrant! What a simply lovely, lovely surprise! Do you know, the gossip network has never been so busy since you arrived? Everyone seems to think you're the best thing since sliced leeks... but I really didn't expect to bump into you up here in the fields.'

Edward rolled onto his back and sighed. He looked up at the enormous muddy Swiss-roll that was clearly thrilled to meet him.

What have I done to deserve this?

'The name is Edward... as I have to explain to everybody.'

'Ed - ward, you say? Well... that's even better! Such a fine, strong name... from the Anglo Saxon for 'Rich Guard' it is. Now, let me tell you, Edward, I was out collecting some elf mushrooms when I spotted you. I don't get many visitors up here you know, so I said to myself, 'Aled,' I said, 'you need to be more sociable you do – roll over there and say hello. Now, when I realised it was you, I was so excited that I switched into overdrive, and—'

'Started throwing rocks at me!'

'Ah, yes... the rocks. I am sorry about that, did one of them hit you?'

'Well of course it sodding well did! Do you think I'm lying here sunbathing?'

'Well, no... that would be an idiotic suggestion, but now I feel awful. It was such a surprise to see you there and... well, I got carried away I suppose. You must let me make it up to you in some way...'

There was a brief silence between man and sod as the latter pondered. A large earthworm appeared from Aled's underside; it sniffed the air, looked at Edward, stuck its tongue out, and retreated.

'I know,' the turf announced, 'I recently acquired a leather-bound collection of Romantic poetry... and I hear that you're a big Coleridge fan...'

Edward raised his eyes. 'So I keep being told.'

'Well, the minute I finish the last few pages, I'll let you have it... for keeps. No... there's no need to thank me – it's the very least I can do.'

There was another silence.

'Now don't get this wrong,' Aled said, 'it's splendid to have you all to myself, but I can't help wondering why you aren't back in the village, joining in with all the fun of the Grunt?'

Edward snorted. 'I'm doing my best to escape 'the fun of the Grunt.'

Aled looked as surprised as it was possible for a roll of turf to look; two earthy mounds raised themselves above where his eyes would have been, had he had any. 'You're trying to escape...? Now look, Edward, I'm sorry to be the one to deliver bad news, but there *is* no escape from Flatpack.'

Edward lifted himself onto his elbows. 'Yes, that's another thing people have told me; I plan to prove them wrong. Now look... errr... Aled, I'm going to stand up now, but don't take that as an invitation to eat me.'

The turf recoiled. 'Eat you? What a disgusting idea. Whatever made you think I wanted to eat you?'

'Well, you ate that sheep.' Edward pointed to a ewe-shaped bulge in Aled's side.

'Ah... you saw that did you? Well I won't deny it Edward, I'm not a herbivore, and the Welsh lamb up here in the fields is so good. But I would never dream of consuming a fine young gentleman like yourself, especially one who shares my passion for the poetry of the Romantics.'

Aled raised his earth-mound eyelids to the sun. 'My goodness, you need to get back to the village as quickly as possible or you will miss the procession. I hear on the gossip network that Primrose Pynching is the Maid of the Grunt this year, and if she doesn't change your view of Flatpack, then nothing will!

'Well Edward, it's been a pleasure, it has. I would shake your hand, but I wasn't blessed as such. Therefore, a cheery 'Hawl Fawr' must suffice,'

Edward sat down and watched the turf as it rolled away, engrossed in an open book which floated inches above it. He could hear Aled reading aloud;

*'She walks in beauty, like the night,
Of cloudless climes and starry skies,
And all that's best of dark and bright
Meet in her aspect and her eyes;
Thus mellowed to that tender light
Which heaven to gaudy day denies.*

'Ah yes – there's lovely, Mr Byron.'

Edward continued to watch until Aled became a pencil line once more. He moved his head from side to side as he scanned the entire panorama. Reluctantly, he felt inclined to believe Angela's words, that 'all you will find beyond the fields are more fields,' and that he only had one option.

#

Her paws pleasantly refreshed by the cool water, Mr Lean jumped back onto the Meander bank and returned to her shady spot next to the empty deck-chair. Having circled the patch a couple of times, she settled down, resting her head on her paws. No sooner had she closed her eyes, than her nose started twitching; she lifted her head, sniffed the air and stood up again. Head down, tail wagging, she proceeded to sniff every blade of grass within a ten-foot radius of the deck-chair. The task almost complete, she stopped suddenly, a bright light in her eyes. Returning to the deck-chair, she placed her paws on the front slat and bounced up onto the canvas. Holding the bun firmly in her teeth, she jumped down again. No longer weighted down, the slip of paper was caught by a breeze and carried skywards, before floating down with the elegant fall of an autumn leaf and making a soft landing on Edward's face.

'Wh... What?' He sat bolt upright.

Shaking his body, he realised that he must have drifted off after his long walk back. He held up the piece of paper and read;

'Ah, Edward - there you are.

I do hope the pair of you had a pleasant walk, I've gone to get you that pint. Try not to be too long – we need you to judge the Who Can Bake the Thinnest Cake competition.

Incidentally, I meant to say to you – Farmer Rosser is planning to lay some turf today, so it might be a good idea to avoid his big field.

Hope you're enjoying your first Grunt,

Maxie'

* * *

17. The Colossus of Rump Hill

'Sister, can you look after the stall for a few moments? I've a mind to go and check on young Dan McGkroid. I want to be absolutely certain that there's going to be no repetition of last year's fiasco.'

Lettie, who was dreamily pulling the petals off a daisy and humming to herself, didn't respond.

'Did you hear what I said, Leticia?'

Little Lettie stopped humming and smiled down at her elder twin. 'You're going to speak to Dan about the pie and I need to watch the stall.' She plucked the last petal and giggled.

'Good. Now, we usually get a run on the Rose-hip Spasm around this time, so I need you to prepare an extra pot while I'm away. Have you got that?' Lettie was humming again, the tune now recognisable as *The Whittler's Hornpipe*, (Fo Riddle me a night-shirt, damsel-do,) and was spinning the depleted daisy around in her fingers.

Hettie rolled her eyes and walked off the green, then turned left up Rump Hill. The simple little shops that lined the hill looked relaxed and at ease, enjoying the one day in the village calendar when they could be themselves, with no requirement to be attractive or welcoming, and free from the endless scrutiny and examination of their wares, the judgemental prodding, the rejection. Hettie stopped outside number twenty-eight, a scruffy establishment with a plaque on the door that read: *'Welcome to the home of The Colossus'*.

Dan McGkroid leaped to his feet as his workshop door scraped open, his head an inch shy of the ceiling. 'Oh, it's you, Hettie... I wasn't expecting you.' He thrust his hands into his grimy trouser pockets.

'That much is *quite* evident, Dan, and there's no point in hiding your hands – I guessed that you would be having a crafty fern instead of concentrating on the task in hand.'

He sheepishly withdrew his hands to reveal his incriminating blue fingertips.

Hettie dragged over the single wooden chair, and produced a small, cotton handkerchief, which she waved several inches above the seat before lowering herself onto it. With legs crossed, and hands in her lap, she surveyed the shuffling youth. 'So, how are you, Dan? You seem to have grown even taller than you were last time I saw you. This has to stop, you know; you'll have all sorts of trouble finding clothes to fit if you continue to expand. My sister made that mistake, and now she has to make all her own ankle-length tea-gowns.'

Dan leaned against his workbench and shrugged. 'Nuffin' I can do abaat it is there? Just a growin' lad, tha's all,' he grinned, 'an' I hear that you laydees really fancy a tall guy.' He raised his eyebrows in a laddish fashion.

Hettie ignored his ocular gymnastics. 'That's as maybe, Dan, but what 'we laydees' definitely do *not* fancy is a guy with a six-inch hair growing out of his chin. It's high time you got that thing under control - you're never going to win the heart of Primrose Pynching unless you smarten yourself up a bit.'

Dan ran his thumb and forefinger down the length of the hair from wart to tip, in a provocative manner. 'Oh, I'll get raand to it sometime... anyway, I don't need to win Prim's heart, do I? She's promised to me - my dad done a deal with her dad.'

'Yes, I know, but agreements that gentlemen make when they're in their cups count for very little these days... and don't forget,' she wagged her index finger, 'you're not the only eligible young man in the village any more; our new Jack's been turning a lot of heads... not least of which that of my dippy sister.' These last few words were muttered to herself with a shake of the head.

'Anyway, the main reason I'm here is because I have some concerns.'

'Concerns... what d' y' mean?'

'Concerns about the pie, Dan. Can you reassure me that these are unfounded, and that it'll be arriving on time this year... and with a full filling?'

Dan dropped his shoulders and expelled an irritated sigh. 'Yes Hettie... I'll wheel the pie onto the green at two o'clock on the dot, an' it'll be filled right up wiv meat, veg 'n gravy. Now will you stop givin' me grief abaat last year?'

Hettie took a deep breath, then continued in her matter-of-fact tone. '*Last year*, Daniel, was a disgrace – I have every right to give you grief about it. It was bad enough that you were late arriving, but then to present the mayor with a half-empty pie...well, that was little short of insulting!

'So, this year is going to be different; I've been elected chairlady of the Scheduling and Quality-Control Sub-Committee, so if you're late and you've got the quantities wrong again, it'll reflect on me! Also, Jack is tall, like you, so it's especially important that the pie's full to the brim. It would hardly be in the spirit of The Grunt to ask a tall man to entertain the villagers with a half-empty pie, now, would it?'

Dan held up his hands. 'Look, Hettie, everything's gonna be fine!' He glanced over at the huge oven door that dominated the back wall of his workshop. 'I got the whole situation under control...everything's gonna be fine.' He turned his back on Hettie and began fiddling with some tools on the bench.

'Oh really?' Hettie folded her arms over her ample bosom. 'So, if everything is going according to plan, why are you repeating yourself and looking so uncomfortable? Come on Dan, spit it out - I know you're hiding something.'

Dan turned around but continued to stare down at the monkey-wrench in his hands. 'Well, i's jus' that... the filling may be a bi' 'ot.' He flinched.

'A bi' 'ot? How can it possibly be *a bi' 'ot*? If you've followed your father's instructions, the temperature will be precisely thirty-four degrees at the moment you wheel it out onto the green.'

'Yeah, I know that, but... well, I tested the meat when I go' up this morning and it was still a bit... well, ya know... chewy, so I pu' it back in the oven for another hour.'

Hettie put her hand to her forehead, 'Oh for the sake of the Lord, Dan, you know how precise the timings are. And, aside from that, what does it matter if the meat is *a bit chewy?* No-one's going to be eating it!' She returned her hand to her lap and sighed. 'So, what's the temperature now?'

Dan stared at his feet and kicked a lump of wood. 'Abaat forty-eight degrees,' he said sulkily.

'What? Are you planning to inflict third-degree burns on our new vagrant? What kind of a welcome would that be?' Hettie stood and began pacing up and down. 'This won't do, Dan, this won't do at all.'

After several minutes, she stopped and stared at the massive oven door, then span around on the heels of her once-a-year camel courts. 'Right,' she said, with purpose, 'this is what we're going to do... and *you* are going to need to move fast. First, you must get the pie out of that oven and wheel it round to old Mrs Trenchant's cottage. Politely explain the situation to her, and leave the pie in the shade of her Mexican Willow – that's the coolest spot in the village. At the designated time, bring it down to the green, position the ladder and wait until Hedley steps forward to make his speech. Now, when he gets to his reprise of the parsnip story, lean in and do the elbow test. It's unlikely that anyone will notice and, assuming the filling has cooled, the crust can be nailed in place as normal. Jack can then do his thing and no-one will be any the wiser. If it's still too hot, well... you'll just have to stir in some frozen beets or something.'

* * *

18. A Primrose by any Other Name

Back at the tea-stall, a neat pile of bald daisies was forming on the trestle table. Hettie arrived back looking flustered. 'Do you know, Sister, I despair of young people; you can't leave them alone to complete the simplest of tasks, they have no discipline, no sense of urgency, no—'

'Oh my goodness!' Lettie squealed, 'there he is!' She pointed to the opposite side of the green, then clasped her hands to her breast, her expression that of a schoolgirl with a major crush.

Hettie was about to berate her twin for the interruption, when she saw the reason for her sister's excitement; there, attempting to negotiate the three-wire perimeter fence, was their new vagrant, a heavily knotted piece of string in hand. He looked dishevelled and oddly brown, his hair all over the place and his jacket missing. The sisters watched as he untangled the excited dog's string, then stood up and scanned the tents and marquees. With a determined stride, he set off towards the one with a banner strung between its supporting poles that read, *'Kafuffle's Ales – fairly proud sponsors of the 59th annual Grunt'*.

Hettie noticed a second figure walking towards Edward, clearly intent on intercepting him before he reached the beer tent, an arm outstretched in greeting. 'Oh for the love of God, that's Bedford Trite! After the sort of morning Jack's had, the last thing he's going to want is to be man-handled by a naked octogenarian!'

Lettie looked down at her sister, 'What do you mean, 'after the morning Jack's had'?'

'Oh Leticia,' Hettie sighed. 'You can be very dim sometimes. It's plain that our new vagrant isn't exactly enamoured with his new home, and has made an attempt to escape from the village. I had a feeling he would, that's why I gave him two of our *special* buns to lighten his mood on the futile journey.'

At that moment, the green went silent as the PA system crackled into life and a nasal, man's voice announced: 'Could Mr Trite please make his way to the Jams, Preserves, Curds, Confits, Coulis, and Chutneys Arena where his wife is involved in an altercation with Mrs Git from the Greengrocers, following the rosette ceremony.' There was a pause, the sound of papers being rustled, then the voice added: 'It doesn't say as much here, but I suspect that it would be beneficial if Mr Git could also go to the Jams, Preserves, Curds, Conf— what's that...? Oh, I see. Apparently, Mr Git is dead, so please disregard my latter request. Thank you.'

Bedford dropped his shoulders and slouched off in the opposite direction, all spring gone from his step.

'Well, that was timely.' Hettie took a sip of her tea. 'Thank goodness for Trudy Trite's inflated opinion of her gourd and garden-peas puree.'

#

An arm clutching an opaque and unevenly-shaped pint glass appeared through the tent flap as Edward approached. He took the glass, stepped inside, and was astonished to find himself in the unique gloom of an English pub.

The room was filled with activity; huddles of cheery drinkers laughing, singing and clinking their glasses, a fruit machine noisily regurgitating winnings and a red-faced woman producing an eerie melody by blowing and plucking a stringed, woodwind instrument. A bar that accommodated around a dozen hand-pumps ran the back length of the room, and three pretty young ladies attended to the thirsty punters. A St Bernard was sleeping in front of a blazing log-fire and, standing astride the dog, a young man in a flat-cap was taking careful aim at a dartboard. The walls were barely visible due to a clutter of horse-brasses, faded photos of moustachioed men, and cobwebby lamps. A rickety play-pen confined a group of small children and an inflatable dinosaur to a semi-circular area away from the main drinking area.

Edward felt a brief flash of euphoria.

I've stepped through the gateway!

His jubilation was short lived as his eyes adjusted to the gloom, and he realised that the only people in the tent were Maxie, the mayor and a very old man who stood behind a modest bar polishing a tankard. The remaining people, fixtures, dog etc. had all been painted with remarkable skill on the inside of the tent, and the sounds of jovial banter emanated from a record player. He span around, disbelieving that his eyes could play such a cruel trick.

Maxie stood beside him, admiring the work. 'It's rather good, isn't it? And all the work of Maynard's assistant, Jenny. She wanted to produce an accurate representation of the Anxious Flounder lounge bar on a typical Friday night. She made one tiny omission - the 'Ladies' Shove the Slack Club meeting'.

'Now... Edward, I need to introduce you to the mayor, so best behaviour please.' He led the younger man to the bar where Mayor Gerald-Hedley was perched on a worryingly bow-legged stool. 'Mr Mayor, I want you to meet Jack St Claire, our new vagrant.'

Edward looked the man up and down. In terms of physique, he and Maxie were similarly expansive, but there the resemblance ended. Whilst not easy on the eye, Maxie's shorts, vest and tea-towel look was better suited to the heat of the day than the mayor's tweeds and robes. It was clear that the man was suffering somewhat, as evidenced by a spreading ring of sweat from his neck-overhang.

Edward had grown weary of correcting people about his name, but each time he was introduced as 'Jack' his hackles rose. 'It's *Edward* St Claire actually.'

'Of course it is.' The mayor put his glass down. 'And it's a great pleasure to meet your acquaintance at last, Jack.' He slid off the stool and offered his hand. Then, on observing the other man's muddy state, quickly withdrew it. 'You can call me 'Mr Mayor,' Jack.' I may be the most impotent and influential man in the village, but I don't like people to stand on celery... we're all clogs in the great wheel of time, isn't that right Atticus?'

He didn't wait for a response. 'And I must say, you're looking absolutely disgusting, Jack – truly filthy – mud, stubble... everything!' He leaned in and sniffed Edward. 'You're even starting to smell like a filthy tramp - this is splendid!' He turned to Maxie. 'You've really excelled yourself this time!'

Maxie puffed his vest out.

'So, how are you finding our little village, Jack? Atticus tells me you're settling in well.'

'Oh, I can't imagine *ever* living anywhere else.'

'Well, isn't that super? And it's good that you feel that way, because.... you never will!' He burst out laughing at the cleverness of his comment. Maxie obediently joined in, whilst Edward remained granite-faced.

The mayor wiped his eyes and drained his glass. 'Now, if you two will excuse me, I need to give my pie-speech a couple of final tweaks.' He turned to Edward. 'The villagers insist I say a few words before you take to the stage.' Turning to Maxie, he whispered, 'Or should I say 'Take to the *pie*'?' The two men chortled conspiratorially. 'I'll catch up with you both later. Looking forward to your first hanging, Jack!' the mayor called back before disappearing through the tent flap.

Edward put his brimming pint glass on the bar.

Within seconds, Maxie was pinned up against the tent-pole, Edward's hands clasped around his throat. 'Now listen... Malleable – you're going to tell me where this sodding gateway is, right now!'

'You know I can't do th—'

Edward tightened his grip, raising Maxie higher up the pole. The old man behind the bar looked alarmed, but continued to polish his tankard. Crouching, and with her ears flat to her head, Mr Lean joined him.

'Okay, okay!' Maxie spluttered, and Edward released him.

Maxie slid down the pole and settled in an untidy heap on the grass. He rubbed his neck and looked up at Edward, an expression of hurt and anger on his face. 'There's really no need for that kind of behaviour, young man - you're a guest in this village and I expect you to behave in a civilised manner!' He got to his knees, brushed himself down and straightened his vest. 'Maybe I've been wrong about you all along.' He reached out his hand. 'Now help me up.'

'Oh, don't give me that crap about being a guest in this dump – I never asked to come here. And right now all I'm interested in is getting out.' He pulled Maxie to his feet. 'So where is it?'

Maxie sighed deeply; the uncharacteristic expression of anger had been replaced by one of sadness. He looked deeply into Edward's eyes.

Oh for God's sake, the old git thinks he can get me to feel sorry for him. Well, think again...

Maxie spoke softly, 'You really *do* want to leave, don't you?'

'Oh duuh! Have you only just worked that out?'

Maxie looked down at the ground and remained silent for a moment. Then his eyes bulged and a tiny smile tickled the right side of his mouth. 'I'll tell you what, Edward,' the bounce had returned to his voice, 'let's do a deal shall we? Seeing as you're so determined to leave, I'll show you where the gateway is, but in exchange I want you to do something for me.'

Edward eyed Maxie suspiciously. 'And what would that be?'

'Watch the procession with me.'

'And that's all?'

'That's all I ask, Edward... and I believe I can hear the floats approaching now, so we'd better take our places.' He gestured towards the tent flap.

Outside, the first of a collection of heavily-decorated farm trailers was rolling towards them with no obvious means of propulsion. Excited crowds encircled each float, and a metal, Vshaped frame attached to the front of each vehicle acted like a cow-catcher, gently flipping the odd child to one side.

A banner above the first float read, 'The 1st Flatpack Brownie and Cub Packs proudly present: A Midsummer Night's Toolbox'. The float was crammed with young children dressed as hammers, spanners, wrenches, fairies and donkeys.

Maxie leaned towards Edward. 'The subject matter may seem a little incongruous, but I understand that the cubs' vehicle is out of action, so the committee agreed to a trailer-share and an amalgamation of themes. Works rather well, I think.'

A sad-looking rawl plug scanned the crowds from the deck of the float. Its expression lit up when it saw Maxie by the beer tent. The plug nudged a neighbouring putty-knife, pointed, then both waved excitedly.

'That's my youngest, Byron.' Maxie returned the wave with equal animation, beaming with pride. 'Mrs Malleable spent weeks making that costume.'

The second float came into view. Edward read the banner:

'Fanny's Ferns;
Don't fanny about,
Roll a doobie and shout –
'Ferns Means Fanny's!'

The float resembled a rainforest on wheels; it was an impressive construction comprising delicate blue blooms shaped in crepe together with thousands of glossy fabric leaves that had been painstakingly wired to cane frameworks to form thick, impenetrable bushes. At the front, two bulbous hands parted the undergrowth to reveal a giant plaster head with a maniacal grin. Clenched between its discoloured teeth was a bulging cigarette.

A villager dressed to resemble some kind of jester or minstrel was prancing around the float's perimeter, tossing what Edward took to be free-sample packets from a bucket. He noted the squeals of delight from the lucky catchers, mainly children.

'You let your kids get their hands on that stuff?'

A furrow of confusion formed on Maxie's brow. 'Why ever not, Edward? It's simply dried vegetable matter... a harmless mood-improver, invaluable in the battle to get our youngsters to eat their greens. Do you know, Frank and Fanny Fatuous have spent most of their lives producing more and more exciting varieties.

'Plus, it's such versatile stuff – you can smoke it, gum it, chew it, cook with it...' He lowered his voice: 'a good handful makes Mrs Malleable's swede stroganoff almost tolerable.'

The third float came into view: *'The Maid of The Grunt, Primrose Pynching, and her hand-maidens.'*

Edward smirked.

The Maid of the Grunt, what a title! They've probably put a crown on a pig.

The hand-maidens sat like the petals of a daisy around the Maid's hay-bale throne, waving at everyone and everything; Edward recognised at least three of the Plenteous girls. As the vehicle approached the beer tent, the Maid had her head down, and appeared to be adjusting her footwear. All he could see of her was a huge mass of curly red hair that tumbled over a silky, white dress. The shoe-adjustment complete, she brushed an invisible speck from her lap and tossed her glory of thick curls up and back. Her green eyes were instantly locked onto Edward's. Not for the first time in recent days, he saw recognition in the eyes of an individual who, to him, was a complete stranger.

Oh my god! She is... angelic!

Even as the thought formed, Edward knew that he had never before used the adjective to describe a woman... even in his thoughts. He also knew that, for Primrose Pynching - the Maid of the Grunt, there was no other.

He tore his eyes away to look behind, in case he wasn't the intended recipient of her attention. There was nobody there; even Maxie had departed on a quest for a top-up.

He turned back to face Primrose once again; her eyes were still fixed on his, having never strayed. The intensity of her stare was softened by the most personal and personable of smiles, a smile that Edward now knew was for him, and it felt wonderful. As he gazed on her lovely face, he could feel a lifetime of tension beginning to depart his body, like he was sinking into the softest bed. In that face, he saw admiration... that was nice - he liked being admired, but there was more - a knowing - an intimacy with aspects of himself that he had kept locked away - his faults and fears, weaknesses and insecurities, why he was the way he was. He saw understanding in Primrose's face, he saw something that appeared to be adoration, and a joy at being reunited with him. He sank further into that soft bed.

Back in the beer tent, Maxie proffered his empty glass. 'I think I'll go for your session beer this time, Maynard; need to pace myself a little.'

Maynard Kafuffle took the glass and held it under a tap. 'You having a bit of trouble with that one?' He nodded towards the tent flap.

'What, our new Jack? Noo - he's a pussy cat.' Maxie leaned in towards the old man, '*And* he's just clapped eyes on the lovely Primrose, so I don't think we'll hear any more of his, 'Show me where the gateway is!' nonsense.'

There were a further three floats behind the Maid's vehicle, but these barely registered with Edward. Having completed a circuit of the green, the procession was heading back towards the dung-gate, with Primrose constantly adjusting her position in order to maintain eye-contact with Edward; it was becoming increasingly difficult and concern showed on her face.

I can't lose her now.

Edward's arms unfolded themselves and dropped to his sides; he picked up Mr Lean and started to walk, slowly at first but with increasing urgency.

He weaved and dodged around huddles of villagers, women pushing bunting-clad prams and a dance troupe who were performing a spade-dance. He splashed through a paddling-pool of plastic piranhas with hooks in their heads, much to the annoyance of those holding rods. He banged into a brightly-painted dustbin which bore the words – *'Try your luck – 2 dips for a Danish, 5 for a Brogue.'* The bin fell and tipped its contents – sawdust and gift-wrapped objects, onto the grass. A fleeting glance was enough for Edward to identify all the prizes as vegetables. He backed away, mumbling apologies to the stallholder, and narrowly avoided demolishing a table laden with extremely thin cakes.

His path was completely blocked by a large group of villagers facing a curtained stage; noisy, expectant children sat cross-legged, encircled by their standing parents. He made a snap decision and cut down a narrow gap between the makeshift theatre and the neighbouring tent. With Mr Lean bouncing in his arms, he hurdled the guy ropes and caught a momentary glimpse of the Maid's float through a plastic tent window. The brief reconnection spurred him forward, but also meant that he didn't see the concrete memorial slab that lay just proud of the grass.

His head stinging, he was able to lift himself up and remain conscious for long enough to read the words: 'This is the spot where Vagrant Ichabod 'Jack' Groove was found, having expired in mysterious circumstances, possibly tart-related. Flatpack's resident vagrant for seven years, Ichabod is sadly missed by several people.'

Then, for the second time that day, all went black.

* * *

19. Naked in the Nettles

Edward opened his eyes and looked up at the tent ceiling.
Canvas... bloody canvas. I just don't get it; what do people see in the whole 'tent' thing - sleeping on rock-hard ground... cramped... draughty... eating godawful 'primus' food. Mind you, Timmy Flanders used to love it – 'Hey Eddy, we're taking the tent to the Lake District again this year' – what a dick... he would get so excited at the prospect... it never seemed to bother him, the idea of sleeping next to his snoring parents... gross. Oh God... and that cub camp, I've never been so bored – who in their right mind would sit around a bonfire of flaming pallets, holding a hot dog on a stick and singing 'Ging Gang bleeding Goolie'? I mean, what the hell is that stupid song supposed—

A woman's face came between his and the canvas roof, cutting through his rambling memories. Her curly, red hair brushed his cheek; she smiled, but said nothing. She was familiar, but Edward couldn't remember why, or put a name to her. He threw back a blanket that had been draped over him, lifted himself into a seated position and immediately became aware of a thumping pain in his head. He saw the woman give him a look of sympathy, then walk to a table in the corner of the tent and begin mixing something in a bowl. She returned, and knelt down next to him. As she did, Edward distinctly heard a 'pop' come from her direction. It resembled the sound produced when a cork is removed from a half-bottle of dessert wine. She smeared something green on his forehead; it smelled herbal, but in a culinary way, rather than a medicinal one. He studied her; she was startlingly beautiful, with perfect, petite features, almost-translucent skin and a jawline that most women would give their right arm for. She had no need of make-up, and wore none. And yet, he couldn't remember who she was... how could he forget such an angelic creature? The word 'angelic' started the ball rolling.

Yes, of course... she's angelic, she's the Maid... and I was chasing her.

The ball hit other balls and soon there was a spherical stampede.

Primrose... Maxie... the turf... The Grunt.

Primrose was looking into his face, silent, an expression of fascination and curiosity; she seemed to be observing the memories returning. Edward was conscious that he was a total mess; he could smell himself and it wasn't pleasant. He needed to break the silence...

'I'm really sorry to put you to this trouble. I think I must have tripped and banged my head.'

There was no reaction or change in her expression.

'I'm not normally like this; I haven't had a chance to take a shower since I arrived, and I have no change of clothes... plus, I had an altercation with a roll of turf earlier.'

What a stupid thing to say; you're beginning to sound like the village idiot!

Again, Primrose said nothing.

Edward tried once more. 'I've heard all about your mother; I understand she resolves village disputes using anchovies...'

Smooth Edward, really smooth.

As before, there was no reaction.

Maybe she's deaf... and mute, or mentally—

'You're uncomfortable with silences, aren't you, Jack?' Primrose's voice was like melted caramel poured over organic compost – smooth, yet earthy. It wasn't said as a question, but like a gentle observation to someone she had known for years.

As Edward considered an appropriate response, she got to her feet... 'pop' and pulled open the tent flap. Staring up at the sky, she announced, 'Twelve fifty-seven... that doesn't give us a lot of time.' She knelt down again, 'pop', then put a soft, fragrant finger to his lips. 'I've got three stories to tell you Jack, very important stories that add up to something very worrying. Now, you're going to have a lot of questions, but I need you to keep them to yourself for now... Do you promise?'

Edward had much greater difficulty resisting the urge to kiss her finger. 'Okay,' he breathed against it. At that moment, he would have agreed to anything she asked of him.

'Good. Now, firstly I need to ask you if you've seen the foxgloves down by the river.'

'What, foxgloves... the flowers?'

Primrose gave him a look that suggested it was the stupidest question ever. 'Yes Jack.'

'Well... err, no I haven't.'

'Oh you must! They're such cheery little guys... we're the best of friends, and I visit them every Monday at noon. Be warned though,' she leaned closer to Edward, 'they can get very grumpy if you're not punctual.' Edward used their close proximity as an opportunity to inhale her fresh, natural aroma, and there was something more - something that took him back a very long way to a happy, innocent time. He closed his eyes and, after a moment announced, 'Rosemary!' Feeling pleased with himself, he allowed the distant memories of his mother's herb garden to fill his head.

Primrose smiled. 'Very impressive, Jack! It's called 'Rosemary Rapture.' Hettie and Lettie make a wonderful range of herbal fragrances, but Rosemary is my favourite. It has an intensity and passion... and is just a little dark. Remind you of anyone?' she teased.

Is she flirting with me?

Edward wasn't completely convinced, and opted for his best wicked smile by way of response.

Primrose slapped his leg. 'You behave yourself, Jack St. Claire... and stop distracting me, this is important. As I said, I call on the foxgloves every Monday, and I can tell by the look of delight on their little faces that they really look forward to my visits. Sometimes I read them one or two of my poems... or I do a little jig… or I just tell them about things that have happened in the village since my last visit. They're very perceptive, you know; they recognise if I'm feeling a bit down and always find a way to cheer me up. Do you know, once they all collectively barked like a dog! Oh, how I laughed.'

Her smile dropped, and she sighed. 'It was the foxgloves that first alerted me that something dreadful is going to happen to the village. I went to see them last Monday, and they were, well… different from usual; they showed no pleasure at my arrival, and appeared distracted and sullen… their vibrant colours looked all washed-out and sickly. I tried to cheer them with their favourite song, 'Way-Hay, The Whittler's Wimple!', but they didn't seem to want to listen, and I gave up after two verses. I went back the following day hoping that maybe I'd been mistaken, but their attitude towards me was the same – moody and disinterested… and I could tell that they were troubled. Worst of all, their centre-stalks were all bent and twisted together… many of their blooms had dropped, and the few that remained were closed in a sort of grimace. I stroked their little heads, trying to sense what was disturbing them. They raised their faces to me as one and, do you know, Jack, I have never seen such fear.'

Edward had only been half-listening. Plants, flowers, and gardening were subjects that caused a power-switch to trip in his brain, greatly reducing his ability to pay attention. Instead, he'd been bathing in Primrose's rich tones, admiring her figure and wondering what the 'pop' could be. She'd been saying something about flowers giving her a warning. And now she was staring at him, waiting for a response.

'Err… maybe they just needed some water.'

Primrose sat bolt-upright, her eyes wide. 'I beg your pardon, Jack St. Claire; are you seriously suggesting that I am unable to tell the difference between a plant that 'just needs some water' and one that is doing its best to warn me of some terrible event?'

'No… no, I didn't mean that.'

'Well, I should hope not!' She took a deep breath and continued in a calmer tone. 'But... I suppose it's unreasonable of me to expect you to be convinced by the foxglove incident alone... but wait until you hear what happened with the nettles!'

Edward let out an involuntary snort.

She's an even bigger fruitcake than the rest of them... but I think I'm falling in love.

'You see, Jack—'

Edward raised his hand. 'Can I just ask one small favour?' Using his thumb and a curled forefinger, he indicated just how small the favour would be. Primrose folded her arms and adopted a long-suffering expression.

'Is there any chance of you calling me 'Edward'?'

Primrose furrowed her brow. 'Why on earth would I want to do that?'

'Because it's my name.'

'Oh no, the Flatpack Vagrant has always been called Jack; it's one of our oldest traditions. I couldn't possibly call you something different.' She grinned. 'Did you know that one of our early vagrants only ever spoke two words—'

'Yes... Cumbersome and Twat, I know. But he was mad, and I'm not... and it would mean a lot to me.'

Primrose thought for a moment. 'So you want me to call you 'Wedwood'?'

'No... *Edward*.'

'Edgwood?'

'There's no 'g' in it... Ed...ward.'

'Ed Wood?'

'Okay, that's near enough. Will you do that for me?'

'Well, it's very unorthodox, Ja... err... Ed Wood, but I suppose it can do no harm... just so long as the committee doesn't get wind of it. But I have to say, it is a very silly name.

'Now, Ed Wood, will you please stop interrupting me or we're going to run out of time.' Primrose cleared her throat beautifully.

'Okay... now where was I? Oh yes, the nettles. Well, most people see nettles as nasty, spiteful plants that inflict pain for no good reason and serve no useful purpose. But really, they're not like that at all; they're gentle, sensitive souls whose feelings are easily hurt. They see how people shun them, and it makes them sad; nobody ever compliments their rich colour, their little white bells in April, or the way they share the hedgerows with the horsetail and spindle communities without squabbles or malice. All they really want is to be treated equally - included in bouquets, praised for their medicinal properties, even sniffed occasionally. Really, Ed Wood, they're no different from the rest of us – ultimately, they just want to be loved.'

Edward was suppressing a grin. 'We are talking about stinging-nettles here?'

She looked at him through narrowed eyes. 'Yes, Ed Wood, we are talking about nettles, and you show your ignorance when you choose to refer to them like that. Now button it and let me finish!'

Edward felt duly reprimanded.

'I put my theory to the test last year; I paid a visit to a magnificent nettle bush that lives by the edge of the recreation ground. After introducing myself, I praised the bush for its impressive size and healthy appearance. I told it a little about myself and my desire for us to be friends, and then finished with a funny story that I thought it might appreciate. Then, I just sat there quietly, being companionable, listening and watching. Presently, I started to hear lots of little voices coming from within the bush; they all sounded really excited, but I couldn't make out any actual words. I sensed that a bond was beginning to develop between us, and I said to the bush: 'I'm going to do a little dance with you now, and I'm hoping that you're not going to sting me, not now that we're such good friends.' I took off my clothes, stepped into the centre of the bush and began to move rhythmically to a tune in my head. After a few minutes, I was astonished to hear the bush humming the very same tune. Soon I was leaping and whooping as the bush swayed to the melody. When I stepped out, I felt quite elated, and do you know, Ed, I had not received a single sting!'

Edward had no desire to relinquish the image of Primrose dancing naked in the nettles, but knew he needed to concentrate on saying something vaguely sensible. 'That's...err... remarkable,' was the best he could come up with.

'Isn't it!' Primrose sounded pleased with his response. 'Sadly, there's an unhappy postscript to this tale. I went back to see the nettles this week; we had a pleasant enough time, but as I stood to leave, a low branch reached out and wrapped its leaves around my leg, stinging me repeatedly. I was so shocked! The guilty limb withdrew into the bush, shamefaced... but why would it do such a thing to me?'

With the clumsiness of a newly-besotted idiot, and without considering the dismissive nature of his words, Edward shrugged and blurted out, 'Nettles sting... that's what they do. It doesn't mean anyth—'

'YES, IT DOES, YOU STUPID, STUPID MAN! It means everything - how can you not see that? Two plants that I know intimately, start acting out of character at the same time, and you think that 'doesn't mean anything'?'

She stood up, 'pop,' and walked to the corner of the tent, her arms wrapped tightly around herself. 'You should believe in me, Edward St. Claire,' she said, pronouncing his name perfectly, 'I believed in you.'

She believed in me? What does she even mean by that - she'd never met me before today? ...oh bloody hell, is she crying?

He tossed the blanket aside and stood behind her; gently he placed his hands on her upper arms. 'Why don't you tell me the third tale, Primrose?'

She shook his hands off her. 'That's all you see them as, isn't it – tales... tales to tell my class of under-fives! Oh... why don't you just go back to your old life?'

This last comment stung Edward; he sat back down on the hard ground and started to think about his old life.

The lies... the lies he told clients to close lucrative sales deals, the lies he told Veronica about his whereabouts during his affairs, the lies he told Ptolemy and Veronique to excuse his absence from their school performances.

Then there was the marriage itself - doomed from the start. Physical attraction had been his only consideration, and Veronica was tall, slim, blonde, leggy and busty. They were married after the briefest of affairs and Edward couldn't wait for the honeymoon to end to show off his smokin' hot wife. One day, after a month of marital bliss, he noticed that he was married to a vacuous airhead who irritated the hell out of him, and had a voice like a rusty hyena. Increasingly, that voice would drive him from their home into the sweaty embrace of the gym, where he would pump iron until his muscles screamed at him. Anything rather than return home.

Like everything else, the children were unplanned. Edward cringed as he recalled how he had sworn to be a proper father, how he would read them bed-time stories, help with their homework and win the Fathers' Race at sports day. The reality had been so different - no wonder they hated him.

Enough!

He looked over at Primrose, who still had her back to him.

If she knew what I'm like, she'd run a mile...

'I'm... no saint, Primrose.'

'Ha! No manure, Ed Wood!'

This made Edward smile. 'I... don't think I want to go back,' he heard himself say.

Primrose turned around; her eyes were red and puffy but, to Edward's relief, she had the broadest of smiles. She sprang forward and launched herself into his lap with a rather louder pop than before. She pressed her cheek against his, and whispered in his ear, 'Of course you don't.'

Edward wanted to hold her close but she shuffled backwards on her knees until she was out of his reach.

'I'm sorry for what I said; of course I don't want you to go back, Ed Wood. That was a stupid thing to say. But you have to trust me when I tell you about the messages I receive. Today is possibly going to be Flatpack's last, and you are the only one who can prevent it.'

'I do trust you, Primrose, but—'

'No!' She grasped his stubbly chin. 'You don't! But,' she calmed herself, 'you must try, you absolutely must. You really are our only hope.'

He looked into her huge, pleading eyes.

I don't know what you expect of me. I don't understand what you think is going to happen but, if I'm your only hope, then Flatpack is in big trouble.

Outside the tent, a chant was building;

'We want Jack!
We want Jack!
We want Jack!
'But we don't mind waiting a little longer if it's inconvenient!'

They both sank into a pool of giggles. Edward had never been 'wanted' before; it was a nice feeling. He turned to Primrose and, trying his best to sound strong and self-assured, said, 'Everything's going to be alright.'

'Thank you,' she breathed and kissed his lips, 'and it's time I told you that third tale. Oh! But before I do, there is something I want to bring to your attention, Mr Wood. Now, I'm not going to make an issue of this, but it needs to be said. You're a very charming man in many respects, but if you really want a girl to fall for you, you do need to mention her ankle-pop occasionally. You haven't complimented me on mine once and, I've been told, it's one of the finest in the village. We girls like our assets to be noticed, you know!' She looked expectantly at Edward.

'It's... err... lovely!'

Ankle-pop?

At that moment, a plump face appeared at the tent flap. The tea-towel had been discarded, and in its place, the centre pages from the day's Observer – a special 'Grunt down the ages' pull-out feature, had been neatly folded and was held in place with a rubber-band under the chin. 'Honestly Edward, can't you hear them calling for you? The pie's here, so I hope you've been practising your pliés.'

Maxie turned to Primrose. 'Primble, could I have a quiet word with you?' He indicated the corner of the tent with a jerk of the head.

Primrose bounced over and Maxie whispered something into her delicate ear. 'Oh!' She glanced over at Edward with a look of surprise. 'I'll see what I can do.'

'What was that all about?' Edward asked once Maxie had departed.

'We have a bit of a problem, Ed Wood.'

* * *

20. Oscar Revisited

There was more than a hint of exasperation in Primrose's voice. 'So why do *you* think the committee has extended your probationary period?'

'I can't imagine,' Edward shrugged. 'I didn't even know that I was *on* probation!'

'*That* is because you never bothered to read the job description and contract!' She let out a gasp of frustration. 'You would have been given the same forty-seven minute trial period as all new arrivals, but in your case the village committee have decided to reinstate yours and extend it till the end of the day... and I'm pretty sure that it's due to 'the issue'.

'And you're seriously telling me that 'the issue' is my dislike of tea?'

Primrose stood up and returned to the corner table on which Edward had noticed a teapot and two matching cups; she lifted the lid and stirred the contents. 'The villagers will never fully accept you if you fail to embrace the aromatic leaf, Ed Wood. To make an announcement that you don't like tea on your first day here was the height of bad manners, and will have offended many of the older villagers.'

'But how would they...' Edward began, then stopped himself. 'Ah yes, of course – the gossip network.'

'You're learning,' Primrose smiled. 'And I hear that you asked Hettie for an espresso! I did laugh when I heard that.' She gave the pot another stir. 'This looks nicely fused.'

'You mean '*in*fused,' Edward muttered.

'Now don't start correcting me, Ed Wood. I know what I mean.' She poured, and passed him a cup. 'Let this be lesson one.' Edward looked at the liquid in his cup; its colour was not readily discernible due to a rainbow surface-film that suggested that there may be an oil tanker lurking at the bottom.

He looked around the tent, but pot-plants were conspicuous by their absence, and anyway, Primrose was watching him closely. He sniffed the steaming liquid; there was an aroma of rubber, prunes and gently-poached bark. He raised the cup in a toast then took a brave gulp; it tasted of rubber, prunes and gently-poached bark. Despite the considerable efforts of his pharynx and oesophageal muscles to resist the swallowing process, the liquid passed into his stomach.

'There, now that wasn't hard was it, Ed Wood? You will get a taste for Hettie's brews; I know you will. Some are really quite uplifting!'

Edward recalled the euphoric effect of the Ladies 'Pagan Infusion.'

'So,' she said in a back-to-business tone, 'the third tale.' Once again, she performed the most feminine of throat-clearances. 'You see, I have a gift - well, everyone calls it a gift, although sometimes I think of it as more of a burden. What happens is, every night I dream about our beautiful village, this place where I was born and which I love so much... and so will you, Ed Wood, in time. Now, the thing is... my dreams aren't really dreams at all, but premonitions.'

'What do you mean?'

'What I mean is, I dream of what will happen in precisely six days' time.' Primrose paused, and Edward realised that his face was being scrutinized for even the smallest smirk.

Remain impassive... dead pan.

Satisfied with what she saw, Primrose continued. 'Say, just for example, there's going to be a shortage of blackcurrant boiled sweets, I would dream about it six days before, and be able to forewarn Mr Molar. He would have plenty of time to boil up a batch of gooseberry sherbets, and the children's wrath would be avoided. The same applies to Mrs Plenteous who is expecting another baby –

I'll be able to let her know the precise delivery date six days in advance.

She took a sip of her drink; Edward felt duty-bound to do the same. 'Do you know, last year, I dreamt that Mrs Malleable would have a nasty fall. I told Uncle Max and, bless him, he didn't let go of his wife's hand all that week and, when the moment came, he was there to catch her.' Primrose beamed. 'It's so nice to be able to help my friends like that, but,' a sad look crossed her face,' it means that I have few surprises in my life.

'Anyway, six days ago, I dreamed about The Grunt; the whole village looks forward to our big day, and I'm no exception. However, the following night I had the same dream! Now *that* is not right, Ed Wood! I should have dreamt about the day after – all the clearing up and so on. And, do you know, every night since then, the dream has been the same, as if today is to be our last day.

'Well, as you can imagine, I was worried, so I went and told Maxie about the dream... *and* about the strange behaviour of the foxgloves and the nettles; Uncle Max always knows what to do – he's such a man of action, don't you think?'

Edward covered his mouth with his hand, an act that didn't go unnoticed. Primrose put her hands on her hips. 'Did I say something funny Ed Wood?'

'Oh nothing, it's just the idea of Maxie as some kind of action-hero... in his string vest and chunky brown shoes... I know - he could be 'Tea-Towel Man!'

Primrose looked at him blankly.

'You know... because he wears a tea towel on his head to keep the...' His voice trailed off as he saw the blank look transform into a withering one.

'We're going to have to work on your sense of humour, Ed Wood.'

She gave him a further disapproving glare before continuing. 'I told Maxie how, in my dream, the day goes swimmingly with all the usual larks; the mayor's funny speech, the procession, you challenging the great pie, the egg and drainpipe race. Right up to the moment when you hang Dr Jeffries. Then there's this… blackness, and I get a horrid feeling of finality.'

There it is again – they really do expect me to hang some doctor!

'Well, Uncle Max thought about it for a minute, then said 'Now don't you worry yourself, Primble, I know just the man for the job, and I think it's time I introduced you.'

'Now I have to tell you, Ed Wood, I had some serious reservations the first time I saw you in that horrid man's office.'

'What do you mean? What office?'

'Oh you know, the one that belonged to the man who sacked you.'

'But you weren't there… I would have seen you.'

'Oh, Ed Wood, you can be very dim sometimes… Uncle Max and I were standing next to the window… at an angle of fourteen and a half degrees from the horizontal of course, so obviously you didn't see us. You'd been told not to speak but you still had an arrogant, self-righteous expression, and you showed no remorse for your philandering. 'Serves him right,' I thought, and told Maxie that I didn't like you, and certainly didn't think you right for the job of vagrant, let alone the man to save the village.

'But then he whisked me back a few years… to your garden… to that rainy day when you buried Oscar…

'Hang on, hang on, that was twenty-odd years ago!'

'Oh no, Ed Wood, it was just last week. You see Uncle Max recalibrated the gateway's range function to allow it to travel through time as well as distance.

'I saw you cradling the box, unwilling to put Oscar into the ground… your dear friend, torn away from you so cruelly. I stood beside you feeling helpless; I saw your tears and wanted to put my arms around you, but of course I couldn't. I knew at that moment why you became a bit of a turd in your later years, and I could see why Uncle Max was so sure of your suitability.'

Edward stared… just stared. Twenty-eight years, twenty-eight long years of blocking that memory, that feeling of being so utterly alone. Pummelling it down every time it threatened to re-surface. And suddenly the memory had been re-written, it turned out that he wasn't alone that day – this wonderful woman had been at his side, sharing his grief. His heart was on fire… in a good way.

Mr Lean appeared from nowhere and placed her head on Edward's knee. Edward sniffed back the tears, picked up the dog and hugged her. There was a lot of purring and wagging.

'We need to get moving,' Primrose announced and pulled Edward to his feet; she produced a fragrant hanky and wiped the pesto off his bump.

Edward's was having trouble taking in what Primrose had just told him. He opened his mouth to ask the first of a series of questions, but was interrupted.

The interruption came in the form of an elderly man's voice, frail and muffled, and its origin was directly beneath Edward's feet.

'Ask no questions, Edward,' the voice said. 'The responses may cause you to have doubts. You have been given a gift; cherish it, hold it as close as you did Oscar that day. Be thankful and remain quiet.'

Edward looked over at Primrose, who was humming and tidying up the teacups. 'Did you hear that?'

'Of course, that was Doctor Jeffries. It's usually best to do as he says – he's right about most things.'

'But… he's under the ground! Who is he? And why do you want me to hang him?'

Primrose burst out laughing. 'Oh you are funny, Ed Wood.'

* * *

21. Plié on the Pie

The two men shielded their eyes from the blazing sun.

'Isn't it magnificent!'

'It's... a pie.'

'Pah! You do have a talent for stating the blindingly obvious, Edward – I do like that about you. You're quite correct, of course, it is *indeed* a pie... but I'll wager you've never seen one quite like it.'

It was true, Edward had never seen a pie on such a grand scale, and neither had he seen a wheelbarrow quite the size of the one creaking beneath. The oversized pair had been positioned on a raised crown of grass in the centre of the green, with blocks of wood wedged under the wheel to prevent barrow and pie from making a break for it.

A makeshift platform constructed from a pair of step ladders and a broad plank stood adjacent to the pie. At the base of the hillock, a circle of tiered seating was rapidly filling, from the top down.

'Well, it is a *fairly* big pie,' Edward said mischievously, 'but I've seen bigger.'

Maxie gave him a look. 'Edward, I do know that you're trying to wind me up, but you'll have to do better than that. This diameter of this pie is eight feet, it is crammed with shoulder cuts from Farmer Rosser's Bearded Longhorns, twenty different varieties of late-summer vegetable and some hugely-unattractive mushrooms from his fungal field... and all of this is suspended in Mrs Curvature's signature *sauce glutineuse*. It is a *masterpiece* of culinary excess, and the Colossus is the only oven in existence that could possibly cope with such a giant.' He laughed. 'I've seen bigger', indeed.'

His piece said, Maxie returned his attention to the pie, tranquil admiration returning to his features.

Edward looked at Maxie, and became aware for the first time since his arrival, that he felt real affection for the contented old man with a colour supplement plastered to his head. He reached up and broke off two pieces of the pastry rim; he popped one in his mouth and offered the other to Maxie.

Maxie looked at the offering but made no attempt to take it. 'You'll regret that.'

Curious at the comment, Edward tossed the morsel around in his mouth; it was delicious - buttery and with a minty hint. It was only when he attempted to bite into it that Maxie's comment made sense. In pain, he put his hand to his mouth and spat it out. 'It's like wood!'

'I'm very glad to hear it!' Maxie said. 'Ideally, it should be the density of red cedar or one of those slower-growing hardwood varieties... you look puzzled.'

Edward rubbed his cheek, 'Well, I always thought that one of the pleasures of eating pastry is that it *doesn't* break your teeth!'

It was Maxie's turn to look confused, 'How would it hold the weight of a grown man if... oh, I see – Edward, this isn't a pie for eating.'

'Then what the hell *is* it for?'

Maxie flung his arms wide. 'Entertainment, Edward!'

'You're going to entertain the villagers... with a pie?'

'Certainly not, Edward... you are.'

A cheer went up as Mayor Gerald-Headley appeared in the entrance to the tiered seating. Everyone took to their feet, clapping, whistling, stamping, throwing their hats and colour-supplements in the air. The mayor walked very slowly towards the platform, high-fiving every man, woman and child on the bottom tier. Finally he reached the steps and climbed onto the plank, where he stood, adjusting the microphone and soaking up the adulation.

Maxie whispered in Edward's ear, 'You'll have to excuse me; I need to take up my place.' Edward watched as Maxie positioned himself directly behind the mayor and began a series of warming up exercises; rolling his shoulders, reaching for the sky, running on the spot, attempting to touch his toes.

'Friends!' The mayor began, oblivious to Maxie's exertions behind him. There was still some general hubbub and the mayor waited for complete hush. He leaned on the podium. It may have been less than a second before he realised that there *was* no podium, but in that time, he was well on his way to acquiring a gravy overcoat. Fortunately, Maxie the hero was ready, and lunged forward to grasp the mayor's flailing arms. Hedley's face was perilously close to the glutinous goo, his chain of office having completely submerged below the surface. Being of similar build, the two men were well-balanced and it took the assistance of two younger, fitter men to pull the mayor upright. Once he was happy that Hedley had regained his balance and composure, Maxie released him; they exchanged a firm handshake, an uncomfortable hug and a series of manly back-slaps. Looking pleased with himself, Maxie re-joined Edward. 'Well, that all seemed to go rather well.'

Edward was astonished. 'How on *earth* did you know *that* was going to happen?'

'What? Oh, Primble told me six days ago.'

Back on the plank, the mayor was wiping his forehead and checking his heart-rate; he looked out at his audience with a little more humility than usual, and straightened the tie that he'd removed a couple of hours earlier. He scanned their faces; a number showed signs of concern, a couple of the older women crossed themselves, but no-one looked remotely amused. He pulled the microphone toward himself, and spoke quietly. 'I believe... that I owe a debt of gratitude to my dear friend Atticus.' He turned to face Maxie and started to clap; soon everyone was clapping loudly, including Edward. Maxie waved the praise away.

Returning his attention to his audience, the mayor sniffed, pulled out some crumpled papers, scanned them briefly, then stuffed them back into his jacket pocket. 'Friends... there are few pleasures in life... I might even say that there are no pleasures in life that can hold a shaking candlestick to the pleasure that I derive from welcoming the Great Pie back into our community bosom.' He held his arms wide in welcome to the great pie, and the crowd returned, once again, to their feet. As the applause began to die down, the mayor raised a finger. 'But... I have been thinking some thoughts about the pie's inclusion in our programme of entertainment. It may surprise some of you to learn that this is the forty-third consecutive year in a row that the pie has entertained us on Our Lady of St Gruntle's special day. It's certainly had a good run hasn't it, but... you know,' he came very close to leaning on the podium again, 'I find myself asking myself, 'Mr Mayor, isn't it time for a change?''

There was some fidgeting and throat-clearing in the crowd.

'You see, when the pie entertainment was first introduced, it was never intended as a permanent feature of the day; it was merely a time-filler between afternoon tea and the hanging of Dr Jeffries. But its first outing was such a success, we had to bring it back year after year, and now it's difficult to imagine The Grunt without it. Personally, I think that the addition of the pie to our coat of arms was a step too far, but the village committee overruled me on that occasion.

'What worries me is that, one day I will happen to ask an outsider if they've heard of Flatpack on the Meander, and they will respond with the words, 'Oh yes, I've heard of Flatpack – that's the village that has a pie.''

The crowd fell silent.

Hedley repeated the line to heighten the drama: 'the village... that has... a pie'.

Before he could continue, Maisie Wittering, who had been listening from her seat in tier three with her handbag on one knee and Aldous on the other, sprang to her feet. 'But that's not right, Mr Mayor! Flatpack isn't just a village with a pie, why... we're a community... with schools, a church... and - and butterflies, lot of butterflies...and a cottage abattoir....and four ponds, six pubs... *and* our very own brewery... oh, and a simply lovely bakery. *And* we've got a sweet shop... and don't forget our family of badgers—'

Hedley held up his hand in a desperate attempt to end Maisie's list. 'Indeed... indeed, and I think the rest of you will agree that Mrs Wittering here has just hit the hammer on the head... so what are we going to—'

'And fourteen ducks,' Maisie added.

'Yes, fourteen ducks, Maisie, quite right. In simpletons terms, if our beloved Flatpack is viewed simply as a village with a pie, then we need to accept that the pie has grown too big for its brogues, and it's time for some changes.

'Now, what I am proposing is this; after this year, we put the great pie out to graze amongst the mothballs and introduce something new to our annual celebration... say... a Great Custard Flan!'

It was clear that the mayor had not anticipated the collective gasp, or the unrestrained wrath that followed.

There was anger:

'Is he mad? The Grunt will be completely ruined! What a reckless idea!'

'A Great Dessert?! Does he care nothing for tradition?'

There were tears:

'He can't take the pie away can he, dear? Surely he can't...I don't think I could cope!'

'Calm down dear, it's going to be ok ...'

There was a deep, serious voice:

'The committee will take a very dim view of this!'

And worst of all...

'Maybe what we *really* need is a change of mayor!'

This was new ground for Hedley, used, as he was to universal acclaim for his suggestions, however asinine. 'It... it doesn't have to be a flan of course – the colossus is very versatile... we could have a Great Lemon Meringue Pie if you like...'

This suggestion seemed to antagonise the crowd still further, as evidenced by the bun that flew past the mayor's ear.

He looked round at Maxie and Edward for help.

Edward strolled over to the mayor, and spoke softly in his ear. 'Why don't you let them have their pie, Mr Mayor? The villagers clearly love it, and they'll hold you in particularly high esteem if you show that you're a mayor that listens to his people.'

Hedley nodded and turned back to the baying crowd. 'A minor alteration to my plan has just been suggested in my ear by our new Jack. The suggestion is: we continue with the pie entertainment in its current form for the next few years and... well, see how it goes?'

Without a prompt, the audience huddled together in small discussion groups, and some lively debate followed. After a few minutes, Bedford Trite stood up, clutching a scrap of paper. It appeared that, despite being completely naked, he had been appointed spokesman in this matter. 'The Village has agreed,' he read, 'to the mayor's suggestion that nothing whatsoever will happen, and the pie entertainment will continue precisely as before. In return we, the villagers, feel that that a 'Return of The Great Pie street party' would be appropriate, and show good-will on both sides.'

Hedley looked over at Edward and Maxie, who both gave him a thumbs up.

'Well...err,' the mayor began, 'I'm not entirely sure that the entertainment budget will stretch—'

Both Edward and Maxie expelled loud coughs.

'Err, yes... yes - that sounds like a splendid idea, just what the village needs!'

Huge applause and three cheers for Hedley later, the mayor looked up at the sun. 'Good Lord, is that the time? We must get the pie entertainment started without delay. As you all know, the pie has a new opponent this year in the form of our new vagrant. Jack, will you please join me?'

Edward looked to Maxie for guidance. Maxie gave him a reassuring nod.

As he approached the pie, Edward received lots of back-slaps and shouts of 'You can do it, Jack.' He climbed the rungs, stepped onto the plank and looked down on an ocean of gravy with random floating objects, some recognisable, some not. On the opposite side, he could see a gangly youth with a hairy wart leaning over the pie-side with his elbow in the gravy. Their eyes met and the elbow was quickly withdrawn.

'Now, before I pitch the brogues,' the mayor continued, 'I did want to share an experience that happened to me a few years back… when I found a parsnip by the side of the road…'

The crowd erupted in delight at the prospect of the re-telling.

Oh, for God's sake, is he really going to repeat that dreary anecdote? Doesn't he have any other funny stories to bore the villagers with?

Edward's thoughts went back to the first time he'd part-heard the parsnip story, and he wondered where the Lady Mayoress had got to. He scanned the seats, but there was no sign of Angela Gerald-Headley.

Thought not – a wise move.

Neither could he see Primrose; she had mentioned something to him about not wanting to miss Dahlia Brûlée's performance. Then he spotted her – bouncing up and down near the back of a large crowd facing the previously-curtained stage. This was now occupied by an elderly woman who was strutting around, flapping her arms and making unconvincing bird noises to the delight of the crowd, mainly children. She had a cotton sheet fastened around her neck like a cape, on which many open-cup mushrooms had been sewn.

From his position on the platform, Edward had a good view of the whole green; the mushroom-woman's performance and the parsnip story were failing to hold his attention and he allowed his gaze to drift.

He could see three boys rolling a large round object across the green. In their wake, a swarm of younger children, many still dressed in toolbox-themed costumes, followed the ringleaders of what had the appearance of a prank. Their guilty giggles added weight to this theory, as did the presence of a red-faced, fist-shaking gentlemen a few paces behind.

A conga was being played over the PA system and a number of revellers, fuelled by Kafuffle's ales, had formed a line which twisted and snaked around the tents and stalls, much to the annoyance of those who considered such a thing rather vulgar for the occasion. The 'snake' entered the beer tent and, after a moment, slurred exclamations of disapproval accompanied by the sound of breaking glass could be heard. The snake's head soon re-appeared and scanned the green in search of another target for its mischief.

There was a particularly long queue at Hettie and Lettie's stall. Five small tables had appeared in front, each with an exquisite lacework tablecloth and a tiny vase of seasonal flowers. Well-trousered men with paisley cravats sat in upright chairs and made pleasant conversation with ladies in long floral frocks, whilst impeccably-behaved children played nicely at their feet. Between exchanges, the couples sipped tea and considered the enticing finger-sandwiches, strawberry scones and one-bite sweetmeats arranged on a three-tier cake stand.

Due to her height, Lettie was first to spot the approaching conga-dancers. 'Oh my mother's marrows— Hettie, look!'

Hettie stopped spreading jam and focused on the approaching revellers. She visibly reddened, and hissed under her breath, 'Scone hour will not be disrupted!' She reached for a chair, stood on it and puffed out her bosom to its fullest extent. Holding a flattened hand high in the sky, she cried, 'Be gone! Your childish gyrations are not welcome here! *We*…. are taking scones!'

Whether the participants would have taken any notice, or ploughed on regardless, Hettie would never know. At that moment the conga music ceased and the dancing stopped. After a squeal of feedback, a familiar, nasal voice announced:

'Ladies and Gentlemen, I'm sorry to interrupt this splendid Grunt, but I have a brief notice that I need to share with you.

'We have received some disturbing reports of a theft from Mr Spurious' *'Vast Vegetables and other Outsized Produce'* display. Ethan has reported that his 'highly commended' radish has gone missing. Now, as you know, Mr Spurious is not a vindictive man, and has proposed a 'radish amnesty.' Providing the vegetable in question is returned to its rightful position on his stall, he promises a complete pardon for the perpetrators.

'Also, would all those who wish to take part in the three-headed race make their way to the starting line?

'Than-kyou'

The music started again; this time it was an Irish Step-dance.

Edward smiled as he watched the disappointed conga line disintegrate; then his eyes fell on the gallows. It was *so* out of place; not a quaint relic of a gentler age like the village stocks; this was a well-maintained construction, an instrument of death, ready for use. The strings and garlands of flowers that decorated it did nothing to disguise its purpose.

'…well, that was the last time I wore braces to a funeral!'

These words and the rapturous applause that followed signalled the end of the parsnip story - second telling of the day. The mayor accepted the ovation, but seemed in a hurry to move things along. He reached into his pocket and produced three coins which he cast into the gravy with a theatrical flourish. 'Could we have the pie crust now please?' he called out, long before the applause had subsided.

Four burly young men stepped forward, rolling a huge pastry lid, which they lifted and slid into place on top of the pie. Once happy that it was evenly positioned, they returned to their seats, only to return with hammers, ladders and mouthfuls of nails. With ladders leant, there was a count of four, then each man stamped his right foot on the first rung. Rhythmically they climbed the steps, stepped onto the crust, and then the hammering began; the men sang and banged out the rhythm of a sea shanty that Renston Ardlish had written many moons before:

A pigeon landed on my head,
'You cannot stay,' I told her,
Ignoring me, she pecked my ear,
Then settled on my shoulder.

I put up with some nasty jibes
From many a beholder,
But I was quite enamoured with
That pigeon on my shoulder.

She'd burned a wing and, for a joke –
I thought I'd call her 'Smoulder';
She gave me such a dirty look,
That pigeon on my shoulder.

November was a bitter month,
December even colder;
She didn't like the northern climes,
That pigeon on my shoulder.

She shivered as we neared the pole,
In cotton wool I rolled her,
She cooed to show her gratitude,
That pigeon on my shoulder.

She'd often kak all down my back,
An act for which I'd scold her,
'I do not have a chamber pot,'
Her comment from my shoulder.

Roger Kent

When bored, I learned the paper arts –
Became a master folder,
I made an origami friend
For Smoulder on my shoulder.

We lived on rum and biscuit crumb,
'It's all we have!' I told her,
'Your diet lacks omega 3,'
The comment from my shoulder.

I saw a mermaid on a rock,
My body ached to hold her.
The mermaid said, 'I like you too -
But *not* what's on your shoulder.'

'I do not care about your tail –
We're meant to be!' I told her,
'She hasn't got the wherewithal,'
The comment from my shoulder.

It was a shock to realise
That I was getting older;
I'd lost my hair, my teeth, but not
The pigeon on my shoulder.

At length, she learned to swear and cuss,
And that was when I sold her.
'I never liked you,' she declared,
And shat upon my shoulder.

Each man knew his assigned area and didn't trespass onto his neighbour's patch. At the end of the song, every hammer was held aloft to indicate completion. The men slid down their ladders and performed a backwards roll into a standing position. They gave small bows and received a well-deserved burst of applause.

Mayor Gerald-Headley joined the applause, then gestured to Edward to take a step onto the pie crust. 'Okay, Jack, this is your moment. You have just five minutes on the clock.' He held up a theatrical clock tied to a bit of string.

Confused, Edward looked at the mayor who, once again, indicated that he should take a step forward.

Primrose whistled through her teeth from the far side, where she was straining to peer over the lip, and beckoned to him. Warily he stepped onto the crust, walked over to Primrose and knelt down.

'Whatever's the matter?' she said.

'I don't know what I'm expected to do.'

'Oh Ed Wood... Jump of course! ... Jump until the crust breaks, then retrieve the brogues!'

'What? Swim around in gravy? I'm not doing that!'

Primrose gave him a stern look. 'Now listen here, Ed Wood.' She reached up and wagged a finger at him. 'You've already alienated half of the village with your, 'I don't like tea' gaffe. Do you really want to turn the other half against you? This is the perfect opportunity for you to win their hearts back!'

Edward looked down into her huge, beautiful eyes; he was so in love that he would have dived into twenty steaming pies to please her. He trudged to the centre and made a feeble attempt at a jump. In response to this, the pie lid quivered with mirth. He tried again, this time going a little higher, but the lid was similarly contemptuous of his efforts. He started to hear mutterings from the crowd:

'He's hardly trying...'
'This is disgraceful...'
'I told you he was unsuitable; didn't I tell you...'
'Doesn't like *tea*, you know...'

A woman stood up and started shuffling along her row with her three children, laden with fluffy prizes, in tow. Edward watched them leave.

Right, this is going to be the one, it has to be...

He took a long deep breath and was about to jump when...

'JAAACKK!!!' It was no ordinary summons, but an ear-drum bursting holler from the top tier. It was the voice of Doug Punitive, Flatpack's resident shouter.

'Jaaack!' Doug shouted again. 'You need to plié!'

Edward shielded his eyes and sought the owner of the almighty voice. 'Plié?'

'Yes, you know – Plié! A Grand Plié is best.' The huge man with a full beard and a *'Shout, Shout, let it all out,'* t-shirt stood up in the top tier. Those at the ends of the rows had to lean against their neighbours to let him pass as he walked down the steps. Once at grass level, he faced Edward, stood tall, turned his feet outwards to a hundred and eighty degrees and closed his eyes. 'Plié' he said, in a quiet, instructive voice. Then, like a projectile in a catapult, he launched himself into the air, achieving an astonishing height before making the most poetic of landings.

'Now *your* landing, Jack,' Doug shouted, 'needs to be much more violent, you need to really hate the pie, and I mean *hate* it. Point your heels at it as you descend and kick them out at the last moment. The crust won't stand a chance!'

As Doug climbed the steps back to his seat, Edward returned to the centre of the pie, and attempted to turn his feet as far outwards as Doug had done.

Back in his seat, Doug shouted, 'Don't forget – really *feel* your hatred of the pie, Jack!'

Edward stood in the centre of the crust and closed his eyes. He imagined leaping as high as Doug, and of the pie crust splintering into a thousand pieces on his landing. He imagined the beautiful Primrose bouncing up and down in excitement and pride. He hated the pie... he truly despised it, and then he hated it a bit more. With determination and hatred in every muscle, he jumped. Whilst in the air he knew that this was a far better effort; he continued to hate the pie as he descended and pointed his heels. He landed; the crust let out a scream and split from side to side. The occupants of the upper tiers, the only ones who could actually see what was going on, went into a frenzy. The message was passed down to the lower rows who similarly celebrated.

Edward was standing in an irregular hole at the centre of the split. His descent was now slow, almost imperceptibly slow, and the slither of the gravy up the narrow gap between his hairy legs and the inside of his trouser was actually rather a pleasant sensation, a fact that he would never admit to anyone. As he descended, he began snapping off bits of pastry in order to increase the size of his hole. He reached down and ran his hands through the goo; unidentified slimy objects passed through his fingers.

When the liquid reached his upper chest, he was relieved to feel his feet finally touch base. He attempted to reach down and touch the bottom, but this was going to be impossible without going under, head and all.

Primrose blew him a kiss from the pie side and flashed her eyes at him; the flash seemed to contain a promise of things to come. Edward's knees became weak, but fortunately the viscosity of the gravy kept him upright. It was a testament to his infatuation with the Maid of the Grunt that he took a deep breath, held his nose and, with his eyes tightly shut went under, down into the brown. With great difficulty, he forced his body to the bottom of the pie. Oddly, the meat and vegetable matter had had no such difficulty, and were there to greet him in a congealed base layer. He combed his fingers through the sludge. Several times he was fooled by an undercooked carrot-slice or a deformed sprout, but he persevered until the need for oxygen took precedence over his quest. Just as was about to launch himself to the surface, his finger touched something metallic. He grabbed it and pushed off.

He broke the surface and hauled himself out onto the pastry, holding his prize aloft. He could see that the audience were in raptures – dancing, hugging and generally leaping about, but his gravy-filled ears prevented him from hearing the whoops, cheers and cries of 'Jack... Jack... Jack... Jack.' He tossed the coin to the mayor who, after much fumbling, caught it. The clock indicated that he had four minutes remaining. Edward scoffed.

I can do it in two.

He jumped back into the gravy in much better spirits.

Right, you little buggers – come to Eddy!

He drifted to the bottom, where he was certain that he would find the remaining coins, and began a fingertip search. After four circuits and no success, he pushed off the bottom with a view to taking a gulp of air and continuing his search. Unfortunately, he misjudged his plié, and smacked his head against the underside of the remaining crust. In a panic, he sought out the hole and hauled himself out, gasping for air and with his head throbbing.

He sat on the edge of the hole with his legs dangling in the gravy, feeling dejected. To his surprise, Primrose appeared and kneeled down next to him. 'Now come on, Ed Wood, you need to make a bit more effort - you can't sit around feeling sorry for yourself. You've got forty-five seconds to find two brogues! Now, how hard can that be?'

Edward saw red. 'For your information, I've just banged my head, and it hurts like f—'

Unnoticed by Edward, Primrose had sneaked behind his back, and gave it a firm shove.

Back in the gravy, feeling irritated at the deception, Edward was aware that something was different; he was no longer alone in the pie.

'You know, it's very unpleasant in here.' It was a voice that Edward recognised as belonging to Dr Jeffries. 'I've consumed many a pie in my time, Edward, but I can honestly say that this is the first time the roles have been reversed. Not that this pie is actually consuming us of course, but... Oh, I am sorry, you're probably drowning. Here, take these - I believe they're what you're looking for.'

Edward realised that he now had two coins in his hand.

'Now, I suggest you vacate the pie. I can't imagine that drowning in gravy is any nicer than losing your life in any other way. Oh – and don't forget to hang me later.'

Edward launched himself upwards; his fist, bearing the coins broke the surface first.

The crowd had completely vacated the seating by this time and were mingling around the pie when Edward burst forth. The sight of the coins in his clenched fist sent them into a wild merriment, the like of which Edward had never before seen; they cheered and danced, they banged hollow logs together, sang close-harmony psalms and improvised madrigals; they threw cup-cakes and meringue-balls at Edward, one elderly man produced a dozen juggling balls and demonstrated his complete inability to keep them in the air. In the spirit of the lunacy, Edward swaggered around the pie's perimeter, dripping with gravy and with his arms above his head, stopping periodically to pose like a body-builder. After about five minutes of this nonsense, he felt a twinge of guilt when he remembered the assistance that he had received in accomplishing his task. It was time to call it a day.

He walked to the pie's edge and eased himself down onto the barrow, then jumped to the grass. The crowd had other ideas; they hauled him up above their heads then passed him, flat on his back from hand to hand, round and round the pie, circuit after circuit, like he was a guitar hero in a mosh pit. Finally he was lowered to the ground, but then the back slapping and hand-shaking began. He also received a number of lingering hugs from young ladies, who seemed unconcerned about the inevitable transfer of gravy onto their summer dresses. The intimacy of these congratulatory hugs suggested that they wanted rather more from Edward than his gravy. Primrose looked on, arms crossed, patiently allowing Edward his moment.

Finally, the last of the revellers moved away.

'Now, where can I get a shower and a change of clothes?' Edward was still as high as a kite.

Primrose looked at him and burst out laughing. 'Oh don't be silly, Ed Wood – you're a vagrant... vagrants don't take showers; you need to go and have a dip in the Meander.'

Edward glared at her as if she were mad; Primrose glared back at him. 'Ed Wood, you just swam around in a gravy-filled pie. Are you really going to object to a rinse-off in the river?'

Edward shrugged. 'Guess not.'

'Now, you need to take that road over there.' She pointed beyond the perimeter fence. 'It twists and winds a lot, but it'll lead you to the spot where the dawn-dippers take their morning plunge.'

'And what about a change of clothes?'

There was a touch of frustration in Primrose's voice. 'We *really* don't have time for this, Ed Wood – there've been loads of donations from the men of the village, and Mrs Dullard is working day and night on the alterations, but you're just going to have to make do with your wet clothes for now. I'll see you at the base of the gallows in thirty minutes, and *don't* be late.'

* * *

22. Falling Asleep without a Goat

The dung-gate was particularly aromatic as Edward passed through it and headed in the direction that Primrose had indicated. He walked up and down the outer fence searching for anything that even loosely resembled a road.

'Are you looking for something, Edward?' The source of the voice was low to the ground, and when Edward saw who the speaker was, he leaped backwards, sending glutinous globules in every direction.

Now, as a rule, the sight of something, animate or otherwise, that causes the viewer such an extreme reaction, is unlikely to inspire the same degree of alarm when viewed on subsequent occasions. One exception to this rule is that of talking cats, and if, on the subsequent occasion, the cat is sitting cross-legged, reading aloud from a book, this exception is perfectly reasonable.

Hexagon untied his neckerchief and began wiping the brown blobs from the pages of his book. Once satisfied that no lasting damage had been done, he closed the book, and Edward was able to read the title; 'Falling Asleep without a Goat – A Ridley Practical Guide.' Below the title there was a tasteful representation of a man sleeping soundly in his bed-chamber without the need to have a goat present.

Hexagon tucked the book into his cummerbund. 'You know, you and I could easily fall out, Edward. Last time we met, when you were late for the welcoming committee, you kicked me and called me a scabby feline; this time you shower me with... what is this stuff?'

'Gravy.'

Hexagon looked Edward up and down, noting the extent of the brown covering. 'Ah yes... the great pie.' He held a paw up. 'Further explanation will *not* be necessary. So, Edward, what are you looking for?'

'A road… there should be a road around here that leads to the river… and I'm in a hurry to find it.'

'Ah, you mean '*That* road'.'

'That road? What road?'

'Oh for goodness' sake, Edward, 'That' is the name of the road.' He stepped to one side to reveal the street sign for 'That Road'.

'So where is That Road?'

'It's about a hundred yards in *that* direction, I'll show you if you like.'

They walked in silence, avoiding nettles, thistles and prickly pears, until the frustration became too great, and Edward asked, 'Why isn't the sign at the side of That Road? It's ridiculous to have it a hundred yards away!'

Hexagon raised his eyes. 'Because then we would have to re-name it 'This Road.'' He shook his head.

That Road was more of an uphill track than a road, strewn with ankle-spraining clods, and pot-holes large enough to lose a horse in. Every one of the poorly-constructed little houses that lined That Road was different, although it was debateable whether this was by design or because the builder was inept. The one thing that was clear, was that he didn't possess a plumb-line; the houses leaned towards each other like old friends, sharing snippets of mild scandal and complaining about their aches and ailments. A couple had clearly leaned too far and collapsed, but restoration work was well under way.

The pair continued up the hill until Hexagon held out a paw, and raised his story-telling claw. 'I know you're in a hurry, but I simply can't let you pass numbers fifteen and sixteen without relating the rural myth that exists concerning these two houses. You notice that they are joined at the upstairs level?'

Edward nodded.

'Well, the tale goes that their ground floors were built at a respectable distance apart, but at some point during the construction, a romance blossomed between the two unfinished buildings. One morning, the builder was astonished to find that the two courses of bricks that he had laid the previous day on each of the two houses had moved noticeably closer to each other. These nocturnal shifts continued until the day when full union was achieved, and two became one. Now, Edward, in case you're concerned that the joining might not have been consensual, you will see that the chimney pots are entwined in a loving embrace.'

Edward looked down at Hexagon with a hugely-sceptical expression.

'Okay, it's just a tale… but it *could* have happened!' Hexagon blushed in a uniquely feline way. 'I mean, look at you and the Maid of the Grunt!' He gave Edward a knowing look, and marched ahead with his nose and tail held high.

'Oh come on,' Edward called out. 'You can hardly compare my feelings for Primrose with those of two partially-constructed houses!'

Again, Hexagon held up a paw. 'We've arrived,' he announced, and pointed toward number nineteen.

To say that number nineteen was different from the other houses in That Road would be an understatement. It was a tall, grey angular building with small windows that revealed nothing of the interior. At least twice the size of its humble neighbours, its demeanour was arrogant and unwelcoming. To some eyes, it might have seemed elegant in a sterile and featureless kind of way, but not to Edward's. 'What an awful place! Who lives here?'

'Angela Gerald-Headley,' Hexagon said in a tone that left no doubt about his dislike of the mayor's wife.

'What? And the mayor?'

'Yes… Hedley lives here as well. Look, Edward, I haven't been entirely honest with you; I knew that you were on your way to the river for a wash-down, and thought I might suggest a pleasant alternative. You could use the mayoress's bathroom... nobody's in, and tales of its splendour are legendary.'

The pair approached the house; Edward leant on the front door as he read an adjacent wall-plaque:

> 'No.19, That Road.
> Residence of
> Mayoress Angela Gerald-Headley
> &
> Mayor Hedley Gerald-Headley.
> No take-away menus, flyers or copies of that bloody awful newspaper.'

Silently, the front door swung open.

After his initial surprise and subsequent realisation that it was *he* who had caused the door to open, Edward peered down the long hallway; the walls were plain and a thick green carpet teased the viewer into guessing its depth. The only wall-decoration was a single, large painting that hung close to the front door. It appeared to be completely abstract, although there was a forceful, yellow brush-stroke in the bottom left-hand corner that resembled a banana with a dynamic disposition. Excepting this, there was nothing that Edward could identify, unless of course the whole design was meant to depict a hurl of vomit.

Beneath the artwork, a small, rectangular panel read;

> 'Rimmington Forswipe (b. 1947)
> Adolescent Angst and Banana, 1969
> Acrylic on canvas.'

He looked at the picture again; it reinforced his opinion about modern art and those whose only creative talent was for extracting money from gullible patrons.

'Well go on then!' Hexagon nudged his leg. 'It's the first door on the left.'

'Don't rush me! I'm concerned about dripping gravy all over the place. Besides, they might come back at any moment.'

Hexagon did the best chicken impression that Edward had ever seen a cat attempt. 'Look – I'll keep watch out front, and if Hedley... or his wife, do return, I'll engage them in conversation and you can slip out the back.'

'You *really* don't like Angela, do you? You can't even bring yourself to say her name!'

Hexagon pulled a face. 'She's a nasty bit of work; thinks she's so much better than the rest of us. Hates the village and our traditions... doesn't even like The Grunt, would you believe? Goodness knows why Hedley married her - he could have done so much better for himself.'

Gripping the door frame, Edward stretched as far into the hall as he could manage, and listened for any suggestion of occupation; there was none. He considered the alternative – a plunge in a cold river with loads of gawping spectators.

Oh... why not?

His mind made up, he took a step inside and his gravy-coated shoe disappeared into the carpet pile. Balancing on that one foot, he swivelled and pushed open the bathroom door.

The moment he crossed the threshold, the room was flooded with the light of a hundred tiny bulbs, recessed into the ceiling, walls and floor. The effect was magical, and Edward experienced a rare moment of child-like wonderment. A circular, sunken whirlpool-bath dominated the room, with steps down from the marble floor. Two amethyst-glass swans with entwined necks sat at the far end, ready to dispense water from their open beaks. In contrast to their elegance, two scrawny, red demons sat astride a pair of conventional taps, attached to a tulip-shaped basin. They seemed to be gesturing to Edward to turn the taps, to let the water flow, to wash his face and rid himself of the gravy. Edward looked into their cruel eyes and saw the malevolence that lurked there.

I'll give it a miss, thanks all the same.

One wall of the bathroom was dominated by a paradise-beach mural complete with palm trees, breaking waves and speedo-attired hunks.

Everywhere there was glass and mirrors; Edward caught sight of his full-length reflection and was disgusted by what he saw - his ruined shoes, his trousers - torn and filthy, two days growth of stubble and his hair, plastered to his head with gravy and mud.

'It isn't a pretty sight, is it, Edward? But that's what a Resident Vagrant looks like ... Still want the job?' Angela Gerald-Headley squeezed past him, and tweaked the tips of the swans' wings. Water gushed forth into the bath.

'Angela! I... I'm sorry, I thought you were out. Hexagon said—'

Angela turned to face him. 'Edward, I don't know if you've noticed, but Hexagon is a cat. Do you normally make decisions based on the advice of domesticated animals? Now, take off your clothes and dump them in there.' She indicated a futuristic shower cubicle that looked more like a time-machine than a bathroom fixture.

Edward started to unbutton his shirt. 'Hang on, I'm not getting undressed in front of you!'

Angela lay back on a strategically-positioned chaise longue. 'My bathroom – my rules,' she winked. 'Oh, don't worry dear, I've seen it all before... *many* times.'

'Not mine you haven't!'

Angela raised her eyes. 'Well no, regrettably that's true, but I'm sure little miss plant-whisperer could give me a detailed description.'

'And neither has Primrose!' Edward snarled.

Angela sat up and began rummaging in her handbag. Finding her silver fern-case, she flipped it open and chose a flower. Edward cringed as he anticipated the fern-ritual; the rubbing of the crushed bloom into the gums, the sucking of air through the teeth and the expulsion of a globule of blue saliva. Angela didn't disappoint, banishing the blue spit to the tulip-shaped basin.

Edward undressed down to his boxers and threw the clothes into the shower cubicle. At the sound of the door opening, the multiple shower-heads, previously hanging like end-of-season sunflowers, sprang into life, ready and willing to provide a pleasurable, life-enhancing experience to their guest. The sight of a pile of filthy clothes came as rather a disappointment but, being professionals, they subjected the garments to merciless blasts from every angle.

Once in the bubbling bath, Edward rested his head on a bath pillow and allowed his whole body to relax. He could easily have slipped into blissful sleep, but was aware that his rendezvous at the gallows was fast approaching. Under the cover of a blanket of steaming bubbles, he removed his disgusting pants and slapped them onto the marble floor. A man-size flannel weighed down with a pumice stone served as a replacement.

Angela picked up the garment with a pair of laundry tongs, and dropped them into the cubicle to be savaged by the shower heads. 'Now, Edward, I need to go and pack a case, so I'll leave you to scrub that muck off your body. Help yourself to anything that takes your fancy.' She indicated a selection of expensive-looking toiletries on the bottom shelf of a unit that was within reach of the tub. 'I've taken all the ones that I'm going to need.'

Angela closed the door behind her and Edward listened to the sound of her ascending the stairs. A small rubber duck floated towards him; he retrieved it, placed it on his chest and wondered what such a tacky lump of plastic was doing in this palace of ostentatiousness. He scanned the bottles in search of shampoo, then noticed that the second shelf contained a row of books, the titles of which left him in no doubt about the state of the Gerald-Headley's marriage. A copy of *'The Art of Avoiding your Husband'* stood alongside, *'The Joy of Separate Beds'*, *'The Joy of Separate*

Rooms', 'Kitchen Poisons that Don't Arouse Suspicion', 'The Good Extra-Marital-Affair Guide' and, *'Get Him to Leave the House for Good; 20 Reliable Methods.'*

At the very end of the shelf, a tall, thin book stood proud, notable for the lack of a title on its spine. Out of mild curiosity, Edward reached for the book and read the words on the front cover; *'Edward – will you please stop mucking about with that damn duck and read this book!'*

23. Swell-O-Soil

No sooner had Edward read the words before the dust-jacket disintegrated in his fingers and thousands of tiny pieces drifted down into the water. He was left holding a thin, hardback volume entitled *'Manual for the operation and maintenance of Flatpack on the Meander, by Dr J. Jeffries.'*

Edward opened the cover and began reading.

'I would like to convey my utmost gratitude to those of you who responded to my advertisement in the Leddington Gusset Echo and who subsequently took part in the construction of the village. I well recall those heady few weeks; the excitement we all felt about what we were creating, the good-humoured banter, the beers, and of course the frustration when things didn't go as planned, notably the difficulty we had achieving the fourteen-and-a-half-degree angle. Were it not for your determination and enthusiasm for the project, I do not think that our beautiful village would ever have been completed and, for that, I thank you.'

Edward turned the page.

'A copy of this book is being sent to every household in Flatpack, and I trust that it will prove invaluable as you settle into your new homes. Its purpose is to give you step by step instructions on how to get the most from the village. I have included a troubleshooting section at the back of the book, but if you face problems that are not covered, you are most welcome to visit me in my chamber, (more on this subject shortly,) and I can assure you of a warm welcome and an excellent cup of Broad-Bean Oolong.

'I would like to tell you a little about my own intentions; I shall be joining you in the next few days and intend to reside in a huge apartment that I have had built beneath the village. For several months, I have been carrying-out a series of soil-improvement experiments, and am pleased to report that these have been a great success. Last Thursday, I spent a pleasant night with my left hand buried in a pot of 'Dr Jeffries' Organic, Filter-drained and Stone-free Miracle-loam', or 'Swell–O–Soil' as I plan to market it. When I awoke, I was delighted to see that my hand had grown to the size of a fairly-large dog. Upon removal, however, shrinkage was rapid and my hand was its usual size within a matter of minutes.

'I anticipate that, once underground in my chamber, which is lined with Swell-O-Soil, my body will expand to the length of the village within about three days, thereby ensuring that a part of Dr Jeffries is beneath every citizen of Flatpack at all times. My growth may cause some minor tremors but I don't foresee any structural damage.

'It is important that my expansion is considerable because I am going to need a pair of huge, capacious lungs; during the course of the first year, and every year thereafter, I will be spending a considerable amount of time inhaling through my wall-trumpet. This device is connected to several miles of winding tunnels which eventually come up to the surface at the 'blowhole', which is situated behind St Gruntle's Church.'

Edward stopped reading and considered the passage.

Why would anyone want to live beneath a village and breathe through a trumpet?

He expected an explanation to follow, but there was none.

'I need to move on to your responsibilities as custodians of the village; Flatpack will require annual maintenance if you wish it to maintain its status as the world's only by-invitation-only village. An annual celebration entitled, 'St Gruntle's Day,' will be held on September 12th on the anniversary of the birth of our adopted patron saint, and the maintenance that I allude to will revolve around that special day.

'On the eve of 'The Grunt,' a ballot will be held in the town hall to determine whether you, the villagers, wish Flatpack to remain in its current form, as a completely isolated village, unknown and unseen by the outside world, or alternatively to become an ordinary English village, bland, dreary, and indistinguishable from a thousand other such villages... such as Leddington Gusset, where I was born.

'I feel compelled to hold this ballot just in case the novelty of living in complete isolation wears off. I hope and pray that this will not happen, but have put in place the means to make the transformation happen if necessary.

'Now, I need to move on the 'hanging' stage—'

At that moment, the bathroom door swung open and Angela re-entered dragging a bulging suitcase. 'Oh honestly, you haven't been reading that pile of crap, have you? I've been meaning to throw it out for ages.' She took the book away from Edward.

Leaning her case against the shower cubicle, Angela flopped down on the chaise longue. 'Well, I'm all packed and ready to go; it's a pity you won't be coming with me, but now that you've embraced life in this dreary place, you've become boring. Do you know, Edward, I find it hard to believe how much you've changed in a few short hours. This morning, you were a much-needed hunk of steaming masculinity in this village full of drips. You would have done anything to escape Flatpack, and when I caught you staring down my cleavage, I even dared believe we might have some fun. Either way, I was convinced that I'd found a partner in crime.

'Now I see that you've acquired an embarrassing little dog, you agreed to take part in their ridiculous pie ritual and are all loved-up with the Maid of the Grunt! I have to ask you, Edward, you are aware that Primrose Pynching is 'not all there'?

'And what's that supposed to mean?' Edward said through clenched teeth.

'Oh come on, Edward! Do I have to spell it out? Angela adopted a high-pitched girly voice. 'I think I'll take off all my clothes off and dance around in a bush of nettles. The nettles won't sting me of course, because they're my friends.'

Any semblance of relaxation gone, Edward sat on his clenched fists.

Angela continued, 'I can tell the future you know, because my dreams come tr—'

'Oh, you can mock, but at least Primrose doesn't have blue teeth!'

Within moments, the mayoress was standing over him looking down through narrowed eyes. 'You have no idea what it's like living with these morons and that stupid man! You find my blue teeth funny, do you? Well... if it weren't for the ferns to keep me calm, I would have killed that idiot on more than one occasion!' She took a deep breath. 'Anyway... after tonight you and the rest of the inbred imbeciles will have to find some other figure of fun - I'm leaving Flatpack, and I will *not* be coming back.'

Edward smirked. 'Yeah right, you know there's no escape—'

'Oh, there's a way... but don't think for a moment that I'm going to reveal it to you. You never did ask anyone about The Year of the Big Forget, did you?'

'Err... no.'

'I guessed not. If you had, you'd have some idea of the events you're going to face later tonight.'

'Why? What's going to happen?'

Angela laughed. 'Yeah...like I'm going to tell you! Oh, don't worry, there shouldn't be any fatalities... Well, except for the village itself, of course, and I for one won't be mourning the demise of this dump. The villagers are just going to have to wake up to the realities of living in a normal village. Not that I care, I'll be miles away.'

Edward's head was spinning. 'Fatalities? What—'

'I'm going now, Edward. I would say it's been a pleasure to know you, but we both know that would be a complete lie. Enjoy your bath.'

Number nineteen, That Road shook as Angela slammed the front door behind her.

24. The Cirrus of Pestilence

Hettie Dalliard stared in disbelief at the contents of the tea cup... it wasn't possible!

Twenty minutes earlier, Lettie, in one of her rare forceful moments, had stated, in a manner that didn't allow debate, that she was going to watch Jack perform his first hanging and would not, therefore, be helping with the washing up this year. Hettie had protested a little, but was well aware of how besotted Lettie was with the new arrival, and soon consented.

Before embarking upon the laborious task of cleaning the crockery and storing it in a well-padded tea chest for next year's Grunt, she liked to concentrate on the silver tea-spoons, which she washed and dried individually before applying a little lemon juice and buffing with a silk hanky. 'Tea-spoons should shine like the stars,' she had told Lettie on many occasions. 'A tarnished tea spoon is only fit for digging carrots.'

She held up the first spoon for inspection; her face looked back at her - lined and saggy with many broken veins and a big nose. The big nose was simply a distortion caused by the shape of the spoon, but otherwise, the utensil was telling the truth. Not normally one for self-pity, Hettie felt a tingling sensation in her average sized nose, a pre-cursor to tears.

'Now stop it, you silly old woman!' she rebuked herself.

Once again, she looked at her reflection, but this time her attention was drawn away from her face to the sky beyond. Putting down the spoon, she looked up. The cirrus that she had spotted much earlier in the day was in precisely the same position, it hadn't changed size or shape, but its centre was now as black as coal.

Concerned, Hettie reached for one of the clean cups and spooned in some Honest Malcolm, a rather nerdy blend, but one renowned for its reliable predictions. She added boiling water to the leaves, then stood back to give them some privacy whilst they agreed their message.

Next, she lifted the cup and, holding it about an inch above the table, swirled it three times anticlockwise. When the leaves had settled to the bottom, she drank the liquid, leaving just a little, and placed the cup upside down on its saucer. After a few nervous moments, she lifted the cup and saw that it contained a perfect likeness of the cloud above her head, complete with the sinister dark centre. The blood drained from Hettie's face. 'Pinochet', she breathed. 'I need Pinochet.'

When Pinochet wrote his ground-breaking 'Lore of Tassiography,' unquestionably the definitive work on the subject, he included a chapter entitled, *'Anecdotes, Rarities and Oddities'*, and it was this section that Hettie now sought. Page 468 was headed up, *'The Cirrus of Pestilence'*, and beneath this was a sketch that could have been made of the pattern in her cup, such was the similarity. The text read;

'An appearance of The Cirrus of Pestilence has never been reported to me directly, however the following narrative is based on the written words of a most-reliable source.

'The reason that the pattern has an entry here is because of what occurred on a winter evening in 1765 to a Cistercian Monk, one Brother Albert, who took tea after vespers in his cold, bare quarters in Birstall Priory. He was surprised to see a previously-unknown leaf-pattern appear in his cup when he had finished. He sketched a faithful copy in his diary, and this is shown above. As a mere novice, and due to the strictness of his order, Albert chose not to share the image with his superiors for fear that there may be a ruling forbidding such practices.

'Within a week, a merciless epidemic, characterised by delirium and boils, swept down the stone corridors of Birstall, entering uninvited into the lodgings, refectory, library and places of prayer.

The disease carried away over half the monks including Brother Albert.

'In time, his diaries were discovered, and hence we are able to show you what appeared in the brother's teacup that cold winter night.

'Birstall priory never fully recovered, it was impossible to recruit candidates to a monastery with a reputation of being, 'out of favour with the almighty'. Within a decade, it was a crumbling ruin.

'To my knowledge, the pattern has never appeared again, a fact for which we can be thankful.'

Holding the cup in one hand, the book in the other, Hettie lifted the items for comparison to the cloud; they were identical. She dropped the cup; it smashed into a thousand pieces on the trestle table.

#

Back in the mayoress's bathroom, Edward was lying on the marble floor struggling to pull his sodden trousers up. It was as if they had enjoyed the shower experience so much that they had no desire to return to their day job. Finally, his zip was zipped and the button fastened, but where was his shirt? He found it whimpering in a corner of the shower, clearly having not enjoyed the experience as much as his trousers. 'Now stop that!' he instructed the shirt. 'We've got a job to do and I need you to be tough and brave.' The shirt, uplifted by Edward's inspiring words, formed its cuffs into fisticuffs to show that it was ready for action. Gone were the days when Edward felt stupid talking to inanimate objects.

Hexagon was waiting at the foot of the steps, looking shamefaced. 'I'm *so* sorry, Jack, she must have been hiding upstairs.'

'That doesn't matter now, Hex, but I *do* need to talk to Primrose urgently.'

Hexagon cringed at the truncation of this name, but bit his lip. 'Oh, she'll be at the foot of the gallows waiting for you to—'

Edward launched himself down That Road, defying the boulders and pot-holes to trip him up and knock him out for the third time that day. Coming to a halt at the bottom of the hill, he stared at the row of quaint, terraced houses that stood between him and the village green.

'Where did these come from?' he shouted back at Hexagon who was carefully picking his way down That Road.

'They've been there all along,' Hexagon called out, 'but you were more focused on finding That Road to notice.'

'So how am I going to get onto the green? I can't go back to the dung gate - that would take forever!'

Hexagon put a thoughtful paw to his chin. 'That it would, Jack, that it would, but... might I propose an alternative?'

Edward looked down at Hexagon. 'The thing is, your alternative propositions do *not* have a good track-record.'

'Yes, yes, yes, can we drop the whole Angela thing now? I didn't know she was upstairs...okay? Now look, all the occupants of these cottages will be huddled around the gallows right now, waiting for you to hang Dr Jeffries. All... except the Reverend Carsten Spankie and his family, who never attend the hanging.'

'And how does that help us?'

'Well, Carsten lives at number eight, over there. If you were to ring the bell, explain your predicament, walk down the hall, enter the parlour, make small-talk with the family, then leave by the patio doors, you would find yourself in the Spankie family garden.'

'Go on...'

'Which has a gate that leads directly onto the green!'

Edward thought about it. 'So, what's he like, this Spankie guy?'

'Oh – a real gent and man of God! It's just that he finds the hanging a bit too 'pagan' for his tastes.'

'And you don't think he'll mind me using his house as a short-cut?'

'Of course not, he's been looking forward to meeting you.'

With some trepidation, Edward pressed the doorbell. By the time it had chimed three verses of 'A mighty fortress is our God,' Edward had had enough. 'They're not in! I should have known better than to listen to another of your stupid ideas. Look, the kitchen window's open – I'm going in that way.'

'You can't do that Jack! It's not...right.'

'Just watch!'

Edward dragged over a large upturned flower pot, pulled himself up onto the sill only to topple head-first onto the kitchen floor. It was then that he heard it... 'All things bright and beautiful, all creatures great and small...'

The kitchen door swung open and a huge, bearded man entered mid-verse. 'Jack! What a lovely surprise...Caroline! Caroline!' he called up the hall. 'Jack's just climbed in the kitchen window!'

The reverend helped Edward to his feet. 'Come through and meet the family.' With his arm in Edward's, Carsten led the way to the parlour. All present got to their feet as the pair entered.

'Jack, this is my lovely wife Caroline, and these are our twin daughters Sparrow and Wren who,' he winked to his giggling daughters, 'I am contractually obliged to inform you, are *not* identical.' Edward greeted each family member in turn although, to him, the twins looked as identical as it was possible to be.

'Now, before you girls get too excited, I have to remind you that Jack is on his way to perform the annual hanging.'

'Oh... can we go, Daddy, please?' the girls pleaded in harmony.

The reverend loomed over his daughters. 'Now look, girls, we've been through this time and time again. As a man of God I cannot possibly endorse the hanging of a fellow man as part of a celebration.'

'But he's not a real man, Daddy,' Wren blurted out. 'He's made of old clothes stuffed with scrunched-up copies of The Observer!'

'*And* acorns,' Sparrow added.

The Reverend looked at his adored daughters as only a loving father who had recently become aware that his girls had become young ladies, could. He sighed. 'This year, *if you're good*,' he raised a finger, 'I'll let you join the crowds at the blowhole.'

The girls' reaction was akin to that of a sportsman who had scored a vital goal in the dying seconds of a match. Racing around the parlour, they punched the air, squealed 'Yess!' and climbed up the reverend's back who, it was clear, had not expected quite such a reaction.

'Girls, girls! Remember we have a guest!'

The girls retreated to a corner for conspiratorial discussions.

'Now, Jack, we have a family tradition, and I'm going to need to know your all-time favourite hymn.'

Edward gulped.

'My family and I will serenade you with it as you depart.'

Despite once being a choirboy, Edward was unable to recall a single hymn, let alone have a favourite, but this he had no desire to admit. Then it came to him and he announced, 'The day thou gavest, Lord is ended.'

'What an excellent choice, Jack! A beautiful melody - I often use it as a rousing evensong finale.

'Now come along family, Jack has important business. Open the patio doors please, Wren.'

Edward stepped out onto the grass, whilst the Spankie family lined up on the decking. Edward looked back and noticed that Wren had acquired a guitar, and the reverend a baton.

The reverend raised the baton, and his family sang and strummed:

'The day thou gavest, Lord, is ended,
The darkness falls at thy behest;
To thee our morning hymns ascended,
Thy praise shall sanctify our rest.'

Edward wasn't sure whether it was customary to stay for all of the verses, but the need to escape the excruciatingly out-of-tune guitar made the decision for him. He opened the gate, waved to the Spankies, then strode across the green towards the gallows. He was surprised to see Hexagon at his heels. 'How did you get through?'

'Oh, I just used the cat-flaps at number fifteen. Luckily, old Two-Breakfasts wasn't in or I might have been delayed. We've never really seen eye-to-eye since he accused me of using his litter tray. I mean, as if I'd go near that steaming box!

'Incidentally Edward, you *do* understand why the hanging is so important, don't you?'

Edward thought back. 'Well, not really... I was just about to read that bit when the mayor's wife came back.'

'Ah! So you've been reading The Manual.'

'Yeah, would you believe she has a bathroom bookshelf?'

Hexagon pulled a face. 'Oh, nothing surprises me with that dreadful woman... but look, let's stop for a minute – it's important that you understand about the hanging.

'You know about the ballot that takes place on the eve of the Grunt. Well, around mid-afternoon, a confirmatory signal needs to be sent to Dr Jeffries that all is well, and that it is time for him to exhale into his wall trumpet. The Doctor has stipulated that the signal must take the form of a hanging, but not any old hanging mind, it has to be an effigy of himself.'

Edward considered this. 'So... what if the ballot goes the other way?'

Hexagon looked at him like he was completely mad. 'Do you know Edward, I generally think of you as a fairly educated chap, but occasionally you *do* ask the most stupid questions. Do you really think there is *any* possibility of the villagers voting to give away everything that they have here? Anyway, unsurprisingly, the manual doesn't cover that eventuality.'

At that moment a voice from the crowd shouted, 'There he is!' A roar went up and the crowd parted to let Edward through. Despite her unfortunate leg-to-body ratio, Mr Lean had managed to scale the gallows' thirteen steps and was tearing around the deck in excitement.

Primrose was standing at the foot of the gallows talking to Mrs Git from the Greengrocers. 'Ah! Here's my lovely Ed Wood now.'

Edward put an arm around her shoulder and steered her to one side. 'I need to talk to you urgently, it's about—'

'There's no time for *talk*, Ed Wood.' She removed his arm. 'You're already late; now get up those steps and give the Doctor a good hanging.'

'But—'

'Now!' It was an order; Primrose's fiercely-beautiful eyes didn't invite discussion.

The school children had made a superb job of the doctor's effigy. He stood on the trap-door in a pair of highly-polished black slip-ons, wearing a pristine three-piece suit, a cravat and a broad smile that suggested that he was relishing his imminent demise.

Edward wanted to get it over with. 'Are you ready?' he called out to the crowd and the loud response to the affirmative nearly blew him over.

Well here goes... first time for everything.

Edward operated the lever, the well-oiled trap-doors swung open and Dr Jeffries descended with such velocity that his head was separated from his body. The crowd's appreciation was rapturous... but brief, as they seemed in a hurry to depart, all in the direction of St Gruntle's Church.

Edward descended the steps and retrieved Dr Jeffries' head. 'We'll laugh about this someday,' he said to the head, then tossed it to the approaching Primrose.

She kissed him on the cheek. 'That was a lovely hanging. Nobody could have guessed that it was your first.'

'Yes, but why are the villagers in such a hurry to leave, and where are they all headed?'

'To the blowhole, silly.' She took Edward's hand. 'Come on – I don't want to get stuck at the back.'

Primrose hummed a merry tune as they proceeded across the green with the flow of people.

There was a nasal address over the public address system. 'Ladies and gentlemen, in view of the high standard of our new vagrant's first hanging, the committee have agreed that Jack has passed his probation and should, from this time hence, be referred to as 'Edward'. Than-kyou.'

Those around Edward and Primrose applauded politely.

'Oh, Ed Wood – isn't that wonderful!' Primrose gave him a huge hug.

'Primrose... can I ask you a question?'

'Of course, my love.'

'Will you tell me about The Year of the Big Forget?'

There was an exclamation of 'Shame!' from an elderly resident walking behind them.

Primrose took Edward to one side. 'Ed Wood – it's the absolute height of bad manners to mention... that, especially on The Grunt! Who on *earth* told you about...' she looked around, 'The Forget?'

'It was the mayor's wife who mentioned it; I used her bathroom instead of washing in the river, and she told—'

Primrose dropped his hand and began backing away. 'You've been taking a bath in *that* woman's bathroom?'

'Well, it was a Jacuzzi to be accurate – it was Hexagon's idea.'

'I don't give a tinker's trousers whose idea it was!' Primrose fumed. 'And did Angela share your *Jacuzzi*?'

'Oh, of course not, it wasn't like that.' He grabbed her arm. 'Look, I have no idea what The Year of the Big Forget is all about, but Angela said that something similar is going to happen tonight...'

Edward had never seen Primrose display such rage as she tore her arm away from him and disappeared into the crowd.

Great!

The slate steps leading from the green to St Gruntle's Church high above were steep and narrow, and there was many a slip.

Edward took the arm of an elderly lady who was out of breath and having difficulties, mainly due to unsuitable shoes.

'This is most kind of you, young man,' she said. 'I'm afraid I'm not the athlete I used to be.'

The expression rang bells with Edward.

...not the athlete I used to be.

Then he remembered. 'Maxie Malleable once said exactly the same words to me.'

The lady laughed. 'I'm not surprised, we tend to use the same expressions after spending so many years together - I'm *Mrs* Malleable. I was listening to your conversation with your fiancée.'

Fiancée?

'The Big Forget *is* a very sensitive subject, but I think Primrose was more concerned that you might have shared a bath with the mayoress.'

'But I didn't!'

She patted his hand. 'Of course you didn't dear, anyone can see that you're completely besotted with Primrose – she is *such* a beauty. But you won't make any friends around here if go around asking about The Big Forget - they all, man, woman and dog remember that night and it fills them with dread. We nearly lost everything that is special about our beloved home; you can hardly blame them for not wanting to talk about it.'

'But it's important that I know what happened; I have reason to believe that something similar is going to happen tonight. Are *you* prepared to tell me about it, Mrs Malleable?'

Maxie's wife looked thoughtful and said nothing for a few moments, then a more decisive expression formed. 'Yes... yes, I think you *should* know about it... but let's get to the top of these damned steps first.'

Edward and Mrs Malleable slumped onto a bench that was almost certainly holding the church up.

'What's your name?' Edward asked. 'I can't call you Mrs Malleable.'

'It's Wendy, I was christened Wendy Wheatfield. You can imagine the fun my school-friends had with that one. Getting rid of that surname was one of the main reasons that I married Atticus. Only kidding, I love him more than he knows.'

Edward could tell that this was true.

* * *

25. The Year of the Big Forget

Wendy shifted nearer to Edward to make room for her sizeable handbag. She opened this and produced a tartan rug which she draped over hers and Edward's knees.

Edward reflected on how much more comfortable he felt sitting next to Maxie's wife than he had with Angela. In his previous life, he would never, under any circumstances, have sat on a bench next to an old lady with a rug on his lap. That would have simply been inconceivable.

They watched the excited villagers file past. Wendy took one of her shoes off and rubbed her foot. 'Ooh, I really shouldn't have worn these shoes; I normally wear my Grunt shoes, but Atticus got there first this year.'

Aha – so they were ladies' shoes.

'So...' Wendy began, 'The Big Forget. Well let me start by saying that I blame Maynard Kafuffle more than anyone else for what happened. As you know, he brews a festival ale for The Grunt, and this is much appreciated by the villagers, but *that* year, he decided that he wanted to give it, 'a bit more of a kick.'

'Now, I wasn't particularly concerned when I heard that his plan was to include some excitable molasses in the mix after all – I'm no prude, but I hadn't anticipated the reckless quantity that he added to the final boil. As you can imagine, the finished brew certainly *did* have a kick to it! But... I have to say, the villagers loved it, so I had my usual pint at elevenses with one of Hettie's special buns.

'It was a delicious combination, but I remember feeling very sleepy shortly after. I returned home with the intention of taking an hour's kip.

'I have no idea for how long I slept, but when I awoke it was dark outside; I would probably have remained asleep had I not heard an almighty cry of, 'We've forgotten to hang the doctor!'

'Now let me tell you, Edward, those words made my blood run cold. As I'm sure you know, the whole point of hanging the doctor in effigy was to send a signal to the *real* doctor that it is time for him to exhale. If no signal is send, our dear doctor won't exhale.

Wendy's voice had begun to waiver; she produced a large, man-sized handkerchief with a capital 'A' embroidered on it, dabbed her eyes then trumpeted loudly. 'I'm so sorry, Edward, talking about the near-demise of our lovely village is not an easy tale to tell.'

'That's okay, take your time.'

I don't get it, what's so important about this doctor exhaling?

Wendy composed herself, stuffed the hanky back up her sleeve and sniffed. 'So, you can imagine my feelings of panic when I heard those words. I went to the front door, tugged it open, only to be blown clear off my feet by the strongest gale I had ever encountered.

'I lay on the floor listening to frightened, confused voices outside, some of which I recognised. One shouted, 'St Gruntle's has grown a second steeple!' Another yelled, 'The Meander has started to sing!'

'I kicked the door shut, shuffled over to the window and peered out; I could see flower pots, dustbins, tents, bunting, oh… all manner of things flying around in the wind.

'It was then that I felt a very strange sensation; as if my home was being ever-so-gently lowered.'

'Like you were in an elevator?' Edward suggested.

Wendy looked at him blankly.

'Oh no, you don't have… ignore me.'

Wendy continued, looking a little irritated at the interruption. 'I shivered as I realised what was happening – the village angle was correcting itself! From fourteen and a half degrees, it was returning to…' she looked up at the sky, blinking away more tears, then in a weak, trembling voice said the word '… horizontal'.

'Can you imagine it, Edward… Flatpack – flat?' She ploughed on through the tears, not waiting for an answer. 'And of course you *do* know what that would inevitably lead to?' She looked at him for a sign that he understood.

Put on the spot, Edward blurted out, 'Well yes… of course!'

Wendy produced the handkerchief again and blew loudly. 'Nice try, Edward, but I can see you don't fully understand the implications of losing the angle. You see—'

At that moment, Maxie Malleable staggered into view looking rather the worse for Kafuffle's Muscular Porter. He lifted the rug and shuffled his large bottom between that of his wife and Edward. Raising a finger, he announced, 'I… jusht fell over,' then let out a peal of giggles. His wife looked at him disapprovingly. Maxie leaned against Edward. 'Wedny thinks I'm drunk, but I'm not you know.' He attempted to tap his nose but missed. 'I'm jusht… happy!' He threw his arms wide to illustrate his happiness and knocked his wife's hat off.

'I *am* sorry about this, Edward.' Wendy reached into her handbag and produced a flask. 'A cup of Hettie's Salutary Suspension should do the trick'.

She handed her husband a brimming cup which smelled of summer afternoons and fresh tomato leaves; he downed it in one. 'Delicious!' he announced, and his head flopped down between his knees. Moments later, it sprang back up again. 'Edward! I see you've met my lovely wife Wendy… Wendy, this is our splendid new Jack… no – wait, I don't have to call him that any more. This is Edward, and he's a jolly fine chap! Now come on, you two need to join the others in the petal field – or you'll miss the big moment.'

Maxie stood up and offered his hand to his wife who, having replaced her shoe, took it. 'Thank you, Atticus, you're such a gentleman.' She whispered in Edward's ear, 'Never fails.'

'You're welcome, my dear. Now, Wendy - I do need to have a quick word with Hedley, so I'll join you in a few moments.'

Edward remained seated. 'But I need to know the rest of the story!'

'Oh, I'll tell you later dear – we don't want to miss the petals!'

Edward and Wendy re-joined the chatty surge and soon became separated. Rather than entering the church, the crowds followed a path that turned right at the entrance and hugged the building until they were standing behind St Gruntle's. No churchyard or garden of remembrance faced them, but a sizeable field, bordered by a dry-stone wall. At its centre was a huge dome of sweet-smelling petals around which the villagers were forming concentric circles. Edward found himself standing next to Bedford Trite, who was attired in his usual lack of clothes.

Bedford offered his hand. 'Hello again, Edward - good to see you. That was a splendid hanging, I must say. This,' he gestured towards the petal dome, 'is the blowhole; the exit from Dr Jeffries' tunnels. A mesh has been placed over the hole so that the children can cover it with thousands of beautiful petals for when the doctor exhales. It's a wonderful sight... you'll see!'

The last of the villagers took their place and everyone waited for the big moment. The atmosphere of excitement and anticipation lasted for around ten minutes, with the children singing, clapping and bouncing up and down, their proud parents looking on, pretending not to be just as excited.

On the stroke of ten minutes, boredom set in, as is its wont. Sibling bickered with sibling, bottom-lips protruded and many a parent was subjected to the question: 'How much longer is the doctor going to be?' The standard answer was: 'He waiting for you to behave yourself!'

Soon, it was the grown-ups' turn to grumble; initially, it was just a single voice: 'Ow much longer's 'e gonna be?'

This encouraged another to inform the gathering, 'My tea's gonna be ruined - burnt to a cinder... *and* it's mi' favourite casserole!'

'Lamb?' Another enquired.

'Yup!'

'With mushrooms from the copse?'

'Yup!'

'Sounds delicious... but yeah, it'll probably be ruined.'

From his position in the third row, Edward caught a glimpse of Maxie and the mayor on the opposite side of the circle and, judging by their stern expressions and the amount of chest prodding, they were having a heated argument, although Edward could hear nothing of what was being said. Then both men turned and looked directly at him.

Oh hell, what now?

They set off in opposite directions around the circle of villagers and met up on either side of Edward.

'Edward,' Maxie began brightly, 'we may have a minor problem, and we wanted to have a little chat with you about it.'

'It's probably nothing,' Hedley added.

Maxie continued, 'You see, normally Dr Jeffries would have exhaled by now, thereby sending the petals high into the sky to everybody's delight.'

Edward folded his arms. 'Yes, I've heard all that... but what has it got to do with me?'

Maxie fiddled with a silver curl that was poking through his string vest. 'Well, we'd like you to pop down into the tunnel and have a little chat with the doctor.'

'What? Can't someone else go?'

Hexagon poked his head through Maxie's legs. 'Oh honestly, Edward, didn't you read the job description and contract?'

* * *

26. Play that Funky Elevator Music White Boy

Maxie lifted the edge of the mesh, and Edward peered down into the blackness. As he did, he felt the sides of the tunnel; they were particularly smooth... and particularly steep. 'I'm not going down there—it's a vertical drop!'

Maxie laughed. 'Oh, only for the first ten feet or so; really it's nothing more than a playground slide for grown-ups. I've ridden it loads of times, and I can never resist coming back up for a second run.'

Edward looked at him sceptically.

I don't believe a word of it.

He took a second look down into the hole. 'For a start, how am I going to see where I'm going?'

'Ah yes, now I'm glad you brought that up.' Maxie rummaged in a hessian bag and produced three metal objects that resembled silver ice-cream cones. 'You're going to need these.' He handed them to Edward who inspected them, then shrugged.

'They're torches. As soon as you get down there, jam the pointed ends into the tunnel wall and you'll be spoiled for light.'

Edward put the torches in the pockets of his trousers which, in view of everything the garment had endured that day, were still in reasonably functional condition. He sat down on the lip and sighed. 'So what exactly do you want me to do when I get down there?'

'Okay, Edward, once you've located the doctor, make sure he's not ill or anything, gently enquire why he hasn't exhaled, then report back to me and Hedley. We'll take it from there.'

Edward felt a hand cover each of his eyes; he turned his head and his mouth was kissed by the softest of lips. 'I'm very proud of you, Ed Wood.' Primrose removed her hands and knelt down beside him.

'I thought you were annoyed with me.'

'Well... I was, but I can only stay angry with you for so long, my love, and I know that there could never be anything between you and *that* woman.'

Edward stared into her eyes.

She is so perfect.

For the first time that day, the sun disappeared behind a cloud. It sucked the sun's rays into its depths and allowed little light or warmth to pass. There was a startled, 'Ohh!' from the villagers at being plunged into semi-darkness. Edward and Primrose were too busy shamelessly canoodling to notice.

Hettie Dalliard stepped forward, stood in front of the giggling pair, and coughed. 'Can you two please either stop gobbling each other or book yourselves into one of the guest rooms above The Flounder!'

Edward and Primrose sprang apart.

Hettie puffed out her chest, then folded her arms over her ample bosom; not the easiest of tasks. Lettie stood behind her sister, attempting to look small; an even more difficult assignment. Hettie adopted a no-nonsense tone. 'As you will have noticed, there is now a cloud blocking out the sun; this is no ordinary cloud but the Cirrus of Pestilence, and its presence indicates that something terrible is going to happen. You, Edward, need to get down that hole without further delay, and find out what is wrong with the good doctor. My sister and I will be happy to give you a push if you need it.'

'That won't be necessary ladies.' Edward held up a hand then winked at Lettie, who clasped her hands in joy. Edward shuffled his buttocks forward like an emperor penguin with a chick between its legs, blew a last kiss to Primrose and disappeared into the void.

Maxie's comparison of entering the blowhole with a ride on a playground slide was not strictly accurate. Instead of a pleasant descent down a smooth metal surface, Edward's experience was one of falling, blind and terrified, into a bottomless abyss. The only similarity was that the ride ended with him sitting in a puddle of muddy water.

He cursed Maxie as he picked himself up and felt around for the torches. Having located all three, he jabbed the first into the tunnel wall and was blinded by the intensity of its beam. If anything, the second was even brighter, and he decided to take protective action before activating the third. Burying his eyes in the inside of his elbow, he thrust it home. This proved completely unnecessary as the torch failed to produce any light at all. Edward pulled it out, shook it, and tried again; the result was the same.

Stupid thing. Two torches will be plenty.

He dropped the duff torch on the tunnel floor and shone the remaining pair into the distance. They revealed a sharp bend to the left after about a hundred yards. He sighed. 'And now... I walk.'

There were many twists and turns, not to mention steep inclines and the odd sheer drop; very quickly, Edward had lost all sense of direction.

After about an hour, he heard voices in the distance, and quickened his step. The light from the torches revealed a small object in his path; he bent down to retrieve it and saw that it was the discarded torch. He groaned and looked up - sure enough, the voices were coming from the blowhole above his head; he had been walking in a circle.

#

'Hey up there!' Edward shouted. There was no response.

A second, rather-louder shout achieved an abrupt cessation of the chatter. The edge of the mesh was lifted and a voice called out, 'Who's down there?'

Edward shook his head. 'Who the hell do you think it is? Throw me down a rope or something!'

The mesh was lowered again; the voice was now muffled but still audible to Edward. 'He wants some rope,' it said, '...we haven't got any rope.'

After a moment, a second voice spoke. 'There's that piece of rope from the Curds, Confits, Coulis and Chutneys arena. It's a bit frayed, but it might do. It all depends on what he wants to do with it.'

Once again, the mesh was raised. 'Err... hello, there's a bit of rope down on the green, but it's not very strong. We can get it for you if you don't mind waiting half an hour.'

Edward tried to control his temper. 'Look, all I want is to get out of this damn hole!'

'Oh! Well... we have a ladder.'

#

It was clear to Edward, as he stepped off the top rung, that not a single villager had gone home, a need for news showing on their anxious faces. The sinister cloud was still obscuring the sun and the temperature had dropped considerably. A growl of thunder did a circuit of the village. Edward shivered.

Maxie appeared. 'Well?'

'I've been walking around in a circle... the tunnel doesn't lead anywhere.'

Maxie drew his bushy eyebrows together. 'Round in a circle?' That's impossible... you must have taken a wrong turn.'

'There were no turns; the tunnel's been sabotaged.'

At that moment, a frail voice spoke in Edward's head. *I have a suggestion,* it said.

Edward spun around. 'Who said that?'

All present looked at him blankly.

Frustrated, Edward raised his voice. 'Who just said, 'I've got a suggestion.'?'

Actually, I said, I have *a suggestion*, said the voice.

Seeing Edward's odd behaviour, Primrose took his arm and led him away from the others. 'Are you feeling alright, Ed Wood? Would a cup of tea help?'

Edward exploded. 'That's the trouble with you people, you think the answer to any crisis is a sodding pot of tea! Well, let me tell you – if your village is facing a major emergency, it'll take more than a cup of Hettie's latest blend to save it!'

Primrose turned her back on him, then swung round and slapped him hard in the face, before marching off.

Edward could hear the voice in his head supressing a laugh. *Well... that didn't go very well, did it? She's a feisty one is our Primrose.*

Oh yes, very funny. Edward put his hand to his throbbing cheek. *Doctor Jeffries I presume? Look, is there any chance you could give me some warning if you're planning to enter my head?*

Oh... I'm sorry, did I surprise you? This is the third time we've spoken and I thought you would be used to my funny little ways by now. What say I ring a hand-bell before I speak in future? How does that sound?

Yeah... whatever. So what's this suggestion of yours?

Well, what I thought is - you could ask Mr Malleable if you can use his gateway to reach me; it would allow you to by-pass the tunnels and take you directly to my chamber. Be gentle with him, mind, he's very protective of the gateway, and rightly proud of the way generations of Malleables have guarded it. He may not be terribly enamoured by the idea.

Edward surveyed the villagers' heads but couldn't see Maxie anywhere. Eventually he found him sitting on a log in the adjacent meadow, his head in his hands. He looked up briefly at Edward's approach. 'I just don't understand it; how could you walk around in a circle? And if it's true that the tunnels have been sabotaged, the doctor's breath is never going to make it to the blowhole. This is a disaster!'

Edward sat next to him and deliberately spoke in a calm and reassuring manner. 'I see the problem, but I still think it's essential that we speak with the doctor... I'm sure we can come up with a solution. I've been thinking; why don't we use your gateway to transport us to Dr Jeffries' chamber? It would –'

Maxie sat bolt upright. 'What? Most certainly not! Why, the gateway is ancient... and fragile, and nobody outside my family is even allowed to set eyes on it. If I brought it out into the open, why... it might get broken... or lose its special properties. No, it's absolutely out of the question!'

Edward kept his cool. 'I do understand your concerns Atticus, and I will personally guarantee that the gateway is treated with the care and respect it deserves. But you must see that it's our only way of reaching the doctor.'

'That's as maybe, but the gateway has been cherished by my family for generations and...' Maxie's features softened. 'Did you just call me Atticus?'

'Err... yes, I haven't used your proper name before because you told me that everyone calls you Maxie... it was actually one of the first things you said to me.'

'So I did. Fancy you remembering that. But, to tell the truth, I rather like the way 'Atticus' sounds when you say it.'

I'm making progress...

'If you like, I'll use it from now on.'

'I'd like that, Edward.' Maxie put his hand on the younger man's shoulder who, on this occasion, didn't shudder or flinch, a fact that surprised both men. 'I'll go and get the gateway.'

'Nicely done, Edward,' said the voice in Edward's head.

Maxie returned moments later and announced with great pride, 'Here it is – the gateway!'

Edward stared at the dilapidated object. 'Is that it?'

'Problem, Edward?'

'Well, yes, Ma... Ma... Atticus. That's not a gateway, it's just an old door-frame with flaking paint and rusty hinges! What use is that?'

Maxie folded his arms. 'Oh I see... and you're an expert on items that possess miraculous powers of transportation, are you, Edward? I didn't realise.' He quickly unfolded his arms. 'Look, I'm sorry - that was uncalled-for... I don't normally do sarcasm, and, frankly, I'm not very good at it.'

Edward smiled. 'I thought it was great.'

They both laughed.

'You're too kind,' Maxie said, 'but you must be more respectful to the gateway you know. It was this object, after all, that facilitated our first meeting, and it was the gateway that you need to thank for your imminent wedlock to the lovely Primrose. It may be ugly but—'

'Hang on... my imminent wedlock?'

'Oh yes, I meant to tell you.' Maxie pulled out a crumpled note. 'Primrose has booked Reverend Spankie to perform the service at six o'clock precisely... at St Gruntle's of course. I trust you'll be able to find some suitable clothes by then?'

Edward tried to speak but seemed only able to manage the beginnings of sentences. 'But we... I'm already... She didn't...'

Maxie looked concerned. 'You do *want* to marry Primrose don't you, Edward?'

'Well yes, of course, but...'

Maxie seemed happy with this reply. 'Good, good. Then that's settled. Now, I'd better explain how the gateway operates; it's quite simple - you approach it, thinking respectful thoughts about where you would like to be transported, step forward, and the gateway will do the rest. Incidentally, do you like easy-listening music?'

Edward pulled a face. 'God no, I only listen to classic rock, but I don't see what that has—'

'It's a minor point, you'll understand later. Now, step forward with me, Edward, and let your mind be filled with respectful grovelling.'

The two men approached the gateway in reverential silence; Edward lifted his right foot to step through the opening, but before he was able to move forward, the gateway and the village vanished, the ground melted away, and he was floating in a pink mist. He couldn't see anything, and all he could hear was a tinkling piano playing a criminally-bland version of 'In the Mood'. A hand rested on his shoulder. 'I'm right behind you.'

After a few moments, a disembodied female voice announced, 'You will soon be reaching your destination. Please cross your legs and refrain from ferning.' Edward did as instructed and, after a few more bars of smooth jazz, felt himself touch down on soft earth, with a pillow behind his head. The mist cleared and he saw that Maxie was sitting a few feet away, leaning against an ornate column, one of many around the walls of the massive chamber. He allowed his gaze to climb the column, up and up until its progress was interrupted by an exquisite stained-glass window, at which point the column did a sharp left to avoid the window before continuing its upward journey. The window depicted the village green on the day of The Grunt with the festivities in full swing. Edward was able to recognise the Dalliard sisters serving tea, Caroline Spankie counting peas and the mayor holding aloft a parsnip. From outside, the sun was shining brightly and illuminated the scene beautifully.

Meanwhile, the column continued upwards until it reached the carved wooden ceiling, at which point it splayed out in a carnival of leaves, branches and squirrels. Around a hundred chandeliers, cleverly-crafted from the ice-cream-cone torches, hung down. It was a while before Edward realised that there were no columns, no windows, bookcases, tapestries or statues; they were all painted onto the clay walls. He leaned back against the pillow to admire the artistry; despite having absolutely no interest in fine art, he heard himself saying, 'This is the work of a genius!'

Maxie nodded his head. 'Indeed it is. The doctor will be pleased that you like his work.'

'So where is he?'

'Err... you're leaning against his nose.'

* * *

27. Liberating a Jeffrey

Edward slowly turned his head, emitted an involuntary yelp, and scrambled frantically towards the painted column to join Maxie. He stared at the enormous nose and his mind shot back to his pursuit of the Maid of the Grunt earlier in the day, when he had witnessed the theft of Ethan Spurious' 'highly-recommended' radish in all its sixty-eight-pound glory.

Dr Jeffries was lying on his side, his head resting on his forearm, a pose that afforded Edward a splendid view of the luxuriant hair that sprouted from the shafts of the owner's puce and pock-marked nose. His other features – piercing kelly-green eyes and thin lips that radiated wrinkles wide enough to toboggan down, were in proportion with the nose, and collectively managed to achieve an expression of friendliness and welcome.

Below, the doctor was wearing a rather smart pair of dungarees; they were, admittedly, a little muddy in places, but didn't seem to have suffered as a consequence of the doctor's extreme expansion.

The giant mouth opened to reveal an impressive set of gaps. 'You're wondering how my dungas survived the effect of the Swell-O-Soil aren't you?' The question echoed around the chamber several times.

Edward nodded, too nervous to trust his voice.

'Well, you see, I rather cheated; I gave my predictive measurements to Dahlia Brûlée before I entered the chamber, and this fine garment was waiting for me when I arrived, stark naked. That lady is truly a miracle-worker with a needle and thread; do you know she sews around fifty open-cup mushrooms onto a cotton sheet for her performance every year?'

Oh God yes, she was the lame bird-impersonator.

'Yes, I've witnessed her fine performance.'

'Anyway, I'm sure you're not here to discuss my elegant appearance. Mr Malleable - it is good of you to pay a visit, but I must insist on a formal introduction to our friend here.'

Maxie wearily struggled to his feet. 'Yes, Dr Jeffries, this is Edward – our new village vagrant. Edward, this is Dr Jeffries, our founder.' He indicated to Edward to stand up.

The doctor addressed the younger man. 'Edward! What a pleasure it is to finally meet you in the flesh, after all the 'vocal encounters' we've enjoyed.' He did an air-quotes gesture with his fingers that blew a parting in Edward's hair. 'Do you remember when you were swimming around in the great pie, and I helped you out with the coins? Or the time you were in a tent and the lovely Primrose was nursing a bump on your head? And, of course, I was in your head a few moments ago... Now that reminds me.' The doctor reached into his top pocket and retrieved an enormous scrap of paper and pencil stub. Leaning on the smooth clay floor, he wrote, *'Bring hand-bell when next entering Edward's head.'* He returned both to his pocket and added, 'Just an aide memoire.

'Oh, and let us not forget, I was one of the group that stood beside you on that rainy day when you buried Oscar all those years ago.'

'What... *you* were there as well?'

'I was indeed, standing at the necessary angle of course. There was a good turn-out that day!'

The doctor cupped his hand to the side of his mouth in a futile effort to exclude Maxie from his next few words. 'You'll notice that Mr Malleable and I are rather formal in our dealings. Don't ask me why, but he never uses my first name.'

Maxie could hardly fail to hear the doctor's words, reverberating as they did around the enormous chamber. 'I just thought... well you know - after what happened, you might be a bit embarrassed by it.'

'Really, you thought that? Why nothing could be further from the truth.' The doctor turned to Edward, 'It's Jeffrey.'

'So... your full name is Jeffrey Jeffries?'

'Well, my full *title* is Dr Jeffrey J. Jeffries, but I'm quite happy for you to simply call me Jeffrey, or even Jeff if you like, but I draw the line at Jezza. I'm a bit like Hexagon in that regard – an epithet from a close friend reinforces your bond, but when used by a relative stranger, it suggests a desire to manipulate, don't you agree?'

Christ, and I thought Maxie was a windbag!

'I must tell you,' the doctor continued, 'in my youth, *Jeffrey* was a staggeringly popular name in the village of Leddington Gusset, where I was raised. At least half of my classmates were called Jeffrey, and that included a number of the girls. I believe the name would still be as popular today if the village committee hadn't appointed Jeffrey Singleton as their mayor.'

Maxie raised his eyes to the roof and mumbled, 'Do we *really* have to hear this story again?'

Whether or not Dr Jeffries heard the mumble, he continued without a pause. 'He was nice enough - a decent and respectable chap who never missed a committee meeting, was always scrupulously fair with the other members, *and* he made some hilarious speeches at civic engagements. In a way, he was a bit like old Hedley - immensely popular with the villagers, particularly the ladies due to his dashing good looks.'

Hedley? Good looks?

Edward recalled Mayor Gerald-Headley's glistening overhang of neck-fat at his opening speech.

'Unfortunately, it soon became apparent that Leddington Gusset's new mayor had a weakness that rather detracted from his many qualities. Without wishing to be coarse, let me just say that the new mayor had a problem retaining his natural gases, and this was particularly apparent at public functions. Now, I have to say, the people of Leddington Gusset had none of the refinement of *our* villagers and found this hugely amusing, so initially there wasn't a problem.

'In time, however, the act of breaking wind became so synonymous with Mayor Jeffrey Singleton of Leddington Gusset, that the term 'Liberating a Jeffrey' entered the English language and enjoyed popular usage amongst the masses.

'Almost overnight, soon-to-be-parents dropped the name as their top choice for their forthcoming offspring, and many existing Jeffreys took the drastic step of changing their names by deed poll to...well, almost anything else. Personally, I had no desire to change my name - I liked it, and soon I was the only Jeffrey in the village.'

Maxie butted in, 'Dr Jeffries... Jeffrey, this is a long and frankly rather vulgar story; do you think we could get on to the reason for our visit?'

The doctor sighed. 'Yes, I suppose you're right, Atticus, but it's nice to nostalge occasionally.' He whispered in Edward's ear, an action that caused Edward temporary tinnitus: 'I just made that word up: 'nostalge.' What do you think of it?'

Is this man real?

'It's terrific.'

Dr Jeffries looked delighted. 'Really? I *am* pleased – I must remember to use it again some time.'

'Now listen, you two.' Maxie stepped forward and spoke with more force than Edward had previously thought he possessed. 'We are *not* here to share vulgar anecdotes about bodily functions *or* to make up new words! Jeffrey, we have a serious problem with your breath failing to reach the blowhole.'

'Oh you don't need to tell me, Atticus, I've blown a year's worth of breath into my trumpet twice, and it just keeps coming back to me. Do either of you know what's going on?'

'Well,' Edward said, 'we believe the tunnels have been sabotaged by someone.'

Dr Jeffries bit his lower lip. 'Oh dear... that sounds serious.'

'But look.' Edward opened his palms. 'Is it *really* such a big deal? So Jeffrey's breath doesn't make it to the blowhole and the petals don't soar up into the sky. We'll just have to apologise and tell the villagers that the petal display has been cancelled due to unforeseen circumstances. Sure, the kids will be disappointed, but it'll give us a full year to sort out the tunnels, and next year's display will be outst...'

Edward paused as he noticed that Dr Jeffries was staring at Maxie, his eyes wide with anger and disbelief. He kept his voice low and controlled but the simmering rage was quite evident. 'So you haven't told him. The one most crucial piece of information that you needed to impart to this young man... and you haven't told him.'

Maxie went on the offensive. 'Well no, I haven't... but you don't know what it's like... having to organise the Grunt! All those activities don't just *happen* you know. I have a thousand things to arrange; there just hasn't been the time!'

Dr Jeffries could control his festering fury no longer; he loomed over Maxie's crouched figure. 'But I'll bet you found time to visit the beer tent and sample the Gruntle Gulp! Tell me, Atticus, how *is* it the festival ale this year?'

Maxie bowed his head. 'It's very good,' he said quietly.

'Oh well,' the doctor's response was as bitter as the ale, 'that's alright then!' He backed up and turned away from the smaller pair.

There was a long silence, which Edward finally broke, 'Well look, just explain it to me now, if it's *that* important.'

Dr Jeffries turned back to face Edward, and now there was the semblance of a smile on his face. 'You know, Edward, I have a mind to promenade, will you join me?'

'Promenade?'

'Yes, let's do that - a light constitutional is what we need; I could show you my home town! Let me just get rid of this first.' The doctor shuffled over to the wall-trumpet and blew for several minutes. Stepping back, he wiped his mouth and kicked off his enormous carpet slippers. From a chest of drawers, he produced a tiny denim garment and a similarly-minute pair of walking boots.

'We've got about thirty minutes till my breath comes back, so... let's head for Leddington Gusset!'

Maxie raised his head, his face now bright red. 'Oh come on! Look, I accept that I forgot to tell Edward why the petal display is so important, but this is *not* the time to take a trip down memory lane!'

'That's fine, Atticus, I wasn't inviting you anyway.'

'Actually, I agree with Maxie,' said Edward. 'You need to fill me in on the importance of the petal business, and then we can brainstorm a solu—'

Before Edward could finish his sentence, he was back in the pink mist with *Pennsylvania 65,000* tinkling offensively in the background.

* * *

28. Didn't We Have a Lovely Time

(the Day We Went to Leddington Gusset)

'You bloody idiot, Jeffries!' Edward shouted into the mist. 'We haven't got time for this!' There was no response.

Soon, *'The Elevator Bossa Nova'* started to play, and the disembodied voice began her announcement. 'You will soon be reaching your destination…'

Edward huffed. 'Yes, thank you, I know the routine – *please cross your legs and refrain from ferning.* I think maybe this time I'll cross my arms and light up a spliff just to annoy you!'

'I have to say,' said the disembodied voice, 'I think you would find it singularly difficult to light a marijuana cigarette with your arms crossed.'

Edward laughed and clapped his hands. 'Oh that is so typical of this place! So you're not a recording, but an actual person?'

'Me – a recording?' The voice giggled. 'No, I'm Summer, and this is my third day on work-experience. I hope I'm making a good impression.'

Edward felt rather guilty about his disparaging comment. 'Yes… I'm sorry, Summer – you're doing a splendid job.'

#

Touching down on a hard, unyielding surface, Edward's ears were assaulted by car horns and people shouting, and his nose by petrol fumes. As the mist cleared, a sweaty, face appeared inches from his – a face red with anger and topped by a police officer's cap. Edward was quite unprepared for the broadside of obscenities that accompanied the constable's questions. Essentially, he wanted to know Edward's opinion about whether the middle of the road resembled a park bench and, if not, why he had chosen the sit there. The questions could have been delivered with brief simplicity, but it was clear that the man was hugely proud of his profanity collection, and was using the incident as an opportunity to display as many as possible.

Edward scrambled to his feet. 'No... no it doesn't. I'm sorry, I was... errr...'

'Over here!' Dr Jeffries, now normal size, was waving frantically from the pavement.

Edward turned back to face the policeman who had folded his muscular arms and was waiting for an explanation.

Edward swallowed hard. 'That's my friend... over there on the pavement... which is, of course, where I should be... not sitting in the middle of the road like an idiot. I really don't know what came over me, Constable, but I promise it won't happen again.'

The policeman gave Edward a long hard glare. 'Better not, son!' He leaned in an open car window, and watched as Edward weaved his way past fist-shaking drivers. 'Jeez,' the Policeman addressed the driver, 'I think I've seen it all now. What a jerk!'

Edward finally reached the doctor who was barely visible within the mountainous ring of denim.

'Well, that was most odd,' said the doctor. 'I've never known the gateway to drop a passenger in a dangerous place. You haven't said anything derogatory about it have you?'

Edward recalled his *flaking paint and rusty hinges* comment. 'No, of course not.'

'I didn't think so... rather strange though. Now look, can you give me a hand here?' He indicated the denim. 'I always swap my monster dungas for some smaller ones whilst I'm in the mist, but it means that I'm left with all this material when I reach my destination.'

The pair made a reasonable job of folding the enormous dungarees and laid them next to the gateway which was leaning nonchalantly against a lamppost. 'They'll be safe here – the gateway will see to that.'

Edward felt the gateway - to the touch it was cold and strangely menacing; clearly not an item that endured criticism or suffered vagrants gladly.

'Now, let me introduce you to Leddington Gusset.'

Before the pair could take a step, a tattooed youth barged between them, sending the doctor to his knees. Without turning, the man raised his middle finger and continued up the high street elbowing young and old out of his way.

Edward gritted his teeth. 'I'll get him...'

'No, Edward!' Jeffrey held tightly to his arm. 'This is one of the reasons I brought you here.'

They continued to watch as the man showed a complete disregard for fellow pavement-users, and collisions were frequent. At one point he was heard to shout, 'Well, you shouldn't walk so slow should you... old man!'

The doctor winced. 'We live in an ugly time, Edward; not just in appearance, but in behaviour and language as well. Let's go *this* way.'

They strolled along the main street, past purveyors of coffee, burgers, pizzas, and mobile-phone accessories; past pawnbrokers and betting shops, past boarded-up establishments sprayed with graffiti and plastered with posters advertising long-since-held events. Neither man spoke; Edward's head was filled with images of Primrose smiling. He imagined her visiting her friends – the plants and bushes, and dancing in the nettles. He looked at the tacky, predictable shops and tried to imagine Hettie and Lettie's Herbal Heaven fitting into this dreadful place... not a chance.

A large rat darted out from behind an overflowing rubbish bin, froze at the sight of the two men, dropped a chicken bone in their path, and was gone. Edward looked behind the bin; there were a number of bones wrapped in greasy paper which, in turn, was enclosed in a gaudy box that bore the face of a smiling cartoon chicken.

Up ahead, they could see a red telephone box – charming from a distance, but as they got nearer, the stench of urine detracted from its charm. Once reached, they found it door-less, phone-less and boasting several inches of liquid.

The doctor's expression grew sadder with every step. 'You know, Edward, with a name like Leddington Gusset, one might reasonably expect hanging baskets, charming hostelries, and delightful people that greet you warmly regardless of whether or not they know you. There is no pride in this place... no sense of community.' He stared down at the infinite circles of pavement-gum and added, 'and there never has been.'

They stopped outside the last shop in the high street and the doctor pointed beyond. 'This is something that really gets my goat – surely if you were a developer, you'd want to provide some vaguely-pleasing housing on the fringes to draw attention away from the *ghastly* high-street, but as you can see...'

There was a large modern housing estate, every residence identical and bland. Edward recalled with affection the wonderfully-eccentric houses in That Road, and Hexagon's story about the pair that fell in love.

'So, Edward.' Jeffrey's demeanour seemed to brighten a little. 'Now that you've seen Leddington Gusset, what is your opinion of my home-town?'

A smile tickled Edward's lips. 'You're having a laugh, right?'

'Oh no - I'm deadly serious.'

'Well... it's not great.'

The doctor shook his head. 'Indeed not. It's a complete pig-sty; smelly, miserable and filled with unimaginative dull-wits. I've hated it from the day I was born here.'

'So why bring *me* here?'

The doctor raised a finger. 'Ah now, *that* is an excellent question. But I'm concerned that I haven't allowed sufficient time to answer it before my breath returns down the tunnels. You see, to do your question justice would require a fairly lengthy explanation, and...' he looked up at the sun which, unlike the one above Flatpack which was largely obscured by the Cirrus of Pestilence, was radiating brightness and warmth from a cloudless sky, 'we have a mere fourteen minutes. I can either give you a condensed version here, or we can return to my chamber, I can collect my breath and then delight you with the full narrative.'

He put his hand to his forehead for a moment, then announced, 'I favour the latter; let's head back to the gateway.

#

The music provided on the return journey was *'The Theme from the Pink Panther'*.

'I rather like this,' the doctor announced as he visibly expanded and discarded his smaller dungas in favour of their colossal counterpart. 'Do you know that Summer plays all the music herself, as well as making the in-flight announcements?'

'No... I didn't know that.' Edward heard a giggle in the background.

He landed, cross-legged, in Maxie's lap. There was a lot of embarrassed repositioning until both men were seated, at a respectable distance, leaning against the painted column. Maxie turned to face him. 'You're back then,' he said through grumpy lips. 'Learn anything?'

'I'm not sure.'

The two men pressed their backs against the wall as the Doctor appeared, waving a tiny pair of dungarees in an effort to clear the mist. 'Right, Atticus,' he instructed. 'No time to waste - *you* need to make use of the gateway now... as we discussed.' He gave Maxie a conspiratorial nod.

Maxie got to his feet, stepped up to the gateway and vanished.

The doctor squatted on an enormous rug. 'Now Edward, you asked me why I took you to Leddington Gusset, well—'

There was a rumble above their heads, above the wooden ceiling, above the grasses and fallen leaves... but only a little above the latter; the sound was comparable to a roll of thunder that had fallen from the skies. It grew in volume and menace as, to Edward's alarm, it passed from the outside world into the chamber where it proceeded to tramp and roar around the ceiling, causing the chandeliers to shake and jangle.

'What the hell's going on?' Edward shouted, indicating the ceiling high above his head.

Jeffrey pointed to his ears and mouthed, 'I can't hear you!'

After about ten minutes of stomping, all went quiet and the unseen intruder took its leave back through the ceiling making a sound reminiscent of a large fish slurping tea from a ladle. Once outside it reverted to roar and rumble.

Jeffrey opened his mouth to speak, but Edward was no longer in a mood to listen and held up his hand to this effect. 'No! I don't want to know - I'm out of here. Prim... the villagers need my help.'

Closing his mouth, the doctor watched as Edward strode towards the gateway, pausing to inform it of his desired destination, then stepped forward... and stumbled straight out of the other side with a complete lack of pink mist, music or dignity. Jeffrey maintained a blank expression as Edward gave him an accusing stare, then tried again, with the same result.

'Is this *your* doing?' Edward snarled.

The doctor shrugged. 'Nothing to do with me. Maybe the gateway feels that you should stay a while longer. Why don't you come back and sit down, Edward?' He patted a cushioned stool.

'I can't just sit here! You heard that... thing!'

'But you can't *help* if you don't understand.'

Exasperated, Edward held out his hands, palms up. 'Understand *what*?'

Again, the doctor patted the stool.

Reluctantly, Edward took the seat.

'As you know, I spend most of my time in this chamber; when I'm not painting, I'm inhaling through the wall-trumpet. Now, I expect you think it to be a rather pointless occupation, but there is a good reason for it. You see, Flatpack on the Meander exists on decency and kindness, on empathy and generosity and, as its father-figure, I see it as my duty to ensure its good health. So, whenever a kind word is spoken in the village, I am able to pinpoint the location, and suck up the sentiment. For three hundred and sixty-four days, I inhale compliments, praise, smiles, words of encouragement, acts of kind-heartedness and compassion, and everything that is good and wholesome. I can tell you, by St. Gruntle's Day, I am full to bursting, and when I receive the hanging signal, I am more than ready to let it all go.

'Within a short space of time, my breath exits the tunnels at the blowhole, and a thousand petals are shot into the sky carrying all those wonderful sentiments from the previous year, and they float to every corner of the village, thereby nourishing Flatpack for the next twelve months.

Jeffrey paused to let this information sink in. 'I'm parched, Edward, do you fancy a whet?'

'A what?'

'No, a whet – I need to whet my windpipe.' He reached into a cabinet and produced a vast bottle of Maynard's Merciless Mild. Having extracted the cork with his remaining teeth he poured himself a glassful. 'I have some normal-sized glasses if you care to join me.'

'I won't, thanks.'

'As you wish.' The doctor took a huge swig and placed the glass precariously on the rug, then adopted a serious expression. 'Now... should the villagers decide, by means of the ballot, that they no longer wish to live in a 'special' village, the hanging would not take place, I would not exhale and Flatpack would not be fed. There would be some rather boisterous weather - storms and earthquakes and a number of peculiar events, before the angle reverts to horizontal and, as likely as not, I would expire shortly after.' He spoke these words in a totally matter-of-fact manner. 'Oh incidentally, I understand that you've been told about the night of the Big Forget.'

'Well... some of it, but Wendy was interrupted just as she was about to explain about the angle correcting itself.'

'Ah, that's interesting,' said the Doctor. 'You see, it was Wendy Malleable who averted the disaster by performing the hanging herself whilst everyone else was running around like headless chickens. If she'd left it any longer, the angle would have been damaged beyond repair.'

'So, tell me, Edward, what do *you* think would be the consequences of losing the angle?'

Edward stood up and did a thoughtful circuit of the doctor and his rug. 'Wendy Malleable asked me the same question just before we were interrupted by Atticus. I hadn't figured it out at that point, but now I see it as clear as day. If Flatpack's isolation and concealment is entirely dependent on the village remaining at fourteen and a half degrees, the loss of the angle would be nothing short of disastrous. The villagers would no longer be able to hide from the outside world.'

Jeffrey smiled and nodded. 'Well done, Edward, I couldn't have put it better myself; yes – the village would be visible to everyone - all the riff-raff and undesirables, commoners, criminals... everyone! And they'd march in here like they owned the place, with their loud, brash voices, vulgar language and a complete lack of manners and courtesy. They'd see the villagers as simple and peculiar, and force them to adopt their charmless ways. *And* they'd bring their own set of laws, which we would be expected to follow without question.

'So you see, if you can't come up with a brilliant solution, the actions of the tunnel-saboteur will result in Flatpack on the Meander becoming no different from Leddington Gusset.'

Edward was about to ask why this was solely his responsibility, but then recalled that he hadn't read the job description and contract.

At that moment there was a flash, and Maxie stepped from the gateway. He was smiling from ear to ear and wearing a white bow-tie, tuxedo, cummerbund, and a yellow buttonhole flower with added leaf. Trousers matching the jacket led down to a pair of blindingly-shiny shoes. In one hand he nursed a top hat and proffered a hanger to Edward with the other, which carried a matching, if somewhat slimmer, ensemble.

* * *

29. A Traditional Flatpack Wedding

'Are you sure this is right? Shouldn't we walk up the aisle like everyone else and take our places?' Edward was trying to detect a chink of light in the dark room.

'I can see you haven't attended many traditional weddings, Edward.'

The two men had entered the church by a side door that led, according to Maxie, to the vestry, which had a second door that would lead to the right-hand side of the altar, where they would await the processional. Edward waved his arms around in an effort to locate the second door but found only cassocks on hooks.

'You must remember,' Maxie explained, 'that you, as groom, are largely superfluous, and at no time should you attempt to detract attention away from Primrose and her big entrance. You need to be here, for obvious reasons, but you must make as modest an entrance as possible, preferably unseen by the congregation. Everything is about tradition, Edward, and there is no more traditional wedding than a Flatpack wedding.'

'Oh, I don't think you need worry about the congregation, we'll be the first ones to arrive.'

'I think that to be most unlikely, Edward.'

Edward located and opened the second door, only to be met by the sight of Bedford Trite's backside, bouncing up and down on a piano stool as he played a honky-tonk version of 'Jesu Joy of Man's Desiring' on a grand piano.

Four tall turrets of tallow burned at the front of the church; though impressive, they provided woefully-insufficient light to illuminate the whole nave. This was briefly remedied by a massive flash of lightning, which entered through the Grunt-themed stained-glass windows and flooded the interior in brilliant colours.

The clap of thunder that followed caused the whole church floor to heave, then abruptly drop, and for large amounts of hot wax to be splattered onto the marble. Edward was reminded of the turbulence that he and Veronica had experienced on the return flight from their only continental holiday. He looked around at the sizeable, immaculately-groomed congregation, who were chatting as if nothing had happened. 'Aren't they worried about what's happening?'

'Oh no, they have complete confidence in you.'

Edward recognised many of the faces in the front pew. Lettie Dalliard gave him a little wave from the far end; she was holding a handkerchief to her nose and there was a look of disapproval on the face of Hettie who was at her side. Lettie was getting a severe rebuke from her sister, that much was clear to Edward, but Bedford's murder of 'Jesu Joy' prevented him from learning the nature of Hettie's displeasure.

At that moment, Bedford closed the piano fall-board and, naked as the day he was born, wobbled over to the organ and commenced playing a gentle adaptation of the Air from Handel's Water Music. The reduced volume allowed Edward to hear Hettie's words.

'You're a complete embarrassment,' she was saying. 'I've seen you making cow-eyes at him, and now you're blubbing because he's marrying someone else rather than you! Good Heavens Leticia, you're twice his age plus!'

'I know, I know, but he's such a beautiful man,' Lettie managed between sobs.

'Oh, and I suppose it should have been you rather than Primrose? Will you listen to yourself?'

Edward sauntered over. 'Hettie, I'm so glad you could make it.'

'Well of course Edward, it's not every day—'

Edward had already turned his attention to Lettie. 'Lettie, Primrose and I have been talking; would you do us the honour of being godmother to our first born?'

The beam on Lettie's moist face lit up the church and made a reply quite unnecessary. Edward moved along the pew, but not before catching Hettie's eye and receiving a rather curious look; initially it spoke of annoyance at having her authority undermined, but quickly melted into an expression of gratitude, presumably for Edward's imaginative solution to Lettie's obsession.

But then Maisie Wittering piped up. 'But she can't be preg... he's only been here for a day... they must have had relations... but that's impossible before marriage... and not right...cover your ears Aldous...'

Edward left Hettie to explain that the couple were just planning ahead.

Another front-row occupant was Renston Ardlish, clearly still wearing the fish costume under his suit. An opening had been strategically cut at the pectoral-fin level to allow his head access to the outside world. He gave Edward's hand a vigorous shake. 'Many congratulations, Edward. You're a very lucky man. I expect your chin to hit the floor when you see your beautiful bride.' He laughed and raised his eyebrows up and down in a most annoying manner. 'Look, while we're waiting, I don't suppose you'd like to hear 'The Grernock'? It's my cautionary verse.'

'Oh look, Renston, I'd love to hear it, but there simply isn't going to be time before the processional arrives.'

The funeral director dropped his head. 'Yes, there never is time, everyone says the same thing.'

Noticing the other man's sad reaction, Edward added, 'But... I'm sure there'll be time for you to recite the whole piece after the speeches at the wedding breakfast.'

The smile on Renston's face rivalled Lettie's. 'Do you think so? Why that would be simply marvellous!'

'And you'd have the whole village present! Mind you, I'd get in quick before Hedley starts telling The Parsnip Story again.'

Renston tapped his nose. 'Good thinking.'

Edward continued along the front pew feeling pleased with himself.

I'm getting quite good at this.

Next, he saw Mrs Plenteous, who was cradling a large stomach-bulge with one hand and holding Mr Lean's lead with the other.

'There's your master!' She indicated Edward's approach for the dog's benefit. Mr Lean's eyes widened, her tail started thumping against Mrs Git from the Greengrocers, and she stood up on her back legs, the lead straining.

Edward stroked the dog's head. 'Hello Leany, hello Mrs Plenteous – where are your girls?'

'Well, Edward, I don't want to spoil the surprise, but it's going to take all of them to carry Primrose's train! Oh I do hope they behave themselves, they squabble over the slightest thing, and I'd never forgive them if they spoiled your big day.'

Mr Lean whined for more attention; Edward tickled her under the chin. 'I'm sure they'll be fine, they're just excited about having such an important job.'

Mayor Gerald-Headley had also secured a front-pew seat; it came as no surprise to Edward that he was not accompanied by his wife. Hedley reached out a hand. 'Aha, and here he is – the Bestest Man!'

Edward shook the hand. 'Err... no, Hedley – Atticus is the Best Man, I'm the groom.'

'No, no, no, what I mean is that I consider you to be the bestest man here; better than Maxie, better than Renston and Bedford... were I not the most impotent man in the village, I even think you'd be better than me!' He looked around before continuing in hushed tones. 'Listen, Edward; as your guest of honour, I wonder if I might be permitted to make a brief speech at the reception?'

'Oh, err...'

'Don't worry, I wasn't planning to tell the parsnip story again – you can have too much of a good thing.'

Edward did his best to stifle his sigh of relief.

'No, I have a rather witty tale about a bunch of purple carrots that I'm sure will go down well.'

Edward stared at him. 'Are all your stories about root-vegetables?'

The mayor laughed. 'Oh no... but I can see why you might think that. No, I also have a splendid banana story, but I'm saving that for a christening, for obvious reasons.'

'Of course.'

Edward was enormously thankful when this ludicrous conversation was curtailed by an abrupt change in the organ music to something resembling a wedding march. 'Sorry Hedley, must take my place.'

The church doors swung open. Edward knew that he should keep his eyes front, but that was never going to happen. Reverend Spankie was first to enter, dressed in a dark robe with a colourful stole. Whether or not he was wearing his clerical collar would remain a mystery due to the extent of his beard. Behind Carsten, Mrs Plenteous' youngest, Apple, was scattering petals at the bride's feet.

Primrose entered the church on the arm of her mother Fuchsia, who Edward only knew by reputation as being the person who resolved village disputes using anchovies. The similarity between mother and daughter was remarkable, apart from Primrose's magnificent red tresses which cascaded over her shoulders and the modestly-dipped neckline. They had the same perfect skin, willowy figure, feminine presence and the elegant neck of a mother swan. The dress, white and unadorned with lace or beading, was startling in its simplicity, with the exception of a dramatically long train which was proudly carried by Merry, Daisy, Felicia, Catkin, Daisy 2 and Blossom.

As Primrose stepped into the church, she radiated happiness, sunniness and warmth; all gloom departed.

The processional approached the altar and the participants split off in various directions; the reverend stepped up and bowed to the cross, Fuchsia took her place in the front pew, and the girls squabbled over their seating.

Primrose took Edward's arm and beamed at him. 'Are you ready for this, Ed Wood?'

Am I about to marry this perfect creature?

'I...simply have no words.'

He went to kiss her cheek but noticed at the last minute that her bouquet comprised nettles and foxgloves.

Reverend Spankie coughed; all present turned to face him.

'Welcome ladies, welcome gentlemen...'

Mr Lean yapped.

'And dogs are also welcome of course!'

Everybody laughed, except Hexagon who shook his head but didn't look up from his embroidery.

'We are gathered here today to witness the joining of our very own Primrose Pynching to Edward St Claire, a man that none of us knew until a few hours ago. Before I say a few words about each of these young people, I would like us all to join together to sing Edward's favourite hymn, The Day thou Gavest, Lord is Ended.'

There was a general muttering from the congregation as they thumbed through their hymnals in a frustrating search for the hymn. Word eventually circulated of the correct page number, and soon all stood ready for Bedford to finish his belting introduction.

Primrose leaned in towards Edward. 'I hadn't thought of you as the sort of man to have a favourite hymn.'

'My mother would sing it to me every night at bedtime.'

The congregation sang their hearts out, with Hettie Dalliard's voice rising above all others. Edward looked over his shoulder to observe her filling her ample lungs to bursting point before delivering each line. A thought entered his head.

Awaiting further instructions, the congregation remained standing when the hymn came to an end. Feet shuffled, throats were cleared and toupees adjusted before, finally, Mrs Plenteous sat, mumbling something about being a special case, and the relieved throng parked their backsides as one.

The reverend offered a belated, 'Please be seated.' He shuffled a few papers on his lectern then looked up. 'Thank you, that was beautifully sung. Now I'd like to say a few words about our couple, beginning with Primrose.' He put on a pair of round-rimmed reading-glasses.

'What can I say about Primrose Pynching that you don't already know? She is, quite simply, our princess – dazzlingly beautiful, kind, funny, giving, pure, and a friend to every person, animal and plant in the village.

'I observed from a young age that Primrose took an intense interest in the village flora, spending long periods talking to corn-marigolds and rhododendrons, and telling jokes to painted daisies and cowslips. I remember finding this quite charming, but never once did it cross my mind that any form of conversation was taking place. This, I was to discover much later.

'As many of you know, Primrose also has the gift of being able to predict, with remarkable accuracy, events that will occur six days' hence. As such, she has prevented many an accident, fore-warned us of the onset of seasonal ailments and, of course, always keeps her lips sealed about the result of the annual shove-the-slack tournament. Plus, she was aware that something dreadful was going to happen to the village today. I don't want to dwell on this; fortunately we have Edward here, so we have nothing to worry about in that regard.

'Let me finish by saying that our Flatpack family would be incomplete without the lovely Primrose, and I am honoured to be able to preside over her marriage to the man she loves.'

The congregation coughed and whispered to each other as Carsten adjusted his papers and shifted his stance to face Edward. Primrose elbowed Edward in the ribs, who returned with a poke, and soon both were giggling. 'Will you behave yourself,' Edward hissed. 'I want to hear what nice things the reverend is going to say about me.'

Carsten gave them a disapproving glare before continuing. 'The fact that Primrose has chosen this man as her husband after only one day must speak volumes about Edward's appeal and fine character. I myself have only met him briefly, when he climbed in my kitchen window, but my family and I found him most agreeable. I've always said that you can learn a lot about a person from their choice of favourite hymn, and Edward's was spot on.

'That said, I have to inform all present, that Edward St Claire was a thoroughly unpleasant person in his former life. Self-obsessed, a serial philanderer and a bully, he put himself and his own self-interest before anyone else, including his own children. He thought nothing of mocking those that he considered beneath him, and never felt the slightest pang of guilt for the hurt that he caused to many.'

Carsten paused; the congregation had gone deadly silent, and all blood had drained from Edward's face.

'Now,' Carsten continued, 'you may find my words harsh, but let me qualify them by saying that Edward was not always that way. Indeed, as a schoolboy, you would have found it hard to find a more polite, kind and friendly young man than Edward St Claire. He was admired by his teachers and had many chums, although none came close in his affections to Oscar, his dog. He grew up with Oscar, who was very much *his* dog, rather than the family pet, and they were inseparable.

'Oscar was cruelly taken from him following a road accident when Edward was just ten. One can only imagine what that young man went through, or speculate on why it changed his character so radically.

'Now, however sympathetic you may feel towards the boy and the loss of his dog, you may be wondering why, with the undesirable character traits that he later developed, we would want Edward to be a part of our special community. The answer to that, my friends, is quite simple; to quote our External Recruitment Co-ordinator, Mr Malleable, 'I have never met a man more in need of 'The Flatpack Effect' than Edward St Claire.' Maxie considered it essential that Edward was 'brought in' without delay.

'And I'm pleased to say that the comments I've heard on the gossip network confirm that Edward's transformation is virtually complete… although I think that The Primrose Effect may also have contributed.'

Laughter echoed around the church.

'Ladies and gentlemen, I give you Primrose and Edward.'

Enthusiastic but respectful applause.

#

'And so to the vows; Primrose, please repeat after me, 'I Primrose Pynching, spinster of this village…''

Primrose repeated the line, her lips caressing each word.

'Take you, Edward St Claire, former adulterer and general ne'er-do-well from the outside, as my husband.'

Primrose bit her lip in an effort to restrain a fit of giggles. 'Take you Edward St Claire, former adulterer and general ne'er-do-well from the outside, as my husband.'

'To hold in my loving embrace, to honour and to obey, except when you're acting like a git or being annoying.'

This time, Primrose was doubled up with laughter and it was a while before she was able to straighten up to face Edward's obvious displeasure. She cleared her throat, composed herself and repeated the line.

'To make you blissfully happy, bless you with many beautiful children and never give your eyes cause to stray.'

Primrose paused before repeating this, the last part of her vow; she moved her face closer to Edward's and looked deeply into his eyes. She spoke slowly, her tone seductive yet serious, putting real emotion and feeling into the words. There was complete silence in the church when she finished.

Reverend Spankie looked at Edward. 'Well, let me say, in all my years I have never heard a marriage pledge spoken with such love. You are indeed blessed young man. But now it's your turn, so please repeat after me, 'I, Edward St Claire...'

'I...'

The reverend looked up. 'Edward St Claire,' he prompted.

'I've got...'

Carsten removed his spectacles and spoke to Edward like he was addressing an inattentive child. 'Edward, I need you to repeat each line after me. Do you understand?'

'But I've got an idea!' Edward blurted out. 'An idea of how we can save the village!' He stepped back and turned to face the congregation. 'All of you – I need you to stand up and file out of the church as quickly as you can. Atticus – where's the gateway?'

'Umm, I think it's in the vestibule smoking a fern.'

'Okay, well take it outside somewhere where there's plenty of space; everyone's going to need to step through it.'

The perplexed villagers looked at each other, shrugged, then collected their bits together and headed for the door.

Edward looked back at Primrose, expecting an expression of utter mortification, but she was smiling at him, nodding her head in approval.

* * *

30. Poppy Knapweed's Fragrant Romance Bookshop

Dr Jeffries had nearly finished sketching the outline for a painting of the Flatpack Parakeet on a blank area of wall, when the gateway appeared in his chamber, spat out five rain-soaked villagers and abruptly departed. Moments later, it returned, ejected five more sodden souls, and was gone again. This continued for some time, much to the doctor's bewilderment.

A party atmosphere soon began to develop amongst the rapidly-growing group, who had clearly not experienced this form of transportation before.

'Ooh, wasn't that fun – can we go back and do it again?'

'I loved floating in the pink mist, it was so delightfully ... pink!'

'Oh, and that girl played such bland, insipid, tunes on the piano... why, I could have danced all night!'

There was one disparager:

'Well yes, it was nice, but she was a bit bossy – telling me to cross my legs! I said to her, 'I'm seventy you know!''

They took little notice of Dr Jeffries – he was, after all, just a giant in dungarees doodling on the wall. Of much greater interest was a hastily-devised game entitled 'Name the Next Arrivals,' the rules of which were blindingly obvious. Those who guessed successfully were rewarded with a toffee-chunk courtesy of Mr Molar from the Confectioners.

Shortly, Maxie and Edward arrived by the same means.

Doctor Jeffries put down his enormous charcoal-stub. 'This won't do, Atticus! I simply cannot have my chamber invaded in this way; you know how much I value my privacy.'

'Yes, I'm sorry, Jeffrey,' Maxie said, then quickly added, 'It was Edward's idea – he'll explain.'

The doctor folded his arms and looked down at Edward.

Edward couldn't contain his excitement. 'Jeffrey – I've got it! I know how we can save the village! I can't believe I didn't think of it before.'

Jeffrey dropped his arms to his sides and a huge, gummy grin spread across his face. 'You've solved it?' He began improvising a strange, celebratory dance, careful not to squash villagers underfoot. 'I knew it,' he laughed, 'I knew you would find a way!' After a few near-tramplings, he sat down on the clay floor. 'Now tell me how it's going to work.'

'Well, if you don't mind, I'd rather wait until every person in the village is down here, then I'll make an announcement.'

'*Every* person?'

'Yes, we need everyone for maximum effect. Now, Jeffrey, tell me – are you able to divide and release your breath in four equal stages?'

'I... well, I've never tried, but I suppose I could approximate it.'

'A good estimate would be sufficient.' Edward observed that the gateway had disgorged five more villagers, but had not returned to collect anymore. He called out to the crowd, 'Is that everybody? Can you confirm that everyone is here?'

A voice from the back replied, 'Mrs Elderberry sends her apologies; if she leaves Dribbles on his own, he eats the furniture.'

Maxie whispered in Edward's ear, 'That's her husband.'

Of course it is...

'Jeffrey – have you got anything that Atticus and I can stand on to raise us up?'

The doctor thought for a minute then clicked his fingers. 'How about my pencil box?' He pushed a wooden box towards Edward; it was the size of, and resembled, a garden shed.

'It looks more like a garden shed.'

'Yes, that was its original purpose, but when Mr Overbite announced his plan to up-shed, I stepped in and made him a generous offer. Well, Lanyard nearly bit my hand off, and now it's a perfectly serviceable pencil box. He picked up Edward and Maxie and placed them astride the ridge. Comfortable it wasn't, but it afforded Edward a good view of the villagers' heads; he estimated that there were around a thousand individuals, and hoped this would be enough.

He called out, 'Can I have some quiet please… and can you confirm that you can hear me at the back?'

'Loud and clear,' came back a shout from the extremities.

'Good. Now we're only going to get one shot at this, so I need you all to listen carefully.

'First of all, I'd like you to divide yourselves into four groups.'

Predictably, the villagers formed four hugely-unequal groups. Edward leant down and whispered in Primrose's ear, and she went from group to group using her undoubted charms to equalise their numbers. She gave Edward a thumbs-up when she was happy that they were relatively even, and he blew her a kiss.

'Now, this is what I'd like you to do; the first group will step forward and form a semi-circle around Dr Jeffries. On my signal, I want you to exhale all the air in your lungs, then raise your heads, mouths open when you're done. When Dr Jeffries sees everybody's heads raised, he will release the first quarter of his lungs' contents over you, moving his head from side to side to ensure that everyone receives an equal quota. Your job will be to gulp down as much of the doctor's miracle-breath as you can.'

This instruction was met with a few muted expressions of distaste.

'The next part will require some discipline on your part; holding your breath and thinking about your favourite place in the village, I need you to step through the gateway in groups of five. You will be whisked to your favoured spot and only then should you breathe out. The gateway will immediately return to collect the next five, and continue to do so until all group-members have been delivered. The next group will then step forward and follow the same process.

'Are there any questions?'

There was lengthy deliberation amongst the groups, and Edward was sure that he heard the word, 'halitosis,' used on more than one occasion.

There seemed to be no questions, so Edward continued. 'Okay, so if you're clear about—'

A delicate hand rose. 'This isn't really a question, but I think we would all like to show our gratitude to Ed Wood, for everything he has done to save our beloved village and,' Primrose blushed, 'for being so ... wonderful.'

There were two minutes of loud applause, cheers and hat-throwing. Primrose and Edward's eyes met and she blew him a return kiss.

Edward waited patiently for quiet. 'Thank you, that was very kind of you all. Now, will the first group approach Doctor Jeffries.'

The process ran amazingly smoothly... at least initially; the group exhaled, raised their heads, gulped down the wonder-breath, entered the gateway, and 'whoosh!' Seconds later, 'whoosh,' the gateway was back to collect the next five. It was as if they'd been rehearsing all day.

After about three quarters of the first group had departed, Edward heard a frail voice trying to get his attention. 'I'm really sorry Mr Edward, I can't hold my breath any longer.' The old man, clearly ashamed, exhaled.

Edward leaned down as far as he could. 'Don't worry, you've done really well to last this long. Thank you for trying.'

The man nodded and walked away, then stood alone, dejected and with head bowed.

Unfortunately, he wasn't alone – by the time the rest of group one had departed, eleven others stood in a dejection-huddle.

Maxie, Edward and Jeffrey put their heads together.

'This is a problem,' said Jeffrey. 'Some of the most decent sentiments that I sucked up last year have been lost.'

'We could increase the number of groups - reduce their size,' Edward suggested.

'Well, that's all very well,' said the doctor, 'but if I get my calculations wrong, I may be left with all sorts of kindness and goodwill, and nobody left to transport it to the surface.'

'We could try sending the older residents through the gateway first,' Maxie said.

Hexagon had been listening to these unimaginative ideas, then launched himself up the side of the pencil shed. 'Might I put forward a simple solution?' he panted.

Edward shrugged. 'Of course, we're open to ideas, Hex.'

Hexagon gave Edward a look of disapproval. 'You always have to abbrev... Oh never mind, look - all we need is a handful of retransmission volunteers.'

The three men stared blankly at the cat.

'Hmm... you don't understand, do you? Let me explain it in simpler terms: if a villager finds that he or she is unable to hold onto their breath, they will advise a volunteer of their favourite location, then pass on the breath, much like an athlete would pass a baton in a relay race. The volunteer will take their place, step through the gate— '

'Good Lord!' yelled a female voice in group three that sounded remarkably like Maisie Wittering. 'I believe the cat is suggesting a... mouth-to-mouth transfer!'

#

Ten men and women volunteered for the roles, including Edward who was relieved to no longer be perched on the pencil-box ridge; it felt as though a carpenter had been vigorously applying a high-grade sandpaper to his thighs. Group two stepped forward, and again, the process went smoothly at first, with the retransmission volunteers standing in a row, ready to assist.

Lettie Dalliard was waiting to enter the gateway, her cheeks bulging. She was nearly at the front of the queue when she stepped out of the line and announced that she couldn't hold on any longer, and needed to transfer her breath. Renston Ardlish stepped forward to do the honours, but Lettie walked straight past him, bent down in front of Edward and put her lips to his. It seemed to take a surprisingly long time to transfer her breath, and after their lips had parted, she discovered that she hadn't completely emptied her lungs, and reluctantly had to go back for a second blow. Eventually she stepped back with an expression that was hard to interpret, and Edward took her place in the queue for the gateway.

Edward delivered the breath to Lettie's favourite place, which turned out to be Poppy Knapweed's Fragrant Romance Bookshop, and returned through the gateway to Jeffrey's chamber.

The remaining groups seemed to have learned from observing their predecessors and completed the task in a fraction of the time without the need to utilise the services of the retransmission volunteers.

Finally, Edward, Maxie and the doctor were left alone in the chamber. Moments later they were joined by the gateway.

'Well, Edward,' Maxie said. 'We did it... wait - what am I saying? *You* did it - it was your idea, you devised and executed it, and you will be the hero of the hour. Primrose is going to be *so* proud of you.'

'Hang on. We don't even know if it's worked yet...'

'Pah! Of course it's worked. Why, I can feel it in my loins. Come on – let's adjourn up top and join in the celebrations! Catch up with you later, Jeffrey.'

Dr Jeffries waved, then picked up his stub of charcoal; Edward and Maxie stepped through the gateway.

As the pair floated in the pink mist, Summer played 'Me and You and a dog named Boo.' Edward relaxed and stretched out like he was on a supremely comfortable sofa.

'So Atticus, when do I start the job?'

Maxie's brows knitted. 'Job, Edward?'

'Yes, you know - the vagranting thing.'

Maxie laughed. 'Oh Edward, you've been doing the job all day without realising it. You know, you really should have read the job description and contract – I put a lot of work into that! Ah, I believe we're coming in to land.'

#

The mist cleared; Edward was sitting on tarmac with his car in front of him.

'What? I don't want to be here!' He stood up, walked to the roadside and began tilting his head to fourteen and a half degrees. Nothing happened.

'Oh come on – this isn't fair! Atticus, where are you? It's not funny you know! His words were met by silence. 'I need to get back – did the plan work? I want to see Primrose... my wife.' A helpful memory reminded him that he had interrupted the ceremony before either of them had said, 'I do.'

There was the sound of a car approaching. As it drew near, it slowed and the driver turned to face him, then burst into nasty, mocking laughter before driving on.

'Angela!' Edward called after the car but it simply accelerated. He stood in the middle of the road watching it disappear from sight, a growing feeling of panic filling his body.

His sight fell upon the gap in the roadside hedge and he threw himself through it. After a desperate, nail-breaking climb, he crawled to the edge of the grassy plateau. His gaze raced down the hill, over the river, up the bank, tore across the wheat field, vaulted the gate, sprinted through the wildflower meadow, hurdled the copse, and there – next to the heart-shaped lake with the forgotten rowboat was a village where no village should be. He crumpled to the ground, tears rolling down his cheeks, 'It failed...I failed them... I bloody failed them!'

There was a strangely-wooden voice behind him. 'You know, blubbing isn't going to help.'

Edward turned to find himself being addressed by the gateway.

'As you can see, the angle has collapsed and Flatpack is now visible to all. The village has lost its 'by invitation only' status, and will soon be overrun by the unwashed masses. Your plan was a good one, but I'm afraid it failed.

'I brought you here because, as I see it, you have two alternatives: return to Veronica and make up some story to explain your absence, although I suspect she'll be in the process of filing for divorce after the Lysette Mason business.

'Alternatively, you can take the road back to Flatpack on the Meander and face Primrose and all the others who placed their absolute faith in you to prevent this from happening. Your choice... neither option appeals to me I have to say. Oh, I've brought you this.'

A shovel clattered to the ground.

'I suppose that's for me to dig my own grave?'

'Oh don't be so melodramatic, Edward! The villagers are going to need your help – the angle won't re-build itself.'

* * *

31. Trouser-Pressing Matters

Edward stared through the streaky window at a nearly-full moon; the nearly-full moon stared back at him. The Missing-Tiles Lodge had been the first hostelry that he had come upon after driving out of the lay-by and, although it looked totally uninviting, it had one redeeming feature—a 'vacancies' sign.

Room twenty-eight could not have been any smaller, and it stank of marijuana and damp; matters that were of no consequence to Edward - he simply wanted privacy to think. That said, he was surprised and pleased to discover a well-stocked mini-bar. On the bedside table, a lamp with a faded rose-design shade and uneven tassels provided just enough light to allow him to line up the tiny bottles that would serve as his evening meal.

He lay back on the bed and disappeared into a deep central hollow created, he assumed, by some massive individual with a proclivity for sleeping with a cannon ball in each pocket. Climbing out, he went to the wardrobe where he found two tolerably-clean blankets which he lay on the damp floor, not that he had any expectations of sleep.

As he stared at the moon, the words, *Why didn't it work?* dominated his thoughts.

It should have been the simplest thing - to transport the doctor's breath from his lungs to the various parts of Flatpack. I mean... what better, more secure container for the journey than inside the villagers themselves! It should have worked... it really should have worked!

Okay, so Jeffrey said that we lost some of the really special sentiments in his chamber before the villagers got the hang of it, but surely that wouldn't have made that much difference.

He finished a tiny bottle of gin in a single gulp.

Why should it make any difference whether the doctor's breath is carried on petals or inside the lungs of villagers? There's nothing magical about the petals – they were just couriers for the kindness.

Maybe it was something to do with the tunnels... maybe the breath needed to derive something from the clay as it passed through. Only Jeffrey would know that, and there's no sign of him entering my head in the near future, ringing his hand-bell.

Edward reached for the next bottle, and continued to drink until he passed out.

#

Early the next morning, Edward appeared at the reception desk looking and feeling dreadful. It was unmanned and there was no bell, so he rapped lightly on the counter. Immediately, a man appeared; in his mid-forties with a pleasant, oddly-familiar face, and dressed smarter than the shabby hotel merited. 'Good morning, sir. I trust you had a restful night?'

'Yeah, fine,' Edward muttered. 'What do I owe you?'

'Well, let's have a tally-up shall we?' The man started tapping keys.

After a moment, he said, 'I see you hit the mini-bar quite hard, sir.'

Edward gritted his teeth. 'That's what it's there for!'

'Oh absolutely, Mr St Claire, but it's an expensive way to—'

Edward thumped on the counter. 'How the hell do you know my name?'

The receptionist stepped back and pointed at the computer screen. 'The register...'

In addition to being hungover, weary and sad, Edward now felt like a fool. 'Of course... sorry.'

The key-tapping continued; it seemed to be taking an inordinate length of time to produce a bill for a single night. Finally, the receptionist tore off a sheet from the printer. 'Well, Mr St Claire, your total is £53.46.'

Edward started rummaging in his pockets.

'But,' the receptionist continued, 'as you are unlikely to be in possession of any means of payment, except Brogues perhaps, I suggest we waive the bill.' He tore the paper in two. 'Let's call it a freebie.'

In the past, Edward would have reached forward, grabbed the man by his lapels, and ordered him to explain how he knew things that he shouldn't. But Edward was a changed man, a heartbroken man and an intensely hungover man. He glared at the receptionist through tired, red eyes. 'How do you know about the brogues… who are you?'

'Patrick.' The man smiled and offered his hand.

Edward shook his head. 'No, I don't want a formal introduction, I want to know how you know about Brogues – the currency.'

Patrick withdrew his hand. 'It's not my real name, of course. I was christened 'Sandwich' would you believe! That was where my parents conceived me – Sandwich, in Kent. You know, you must go back to Flatpack, Edward.'

Edward feigned tearing his hair out. 'Look, just… stop this! Stop playing games with me!' He put his hand to his throbbing temples, took a deep breath then let it out. 'I can't go back. I've failed them all and now their village is ruined. I expect it's crawling with reporters, banging on doors wanting an exclusive about 'The Village that Appeared Overnight.' The villagers only wanted one thing, and for some reason they chose me to deliver it. Well I failed, so how can I possibly face them now? Especially Primrose.'

Patrick pondered this for a few moments, then said, 'Things may not be as bad as you think, Edward. Why do you feel that you've 'ruined' the village?'

'Because I saw it… in all its glory. And I shouldn't have been able to… well you obviously know how it works.'

'Yes... I do,' Patrick smiled. 'But Primrose will be very sad if you don't go back.'

'Ha! I doubt that – I failed her as well!'

Patrick put his hand on Edward's shoulder. 'She's young and forgiving Edward, and I'll bet that she's thinking of you right now.'

'Really, and how would you know what she's thinking?'

'Oh, I know her pretty well. Primrose is my daughter.'

#

After Edward had picked himself up, he began recalling things:

Primrose never mentioned her father, and I never thought to ask. I should have realised that something was wrong when her mother walked her down the aisle.

'If that's true, then why are you here?'

The expression on Patrick's face turned to one of sadness and regret. 'Fuchsia and I separated after I had a stupid liaison... I feel ashamed of it to this day. That sort of thing is virtually unheard-of in Flatpack, and the village committee felt that it would be best for everyone's sake that I leave the village.'

His face brightened a little. 'I still see Primrose; Maxie arranges visits.'

Edward considered this news for a moment. 'I think I can probably guess who you had the liaison with.'

'Yes, I expect you can. There's really only one bad person in the village.'

'Angela Gerald-Headley?'

'Indeed – the witch of Flatpack. I should never have had anything to do with that damned woman but, of course, it takes two to tango. I hate that cliché.'

Patrick leaned across the counter. 'I have a proposition, Edward; our situations are remarkably similar, never mind the fact that we're talking about mother and daughter – we're both afraid to return to Flatpack for fear of the reaction of our loved-ones. Now,

I've decided that I'm going to go back, I'm going to make things right with Fuchsia, and I don't give a damn if I bump into Angela.'

'Well, I've got some news for you there, Patrick; the witch of Flatpack is now 'on the outside.'

Patrick's eyes grew wide. 'What? You're kidding me! How on earth... no, it doesn't matter, this is terrific news and it reinforces my decision. Come with me Edward!'

'When?'

'Now!'

Patrick picked up his coat and headed for the door. 'I'll tell you one thing– whatever happens, I am never coming back to this godawful place!'

Edward looked around the reception area which was just as neglected as room twenty-eight. 'It isn't good.'

'That's the biggest understatement ever!'

Both men laughed.

#

The blackbirds were singularly unimpressed by the return of Edward's car. They'd gorged themselves on blackberries the previous night and were having a lie-in. The hedgehogs, feeling a bit exposed in the fridge-freezer vegetable compartment, had vacated it in favour of a more traditional mound of rotting leaves and vegetation.

'Why did you want to stop here?' Edward asked.

Patrick replied with a glint in his eye. 'Because I think you may have been a bit premature in the conclusion you drew.' He stepped out of the car, walked to the side of the road and began tilting his head.

'I'm afraid that doesn't work anymore.' Edward called out, guilt in his voice.

'Yes! Yes, it does. Look - there's the village sign!'

Edward rushed over and tipped his head. There it was;

'Flatpack on the Meander.
A warm welcome assured on Tuesdays and Fridays.'

Edward was overjoyed, but confused. 'But it shouldn't work!' He felt something nudge the back of his foot, and turned to see the end of the road urging him forward. 'You're back!'

The two men started walking, the end of the road clipping their heels, and soon the outline of Flatpack's buildings began to appear through the September mist. Between the men and the village, a lone figure stood motionless in the middle of the road. The figure peered at Edward, then sprinted towards him, throwing herself into his arms. Through her tears she cried out, 'Where did you go? Why did you go?'

'Oh Primrose,' was all Edward could manage as he stroked her glorious red hair. Such was the intensity and duration of the embrace that Patrick turned his rapidly-reddening face away. Once, Edward tried to conclude the matter, but Primrose was having none of it.

'Please hold me for a little longer, Ed Wood.'

It took a cough from Patrick to part the pair; they took a step back and looked at each other, the joy of reunion showing on their faces. Primrose turned her attention to her father and cuddled him in a different, but equally-loving way. Over her shoulder she whispered, with a giggle, 'His name's not really Patrick, it's... Sandwich.'

#

The threesome walked towards the village, an unseasonably cold wind blowing in their faces. Primrose was first to speak. 'I couldn't believe it when the gateway returned with just Uncle Max. Even he couldn't explain it. There was a big celebration anyway and everyone toasted you; Hedley made a glowing speech about your achievement and we all expected you to suddenly appear, but you didn't... so it all meant nothing. I walked home and cried myself to sleep.' Right on cue, a tear rolled down Primrose's cheek; even her tears were beautiful.

Edward didn't speak for a moment; he felt guilty and confused. He couldn't understand how he could have seen the village from the plateau when it now seemed that his plan had worked without a hitch. He brushed the tear away. 'You are the very last person I would ever want to hurt... but I thought I'd ruined everything.'

Primrose went to speak but Edward put his finger to her lips. He explained how the gateway had dumped him in the lay-by, and everything that had followed, including how he believed that the angle must have collapsed.

'Oh my dear, dear Ed Wood – the angle didn't collapse... Well, only for a few moments, but then the village was showered with love and kindness and empathy and compassion... and all from the mouths of the villagers, and Flatpack couldn't wait to spring back up.'

'But I did see the village, my love, as clear as I see you now.'

'Yes, Ed Wood – you did see the village – but your timing must have been terrible; as soon as Flatpack saw villagers popping up all over the place, breathing out all those lovely sentiments, it bounced back to its normal gradient. It lay horizontal for such a short time, but that must have been when you saw it.'

'But if I saw it, maybe others did. That could be a real problem.'

Primrose waved Edward's comment away. 'Oh I don't think so – of course some may claim to the papers that they saw a village appear for a few seconds, but such a ludicrous claim would soon be forgotten.'

Edward stared into her huge eyes. 'Do you know, I might have never come back if I hadn't met your father. Patrick needed to see your mother as much as I needed to see you. When he suggested that we go back together, I stopped fighting. I knew that the angle had collapsed, and I no longer cared what you might say to me –

whether you were going to scream at me, call me useless, tell me you hated me, or whatever. I just had to see you.'

Edward dropped to his knees. 'My darling Primrose, will you agree to finish the wedding that I so rudely interrupted?'

'Of course I will you stupid, wonderful Ed Wood!' Another lengthy embrace followed.

#

As they walked up Rump Hill, villagers began to appear in every house and shop doorway, cheering and applauding and overusing the words 'He's back!'

Edward, Primrose and Patrick were soon surrounded by well-wishers. Hettie Dalliard shouted above the din, 'Good to have you back Edward!' She then looked up at her lofty sister and said, 'Come along Leticia, we have roodleberries and blind herbs to pick.'

'No, Sister!' came the surprising response. 'I'm going to have a quick word with Edward and Primrose; it won't take long but I'm going to do that first.' Lettie pushed her way through the throng leaving her aghast sister open-mouthed.

Lettie spoke to Edward, aware that Primrose could hear every word. 'Edward, I want to apologise for taking advantage of you in the doctor's chamber.'

Primrose looked at Edward with an expression of shock.

'It isn't how is sounds, Primrose,' Lettie said.

'Oh yes?' Primrose folded her arms and looked to Edward for an explanation.

Before he could open his mouth, Lettie spoke up again. 'You see, I couldn't hold onto my breath in the chamber so Edward, like the gentleman he is, took it to the surface for me.'

Primrose thought for a moment, then said, 'So let me get this straight, you used my husband-to-be's position as a retransmission volunteer as an excuse for a damn good snog?'

Lettie bowed her head. 'Yes, I'm afraid so. I wouldn't be able to live with myself if I hadn't confessed.'

Primrose looked up at the spinster and felt for her. She wondered how many times Hettie had stood in the way of her sister's happiness.

Primrose gave Lettie a huge hug around her thighs. 'Well, if you're thinking of making a habit of that, we'll have to ensure that you're kept busy with your godmothering duties.' She gave a naughty smile to her husband-to-be. 'Eh Ed Wood?'

'Oh... definitely!'

'Will you please hurry up, Leticia!' came a voice from some way back.

'Coming Sister!'

#

Hedley approached the horde of well-wishers wearing his ever-present chain of office; the crowd parted out of respect for their mayor. 'Welcome back, Edward. I don't know where you've been, but you missed a terrific celebration and one of the best speeches I've ever spoken. Incidentally, you haven't seen my wife, have you? I seem to have mislaid her.'

Edward took the mayor to one side. 'Hedley, I'm really sorry to be the one to break the news, but I have seen her... and she's on the outside now. She must have slipped through while the village was 'down.'

A broad grin formed on Hedley's face. 'You mean I'm free of her?'

'Well... yes.'

'Why, that's a terrific piece of news! We've hated each other for years – I only stayed with her for appearances!' He skipped away in the direction of The Weaver's Slouch.

#

Fuchsia appeared at a doorway. Patrick turned to Edward who mouthed, 'Good luck.' Patrick walked up the path to their once-marital home; Fuchsia smiled, the pair went inside and the door closed.

Moments later, Edward received a hard slap on the back. 'Edward – this is wonderful... but where did you go? One minute you were there next to me in the mist, and then suddenly you were gone!'

'Back to the lay-by, Atticus. The gateway told me the angle had collapsed.'

'The gateway did what? Why, that useless lump of paint-peeling wood! I think it's time we chucked it on a bonfire!

'But anyway, now that you're back, we need to have another celebration – I'll have a word with Mrs Yawn from the chemist – get her to spread the word on the gossip network. I'd better make a list – we're going to need Farmer Rosser to knock up some more fertilizer fireworks, Hettie to bake some of her 'special' buns, Maynard to roll some more barrels down the hill... Oh, and of course Hedley will want to make another speech, I'd better give him some advanced warning.'

Edward put his hand on Maxie's shoulder. 'Atticus, I was rather hoping that Primrose and I could have a bit of time together... alone.'

'Pah! There'll be plenty of time for that, Edward, you old dog. But don't forget... you're not married yet.'

Edward whispered in Primrose's ear, 'I'm never going to get you alone, am I?'

She gave him a wicked smile. 'Be patient my love. When we're Mr and Mrs Wood, you'll have me all to yourself.'

END

Appendix

The Grernock in the Copse

A Cautionary Tale

by

Renston Ardlish

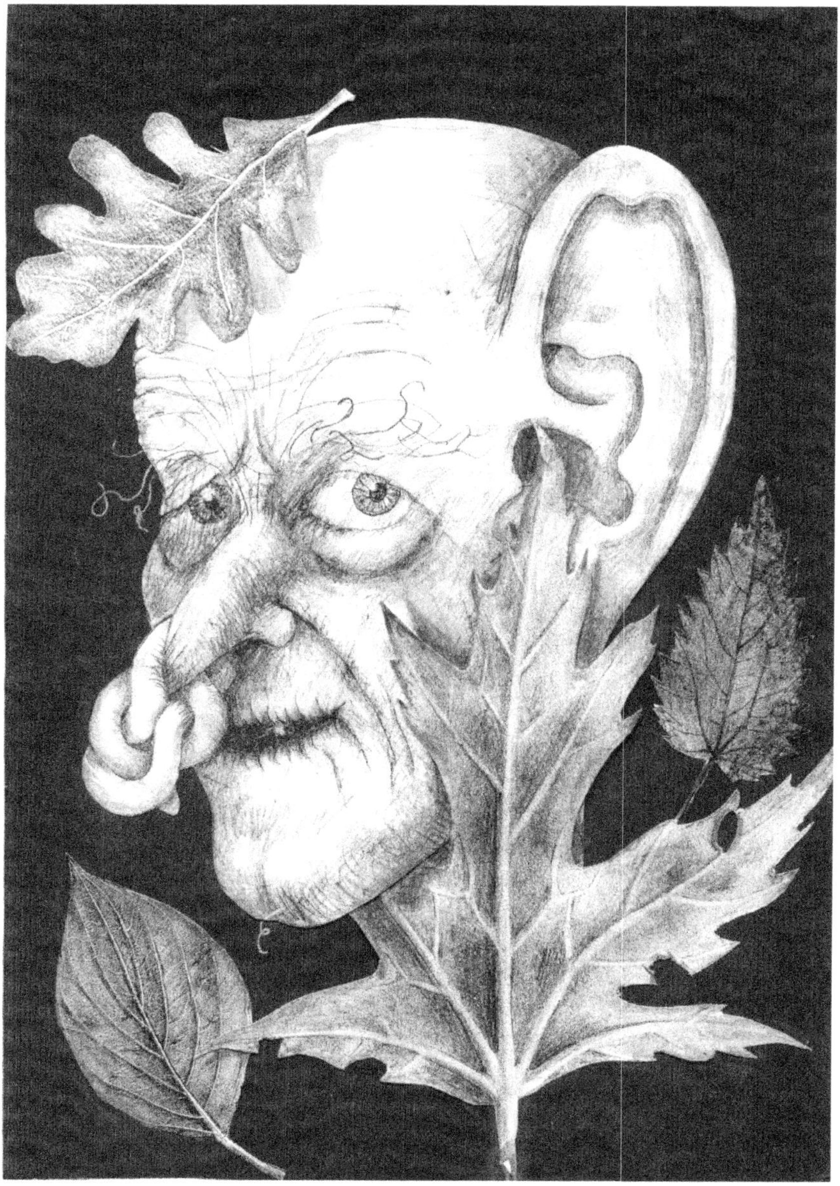

Too Few Trees

With too few trees to qualify
As forest or as wood,
It never had a proper name
Though many thought it should.

The locals called it Skinner's Copse,
A kind and thoughtful touch,
The aim to keep the name alive
Of one they missed so much.

Young Skinner, an apprentice
In the leather-tanning trade,
Had disappeared one afternoon
As light began to fade.

He whistled as he left his house,
He closed the garden gate,
And nothing more was seen of him
And no-one knew his fate.

A major search was organised
With all the town involved,
But to this day, I'm sad to say,
The case remains unsolved.

Roger Kent

The Years Pass

I'd walked that path a hundred times,
I knew each twist and turn,
I knew each overhanging branch,
Each nettle, bush and fern.

I liked to ping the beaded webs
And ring the bells of blue,
Identify the fungal forms
And catalogue a few.

I'd stop to watch a tiny bird -
It's first attempt at flight,
I'd wonder at its willingness
To leap from such a height.

But somehow it was not the same,
That day in early June;
The best way to describe it is -
The copse was out of tune.

The shadows were much darker
And the trees bereft of green,
The daisies and forget-me-nots
Were nowhere to be seen.

No scampering or rustling,
No birdsong filled the skies,
The trees that lined the path that day
Were strangers to my eyes.

Of course, I should have turned around -
Gone back another day,
But I would not admit the fact
That I had lost my way.

The Flatpack Observer

My eyes, they were deceiving me -
A trick of fading light,
Yet somewhere in my consciousness
I knew that wasn't right.

Roger Kent

The Advice of the Trees

I've heard people say, 'If you should lose your way
You should seek the advice of the trees,
They are gentle and wise and they never tell lies,
Though they can be a bit of a tease.

With limited vision I made a decision;
'I might as well give it a go -
They must feel compassion in some kind of fashion
When I, my predicament show.

I turned to their leader, an elderly cedar,
'A tick of your time may I take?'
The cedar looked down with a withering frown
And I knew that this was a mistake.

'I need your assistance - look into the distance
And tell me the way to my bed.'
He thought for a second, then calmly he beckoned
And these are the words that he said;

'The best thing to do is to bury your shoe,
And to bury it deeper than most,
Then wrap up the other in Whistler's Mother,
And send it by registered post.'

Oh give me a break - he's as mad as a cake
And about as much help as a pie,
The next one who spoke was a miniature oak,
And I must say my hopes were not high.

'If you can't write a ballad, pretend you're a salad
With mustard and mayonnaise dressing,
Ordain as a priest, or a vicar at least,
And then give your tomatoes a blessing.'

The Flatpack Observer

'Take a chaffinch's chirrup and dip it in syrup,'
Was the maple's advice on the matter,
I thought, *I'll be found, lying dead on the ground,*
Having drowned in deciduous chatter!

'You're no help at all!' I declared in a rage,
'Your advice is a sack of manure!'
I knew straight away, sure as night follows day,
I'd offended them, simple and pure.

'How very ungrateful, advice by the plateful
You chose to deride and to spurn,
Be gone from this place, you're an utter disgrace,
And make certain you never return!'

Roger Kent

Too Few Ears

I stumbled on through bush and scrub,
My clothes were ripped and torn,
My walk it had become a fight,
With bramble, spine and thorn.

The roots arose above the ground,
Intent to catch my feet,
And creepers curled around my neck
To make the job complete.

I swear I saw a sycamore
Approaching from the right,
With bulging bough and fists of bark,
A look of rage and spite.

To my surprise and great relief,
I stepped into a clearing,
Then turned to see that nasty tree -
All mockery and sneering.

A figure sat upon a log,
His wave put me at ease,
But very soon I wished that I
Was back amongst the trees.

In stature he was rather short,
Yes - *rather short*, is what I thought,
He ought to be less short, I thought,
Less short, I thought, *he really ought.*

His nose it had a knot in it,
(A granny I believe),
At least he'll never need to blow
Or wipe it on his sleeve.

The Flatpack Observer

And then I noticed something else,
I could not help but stare,
An absence of the aural kind -
A pair beyond repair.

He has one ear! He has one ear!
How very queer, he has one ear!
He has one ear, but what an ear -
So grand it has an atmosphere!

'I am a Grernock,' he announced,
'A pleasure you to meet.'
He shook me warmly by the hand
And offered me a seat.

He handed me a plate of nuts,
Some berries, mushrooms wild,
He was a most attentive host...
But then he broadly smiled.

He has no teeth! He has no teeth!
(And precious little gum beneath),
He has no teeth, like Grandpa Keith,
Who buried his on Skinner's Heath.

'You must excuse the way I speak,
My teeth - they are but few,
It would be great to masticate
Or vigorously chew.

'Upon a plate of roasted meat
With sausages and mead,
But feeling sorry for myself
Will not, my stomach, feed.

'I suck on roots and forest fruits

And sup the morning dew,
I close my eyes and fantasise
Of casseroles and stew.'

We spoke of steak and carrot cake,
Then I, the question placed;
'Prey, how can I escape the copse?
It is not to my taste.'

He said, 'I guessed you'd want to leave
And I can help you there,
But you must help me in return -
I think that's only fair.'

The Grernock's Tale

'Now, first you must endure my tale;
A tale of rise and fall,
A tale to touch the hardest heart
And stir your bladder gall.

'I have not always been this way -
The way you see me here,
I had the kind of classic looks
That drew the ladies near.

'With figure slight and buttocks tight,
A mop of curly locks,
I dwarfed my male contemporaries
When only wearing socks!

'That evening, when I left the house,
My girl was on my mind -
I would admit my thoughts were not
The honourable kind.

'I meant to pick some pretty blooms
And place them in her hand,
I knew the copse contained the best,
But nothing went as planned.

'To find the ones I sought, I went
Much deeper than intended,
I didn't even notice that
The day had truly ended.

'A sickle moon provided me
With very little light,
I groped around, my hope to find
Some comfort for the night.

Roger Kent

'I soon became aware of
Something sticky on my hand,
I tasted it - it tasted good,
So good it should be banned.

'I kept on going back for more,
In fact I gorged myself,
I wished I had a jar of it
To keep upon the shelf.

'It had a very odd effect -
A psychedelic high,
The stars above me danced
A Passo Doble in the sky.

'When I awoke, my head was sore,
I leaned against a trunk,
My teeth and ear lay on the ground,
And worst of all - I'd shrunk!

'A silver birch examined me -
'I'm not completely sure,
But I suspect you tapped the sap
From Satan's sycamore.'

'His voice was grave and solemn,
And I knew he spoke the truth,
"That sap has made you hideous
And robbed you of your youth."

'I felt completely desperate,
I couldn't hold it in,
A tear rolled down my knotted nose,
Descending from my chin.'

A Pip in the Hand

'So now I've told you everything,
I hope I didn't bore you,
And every single word is true -
Of that I can assure you.

'I have a plan', he said, and gave
A sly and gummy grin,
'A plan to bring young Skinner back,
... and that's where you fit in.

'This pip is from a napple fruit,
Picked from a napple tree,
The fruit it will return me to
The boy I used to be.'

'I think you mean an Apple tree,'
I said it rather smugly,
He smiled, and in that smile, I saw
The boy before the ugly.

'I may not be the boy I was,
But I am not a jerk,
A napple is the fruit I need -
An apple wouldn't work!

'It will not grow within the copse -
Repeatedly I've tried,
And I am too ashamed to take
A single step outside.

'Be sure you plant in fertile soil,
Protect it from the frost,
A little water now and then,
And keep your fingers crossed.

Roger Kent

'The napples will be at their best
When summer's at its height,
Please bring me four - I must be sure
To get the dosage right.'

He placed the pip into my palm
And closed my fingers tight,
'I put my trust in you, my friend -
I know you'll do what's right.'

He led me to the clearing's edge
And whispered to a yew,
The trees divided to reveal
A pathway straight and true.

I didn't stop to offer thanks,
I simply took my chance,
And raced along that shady path
Without a backward glance.

I got inside, I slammed my door,
I poured myself a drink,
I scrutinized the wretched pip,
And flushed it down the sink.

The Flatpack Observer

More Years Pass

The seasons went past quite remarkably fast,
And I worked every hour I was able,
I pushed myself harder to fill up the larder,
And put enough food on my table.

I scratched out a living from panning and sieving,
The gold from the bed of a stream,
My wages were tiny for something so shiny,
But I caught the occasional bream.

I felt no concern for the hideous grern,
Grew that memory evermore distant,
Till a rap on the door brought it back to the fore,
It was regular, loud and insistent.

It was a surprise of immoderate size
To be greeted by no-one at all,
I fingered the blame at some juvenile game,
Then a napple rolled into the hall!

I smelled it and stroked it and generally poked it -
Cylindrical, shiny and blue,
A thing so incredible cannot be edible -
Not with that indigo hue.

Discarding all caution, I bit off a portion
And, chewing it over, I pondered;
This sensory pleasure surpasses all measure!
Then into the garden I wandered.

I want to relate how I felt as I ate,
As the sweetest of images flowed;
A smile like no other, from baby to mother
At birth, in a humble abode.

Roger Kent

The freshness of rain in an arid terrain,
Or a wave on the muscatel seas,
The caramel kiss of an innocent Miss,
With a melody riding the breeze.

A ripple of silk on an ocean of milk,
Or the mist in the valley below,
An expression of grace on a beautiful face,
With the texture of virginal snow.

It seemed to have suited the tree to have rooted
Within my exterior drain,
A picture of health - just imagine the wealth
If I use it for monetary gain!

Though daylight was fadin', could see it was laden,
And many had dropped to the lawn,
Their blue was inspiring and, though it was tiring,
I didn't stop picking till dawn.

Napple Mania

I wrote a simple business plan
And bought myself a field,
I planted many napple pips
And waited for their yield.

I sent a fine example
To an editor I knew,
Who placed a glowing article
In Fruiterer's Review.

I gave one to the Vicar's wife,
Who shared it with the Vicar,
He gave a shout, 'It's evened out
The beating of my ticker!'

When Sunday morning came
The Vicar told his loyal flock -
By afternoon, the congregation
Queued around the block.

I charged a very modest price -
They mustn't think me greedy,
I need to keep the punters sweet
Until they're good and needy.

A wealthy man enquired if I
Would fill a wooden cask,
'They taste so good I'd pay you
Almost anything you ask.'

A doctor wanted napples
To prescribe instead of pills,
He spoke of healing properties,
A cure for many ills.

Roger Kent

A midwife said, 'Your napples
Are like manna from the gods -
I've seen a sudden increase in the
Instances of quads.'

A 'Napp' became the snack of choice
For pensioner and teen,
One even made the centrefold
Of 'Peelers' Magazine.

I registered a patent with
The office of that name,
Then raised my prices seven-fold
Without a hint of shame.

The napples went on selling
So I raised them even higher,
And never saw a day without
A visit from a buyer.

The balance of my bank account
Was something to behold,
I made some wise investments
In commodities and gold.

I flaunted my prosperity,
Enjoyed a shameless gloat,
I bought a massive property
With gardens and a moat.

I turned my back on friends of old,
I wrote them all a letter:
'I move in higher circles and
My new friends smell much better.'

I thought about the grernock

The Flatpack Observer

As my fortune grew and grew,
I would have gone to visit
But had far too much to do.

Roger Kent

Napple Blight

A balmy summer's afternoon,
A gentle summer breeze,
A time to sit and contemplate
The busy bumble bees.

The breezes carried tiny spores
Of deadly woodland blight,
That blanketed the country on
That balmy summer's night.

The blight just prompted laughter
From the old, established trees,
Who'd long-since grown resistant
To infection and disease.

But not the gentle napple trees,
Who didn't know the danger,
And threw their slender branches wide,
To welcome in the stranger

The savage blight embarked upon
Its grim and germy mission -
To kill the roots and thus prevent
Absorption of nutrition.

And once it had a proper hold,
Its grip, it never slackened,
The napples grew a furry mould
As, on the branch, they blackened.

The crash of falling napple trees
Reverberated round,
I found it such a bothersome
And irritating sound.

The Flatpack Observer

The strongest and the last of them,
At length succumbed and fell,
I didn't mourn their passing -
They had served their purpose well.

Roger Kent

The Visitors

One night I sat up reading,
By my side a candle burned,
I heard a noise outside the door,
And then the handle turned

A couple stepped into the room,
Like Adam with his Eve,
An instance of the beauty
Mother Nature can achieve.

I've met this man before! I thought
And tossed my book aside,
But couldn't place that handsome face
However hard I tried.

'I am the one that you betrayed,
The one who trusted you,
To bring a napple to the copse -
That's all you had to do!'

I felt a blast of icy wind,
A sudden chill within,
A wave of guilt crashed over me
And soaked me to the skin.

He gave a smile I knew so well,
This time with teeth included,
My guilty chill departed with
The warmth his smile exuded.

'I do not harbour bitterness,
I do not seek redress,
I was delighted when I heard
The news of your success.

The Flatpack Observer

'I would admit I plotted,
As I languished in the wood,
But life's too short for such a thought,
Besides, my news is good.

'My lady found me in the copse
And wept at what she saw,
She brought the last four napples,
And the grernock is no more.

'In fourteen days we are to wed
And want you to attend,
Despite the things that went before,
I see you as a friend.'

He then produced a bottle,
And filled three tall glasses high,
We raised a toast to Skinner's Copse,
Then drank the bottle dry.

I marvelled at the grernock,
As the couple slipped away,
Forgiveness of a selfish act -
My lesson for the day.

Eventually I fell asleep,
I drifted out of mind,
And travelled to a world
Of a completely different kind.

I dreamt of Grernock villages,
The stuff of story books,
Where judgement of your worth is never
Based upon your looks.

I dreamt that whole communities

Roger Kent

Felt neither fear nor dread,
Where beauty and deformity
Would share a single bed.

When I awoke, I was at peace,
All thoughts of selfish greed,
Had been replaced by empathy
With those in greater need.

The sun was casting shadows
of an overhanging willow,
Then, filled with fear, I saw my ear,
Relaxing on my pillow.

End